FORBIDDEN FRUIT:

stories of unwise lesbian desire

FORBIDDEN FRUIT:
stories of unwise lesbian desire

Edited by Cheyenne Blue

ISBN-13 978-988-13637-0-1

CONTENTS

INTRODUCTION

There is a charm about the forbidden that makes it unspeakably desirable. — Mark Twain

Why is the forbidden so compelling? What pushes the forbidden into your head and lodges it there despite your best efforts to evict it? Why do thoughts of the woman you cannot have fuel an obsession that burns through your daydreams and scorches your nights?

This anthology collects together erotic stories that sample the forbidden. The women in these stories have tough choices to make, for an illicit taste can put something else on the line: a career, a friend, a marriage, even a life. But when boundaries are challenged, when lines are crossed, and the forbidden fruit is plucked from the bough, lust—or love—can come to the fore.

The seventeen stories in this anthology explore many reasons why a woman might be off limits. In Beth Wylde's *Bachelorette Party* a butch turns her best friend into her lover the night before the bestie's wedding. L.C. Spoering explores the allure of the older woman, and Harper Bliss takes it one step further as that older woman is also her ex-girlfriend's mother.

Duty versus desire is the theme for stories from Emily L. Byrne, when an off-duty cop realizes where she has previously seen the woman she's lusting after, and Axa Lee, whose historical story *The Clinton County Horse Thief Society* plays the theme for the highest stakes of all.

Allison Wonderland romps in her inimitable way through the tale of a fundamentalist Christian and an atheist, and Lisabet Sarai tells a powerful story of a nun working in a halfway house who is beguiled by a hooker in her care.

With settings ranging from a BDSM club to a sports stadium, and timeframes from regency England to a dystopian future, there's a variety of sizzling stories here to satisfy even the pickiest reader.

Go on, pluck the fruit.

Take a bite.

I dare you.

Cheyenne Blue
Queensland, Australia

OUR WOMAN
REBECCA LYNNE FULLAN

When the war started, I was five years old and Sarah was sixteen. When it ended, I was nine and she was twenty-one. The difference contained in those ages cannot really be measured. It is the difference of memory. My memories before the war are fuzzed, and, when they come into focus, they are so particular as to be meaningless outside the context of my life: a red balloon I was given at a party, a pair of blue shoes I found beautiful, the mole on the right side of my mother's jaw. Sarah's memories before the war were clear and sharp, an entire pattern of life formed and removed while still cooling. And Sarah was old enough during the war to make choices, to do things. She did a lot of things. All the information I've found is agreed on that.

Of course, most people wouldn't know her by the name Sarah. She passed the name to me in the dark, with her lips against my neck, a quick and sibilant whisper to my pulse. To call her something else would bereave me further.

When the war ended, my mother was dead, and my father was almost powerful. "To be almost powerful is more dangerous than to be nothing," he would say to me, putting his hands on my shoulders. My father was a serious man, and he always spoke to me as though I could understand. And yet Sarah was with us four years before I understood she was a slave.

We called her Our Woman, and out of the scraping, dripping grief for my mother, I emerged into her care. It did not occur to me to ask where she had come from. She was short—by thirteen I had passed her in height, and when she came to us she was as thin as a rail, but she soon grew softer, more rounded. She would pass her hands over her stomach as it grew and say, "Lacey, I am going to be as fat as a beach ball."

The thought seemed to please her, and it made me giggle. She seemed to like making me laugh, looking at me with a slanting, slight smile and a shine in her eyes. Her eyes were black and expressive, but what they were expressing was often hard to pin down. After the war, we moved to a new house: small, isolated, and pretty, tucked into a curve of the riverbank. We had no neighbors. Our Woman would walk with me along the riverbank and tell me stories of river fairies. She had a thick, deep voice, and the fairies she spoke of were capricious and reticent, peering out of the folds of the river to watch us as we walked. She gave me nightmares by telling me they had been known to eat children, not from the outside in, but from the inside out, so that you would not see fingers and toes disappearing but rather notice that a child had less and less inside them, until they lost a stomach and could not eat, or lost a soul and could not see.

I wanted to be brave and earn her stories, so I tried to hide my fear from her, even when it woke me stark and sweating in the night. She would always hear me wake, though, and rise from her mattress at the foot of my bed, and stand in the dark with her bright black eyes fixed on me. Finally, after a week of nightmares, she swung a shawl from around her shoulders and laid it over me, and she sang. The words were jumbled syllables of nonsense, but the music both ached and soothed, quieting me. Her singing was more threadbare than her speaking, but also more beautiful.

"What are the words to that song, Woman?" I asked her. "I can't understand them." She stayed still for a long time. I recognized the tactic as something my father had done before she lived with us and assumed she was waiting for me to go to sleep. I hardened my body against sleep and held my breath to keep myself from drifting. Finally she spoke, flatly and clearly, the same sequence of sounds she had made in singing. I laughed aloud, thinking it a joke. "But those aren't words," I protested.

She went on. She went on so long that it wasn't funny, and I began to be frightened. A tone of passion crept into her voice, and the not-words quivered and shimmered around the edges, as with heat. I thought she was angry. I thought she was crazy.

The next day, I went into my father's study while Our Woman prepared dinner. It was a good sized room, given the smallness of the house, and lined with bookshelves, all full, and further made into a pleasant maze by little stacks of books scattered about the floor. He looked up at me with a worn and weary smile.

"Lacey," he said. "Come to find a new story to please you?"

"No, thank you," I answered. My father had never really been angry with me, but I understood, on some basic bone-deep level, that it was important always to remain polite. "I would like to use a dictionary. I want to look up some words I don't know."

My father swiveled around in his desk chair and pulled his big, dusty dictionary off the shelf. "I'll look them up for you. Do you know how to spell them?" I shook my head no. "Well, repeat them to me, then."

I thought hard, but although I could still hear the strange words echoing in my brain, I couldn't bring them to my tongue. "I—I can't," I said. "They're too different. They're different from anything I've ever heard."

My father didn't move an inch, but he sucked in a sudden and shallow breath. He asked me again to try and repeat the words. I could tell it mattered. His whole body had changed without changing at all, like the moment when you realize a river fairy has eaten away your bones. "There are other ways of making words aside from ours," he said, "but they are forbidden by the Good Government. I won't be angry, but I need to know what you heard."

"I can't," I said, and I started crying. "I can't remember." But when he insisted, I lied instinctively and told him I'd heard the words from an older cousin who had visited us for dinner the week before. It was the first time I lied for Our Woman's secrets.

Our Woman braided my hair and made food for us. Later, she told me that the river fairies wouldn't want to eat anything inside me, that they were on my side. She said they had come to her in dreams and told her so, and I believed her.

When the weather was beautiful she took off her socks and shoes and rolled up her pants and walked in the river. She didn't get angry when I splashed her. Her smile burst through like sunlight and her laugh chased the ripples of the water. When she rolled up her pants I could see the X branded on her calf. It was smooth and beautiful. I loved to put my hand on the scar. The first time I touched it, she looked at me in startlement.

"It's pretty, Woman," I explained. "I'd like one, when I'm grown up."

She lowered her eyes and laughed, but her laugh was slanted and sharp-edged. "You will have to earn it," she said.

"How?" I asked. "Is it a prize? Do I have to start training now?"

"Yes," she said, and wouldn't elaborate. She bent and picked up a sizeable rock from the river. She held it in her hand and looked at me. Then she turned and threw it, violently and far, so it splashed hard in the water farther downstream.

"You're very strong," I said.

"I used to be stronger," she answered. "Come and walk with me; the river fairies will bless you."

I didn't want to show fear, so I went to her at once. In my haste I forgot to take off my shoes, and the river soaked through them. We walked, in sunlight and water, stopping before it got too deep and swift. Later, I heard my father scolding her for letting me ruin my shoes.

"I trust you to take care of these things," he said. I felt her silence spread around her like an ink stain.

That night, she sat on the side of my bed and ran her fingers through my hair and hummed. I felt my skin grow swollen with feeling.

"Thank you for being Our Woman," I murmured. Her fingers and her music stopped and her body stiffened.

"I can't say you're welcome for that, Lacey," she said, steady, careful. Something rumbled deep beneath her words. The surprise and sting of them took my breath, and I never spoke of it again, but from then on I was desperate to understand.

When I was fourteen, someone said the word to me. From time to time, Father had guests, men and women with better clothes than we had and a brisk energy that I also felt we lacked. One of them, a man with a beard who wore a very large wristwatch, said to me that I was lucky to have such a fine and useful slave. Our Woman seemed unfazed, but I was startled. I knew the word slave, and my father had explained the concept to me, but his examples were all drawn from the past.

"Our Woman is not a slave," I said. "She wants to be here with us."

The man chuckled and didn't say anything else on the subject. The next time Our Woman and I were alone, I burned with shame and questions and startled visibly when she said my name.

"Lacey, will you help me peel these potatoes?"

I walked over and picked up a potato and a knife. My hands shook. I set them down again. Our Woman was peeling steadily, not looking at me.

"Why do you think I have a brand?" she said at last. Her voice was calm and almost kind. "Why do you think I am called 'Your Woman,' instead of by a name? You have heard other people speak of their Women and Men. You must have understood before now."

"I didn't," I said. It was a lie, but it was also not a lie. Our guests were so infrequent; the whole pattern of life I understood was contained among my father and Our Woman and me. "I thought... I thought you were Our Woman because you loved me. I thought you wanted to take care of me." I heard my own words in the silence, childish, need-swollen. I picked up the potato and the knife once more and began to peel. "Please tell me the truth, Woman. Do you—" I was struck with the horror of it, the obviousness of it. "Do you have a name? Have you had a name all along, for years?"

"Yes," she said. "I have a name. I had one. I haven't heard it since the war."

I peeled furiously and sliced the top layer of skin off a finger along with the potato peel. Our Woman put her hands on mine. She took the knife from me and laid it down. My cut finger burned and stung where she touched it. I looked at her face, and while her voice and hands remained so steady, her face was not calm. It was a wilderness of feeling. She squeezed my hands hard and I gasped with the pain. I thought of how she was always near me, with knives, with fire, with water, with rocks.

"My father trusts you," I said, wondering.

"To an extent," she answered.

"To the extent of me." I paused, trying to choose my words carefully. "And I trust you to the extent of me."

"Do you?" she said. "You trust me, or you trust Your Woman? The one is impossible; the other unwise, though I understand that it may be hard to break the habit right away."

I began shivering with tears unshed and words unspoken. "What's your name?" I whispered. "I could trust you if I knew your name."

She did not answer. She let go of my hand and carefully dampened a cloth with warm water to clean my cut, and then she bandaged it. She worked methodically and gently. I watched the motion of her hand and the concentration of her face and I was struck, suddenly, with the thought that she was beautiful.

"Now that you know I'm a slave," she said, "You needn't help me anymore with the potatoes." A swift shadow of humor passed over her face.

I learned more about making potato soup that day than I had ever thought to know. She taught me how to do each step with a hungry patience and I worked to understand spicing and mashing as though they would fix everything out of balance, in our home or in the world. When we sipped from the ladle at the end of preparations, the soup was delicious. Our Woman laughed. She set down the ladle hard in the soup and laughed and laughed, leaning against the counter, and I saw tears sparkling in her black eyes.

"I hate cooking," she said through her laughter.

"I'll cook from now on," I said, reaching for and gripping the ladle. "I'll tell Father that I want to."

That was the beginning of our conspiracy of shared labor. Over the next few years I watched Our Woman incessantly, trying to read in the line of her elbow whether a task pleased or disgusted her. I watched her feet when she slid them out of her shoes and rubbed a strong, broad foot with a skilled, calloused hand. I watched the changing moods of the branding scar on her leg, its varying whites and pinks and sometimes even a livid purple-red. I watched the curve of her shoulders while she worked, the roundness of her belly that pleased her. I drifted from my intention to read the needs she could never speak and began to see an artistry in her body that left me mesmerized. The rise of her breasts carried the songs she would no longer sing to me, and the sly mischief of her smile transformed her otherwise often-brooding face. I watched her long after I could no longer have said what I was learning.

Father perceived some of these changes and attempted to take in hand those aspects of my education that he had let fall through diffidence and discomfort. At some point after I learned that Our Woman was a slave, he sat me down to speak with me. His eyes never left mine, sharp and precise even though his words were vague and his voice passionless.

"Slavery was different in the old days. It was based on race or on economic status. Now, under the Good Government, slavery is based on politics. People's choices bring them to slavery or to freedom, not things beyond their control."

"What were Our Woman's choices?" I asked. He didn't answer. "What were yours?"

"I chose freedom itself," he said, and for the first time in the conversation, his voice matched his eyes in intensity. "For me and for you."

It was several years before I understood that my father had been given Our Woman as a slave precisely because he was not entirely trusted. She was his test, and by keeping her docile, he'd passed. The arrogant visitors in good clothing were not his friends, although they were not his enemies either. They were the people he had to please to keep this small, isolated house ours. I figured out what I could on my own, and I asked Our Woman to confirm the rest.

"You're too curious, Lacey," she told me when, at nineteen, I had come to her with my latest theory on the details of the war, the politics behind it, and her role and my father's role in the whole thing. "I was younger than you are now when the war started, and I wasn't much older when it ended."

"Why do you stay here?" I asked, carefully casual, aware that it was a lit match tossed on dry wood. "You are stronger than my father."

She looked at me, calculating and sharp. "I stay because I am compelled to stay. I have been hunted once, and with teeth. Your father's chores are better than that life."

I lost my breath, though I couldn't have expected another answer. I looked at my hands, my whole body tensing.

"You want me to say I stay for you?"

I raised my eyes to hers, feeling hot and desert-dry. She must have seen something there that surprised her, because her expression lost its irony and became quite thoughtful. I watched the shape of her face with a connoisseur's habit while a terror I had hidden for years gripped my center and squeezed.

She tried again. "Lacey, the war was like the river fairies when they're being nasty. It ate me hollow before it had really begun."

"I just want to understand it," I insisted.

"Then you'll have to ask someone else."

Father mostly liked to keep me (and himself) at home, away from people and influence, but I convinced him to let me go to the nearest city in order to find a book he was missing from his personal library and deeply wanted. He gave me a flood of instructions: how to behave (quietly), what to do (little), and whom to speak to (no one, if possible). I absorbed his instructions obediently, thinking I would toss them aside when I arrived in the city. Instead, I was dazzled. The city was a mess of ruins, but also a mass of bustle, as people hurried back and forth between the remaining buildings. I had never seen so many people. I stood dizzily on corners and watched the flow, like leaves tumbling along when the river was swollen with rain. Someone's shoulder brushed mine and I sprang away, only to bounce into another frame, murmur apologies, lean breathlessly against a street lamp. I sank into my father's rules willingly.

I found my father's book in a bookstore as quickly as I could, and then I stayed for an hour before I had the courage to ask for things to read about the war. The bookseller gave me a thick and heavy book with a dark green cover. I sat in a corner and read throughout the day. When I had given up hope of learning anything specific, I turned a page and saw a picture of Our Woman, standing in front of a microphone, her mouth open, her hair blowing, and her fist in the air. "Student Leader of the November Resistance," the caption read. I tore out the page and tucked it in my bag.

Back at home, I went looking for Our Woman. She wasn't in the house, and my father said she had gone for a walk along the river hours ago. I took the picture with me and set off. I followed the path we used to take when I was little, looking for some sign of her. I found farther downstream than I expected, leaning back against a tree. Her face was open and her eyes were closed. Her lower lip was caught between her teeth, and I saw her bare feet shift against the ground, toes curling and uncurling, hips rising off the ground to meet her sure, steady hand tucked deeply between her legs. I moved closer, holding my breath. I drew close enough to see the small bones in her wrist moving in their own tiny rotations, as she played her body like an instrument. Her breathing was rapid and uneven. Her mouth opened and closed in a rapid sequence of strife and bliss, strife and bliss again. I had the page with her picture on it crushed into my sweating hand, and I felt my own lips trembling. Her throat worked, her round belly rose and fell, and her other hand moved with certainty under her shirt, finding a nipple and squeezing it between her fingers. A deep, quiet ghost of sound came from her throat and she thrust her hips up against the movement of her hand, opened her mouth wide, and shuddered from head to toe. And opened her eyes and looked at me.

I froze. She stared right back, her pupils dilated and open. And then she smiled, full and rich and beautiful. She didn't say a word, but pulled her clothes back into their proper places, raked her fingers through her hair, and got to her feet. I held out the page of the book to her and she took it, our fingers briefly touching. She looked at herself in the photo.

"Life is strange, Lacey," she said at last. "I have always been hungry for things that are hard to get."

"Is it over, then?" My voice was unsteady. "Your war? What was the November Resistance?"

"It is over," she said. "I have been made a slave."

But that night, as I lay in my bed not sleeping, she rose from her mattress, pulled the blankets from behind me, and pressed her lips and her tongue against the back of my neck. She caught my skin in her teeth. I shivered.

"The November Resistance was our last great push against what you call the Good Government," she said to my neck. She reached her lips up and sucked and bit my earlobe. "Your father used to speak and write of what he believed and now he is silent. I used to make speeches and burn down buildings and now I make soup and am

11

burned with a brand. That is the Good Government."
She reached her hand down my body and began to rub
my clit, roughly. It sparked and ached for her.

"Tell me your name," I begged, my voice unsteady.
Tears spilled down my face and we both tasted them.

She turned me on my back and held my shoulder
down with one hand while the other still worked between
my legs. I shook and stared into her eyes. My body was
swollen, burning, turned into an arrow that ended at my
clit and pointed straight to her. I choked back sobs and
reached with my free hand to press it tightly to her chest,
to squeeze her breast and find the pounding of her heart.

"When I first learned I would be enslaved by your
father—wordsmith and traitor, slippery quiet stooge of
the Good Government—I thought I would kill you. I
thought I would bring you up stunted, crippled,
frightened of your own shadow. I thought I would get
you to trust me and then poison you when you were old
enough to understand." Her voice was hoarse, and,
despite its words, the rhythm of her speech and the
movement of her hand opened widening circles of
pleasure in me. My tears slowed and I felt a strange, wild
joy move up to take their place.

"Put yourself inside me," I said hoarsely, "Fuck
me."

She laughed. Her fingers moved to find my slick,
wet opening, and she played there, lightly. I quivered
harp-like, feeling the resonance all through my body. She
slid one finger in, then two, and I clenched and rose and
fell around her. I covered my face with a hand, and she
released my shoulder and took my hand away.

"I'm going to look at you," she said. We stared at
each other while she fucked me. I put my hand over my
clit instead of my eyes, and rubbed in eager circles. She
slid her two fingers out of me, tucked a third beneath
them, and pushed all three inside again. I bit back my

cries. My whole body was throbbing, radiating out from where she touched me. Sweat gathered on my forehead and dripped back onto the pillow, and I raised my hips up and thrust to push her more deeply into me. She found a pulse inside me and pressed her fingers tight against it. My eyes widened and lit.

"More," I growled, in a voice I could barely recognize, "I want to swallow you."

"I want to break you open," she countered, and she pulled her fingers out with a wicked smile. The middle three were slick with stickiness and juice, and she tucked in her pinky and her thumb, making a sort of lily with her hand, which she showed me, raising an eyebrow. Then she put her other hand over my mouth, and pushed that lily slowly, carefully, excruciatingly inside. Up to one set of knuckles, and I vibrated like a string. My clit pulsed against my fingers, and I touched it desperately and gently, while I felt her fingers working their way into my center. It hurt. My vision blurred. And then she began to move, slowly, a little awkwardly, in and out. My vision exploded and my clit throbbed and I came before I could think, my mouth stretched wide, biting and grabbing at the hand she'd placed over it to catch my cries.

She slid herself out of me as I came down, and it was a relief and yet so lonesome that I nearly wept. Then she tucked herself sweetly beside me on the bed, fitting there as though we'd done this many times before, and whispered softly but clearly against my throat between kisses, "My name is Sarah."

The next morning, she was gone. She took with her some warm clothes and some food and an extra pair of shoes. She left a note for me. "You are right. My war is not over. Perhaps uncertainty is not the same as being hollowed, and pain is not the same as surrender, and even surrender is not a permanent condition. Don't stay forever alone here—your father's refuge is not necessarily yours." There was another line below this, in letters I could not read.

My father and I stared at each other over the breakfast I prepared, and I tried to gather myself together enough to lie for her, to invent an errand I'd sent her on. My father cut me off.

"I can keep quiet for three days," he said. "After that, I'll have to report her. There are rumors of resistance operations in the mountains a few miles from here. I have been fabricating these reports for years; they are not true. I do not know where the resistance is, but it isn't there. I think my story will be convincing. You can help me form it, if you like. There are records I've kept hidden from you, but you can read them now." He was matter of fact, nervous, dry. I didn't know if I loved him or hated him.

I spent the next three days alternately working with him to make the story right, and trying to convince him not to make the report at all. He opened his records to me and I read. I read his articles from the early days of the war, hopeful for change but critical of the Good Government as it formed. There were articles I could not read, written in the same letters as the end of Sarah's note, but he wouldn't say more on that subject, and I didn't show him what she'd written. I read of my mother's death, so carefully eulogized as an accident, but after which my father wrote only in praise of our new leaders. He gave me the writing about my mother as he gave it all, without comment, and I stared into his face, trying to read him like a forbidden language.

At last he gave me a thin sheaf of papers, saying, "This is Our Woman." I read of Sarah, who in these records was called the Rose of the Mountains, a persistent dissident who had eluded capture for nearly a year of searching before being sentenced to a life enslaved. I spent the nights mostly sleepless. I brought myself to one orgasm after another, easily, desperately, trying to find Sarah on my skin.

On the third day my father took his bundles of paper into the city and he made his report. I walked along the river while he was gone. I walked as far as I could, farther than I ever had before. I made it to a small waterfall and stood beneath it, the water thundering over me, drenching me to the bone.

Then I saw them. Forty or more tiny faces, eighty or more tiny eyes, moving here and there, up and down, in the cascading water and climbing over the slick brown rocks. I saw their limbs like sticks, and their blinking, insect-like eyes. River fairies. Sarah had told me the truth. I opened my arms, whether they had come to help me or to hollow. I sang to them in words I never understood, that I thought I had forgotten, but which remained, hidden, in my memory and my mouth. I felt their feet against my skin and I sang them Sarah's song.

HANDS OFF
AVA-ANN HOLLAND

When Marianne walked into the hotel lobby, she instantly felt out of place. It was exactly the kind of establishment she had always avoided at all cost. While she waited for the receptionist to deal with a young couple who had financial success written all over them, yet no discernible taste, she took stock of her surroundings.

The lobby was a faceless, enormous box decked out in the cream, brown, and beige tones of expensive corporate interior design–light, but easy to clean and forgiving where it mattered. Soft, ambient lighting along with regular puffs of pine fragrance pumped through the air conditioning dulled the senses and made her feel even more unreal than she already had on the way here from the airport.

If it had been up to her, she would have chosen an entirely different type of hotel. Somewhere small, possibly slightly dilapidated, with creaky stairs and a big, loud Italian Mama behind the desk. Somewhere with a heart. But she understood that Irene's fortune in life limited her to staying in faceless, discreet places like this one. Although she was not exactly hounded by the paparazzi any longer, now that age had crept up on her like any other mortal and the movie parts had dried up significantly, Marianne's childhood friend was nevertheless not un-famous enough yet to warrant staying anywhere *nice*.

A flutter of excitement winged across Marianne's belly and did a loop-de-loop. She had been nervous all day, kidding herself at first that it was her old fear of flying raising its ugly head, but knowing full well it was the impending reunion with the most beautiful girl she'd ever known that was giving her butterflies. It had been twenty-seven years since she had kissed her best friend goodbye at London Heathrow—a long, sloppy kiss, officially for the benefit of the two guys who'd been standing behind them in the baggage drop off queue trying clumsily to chat up the girls. Unofficially, the kiss had gone much deeper, leaving her breathless and wet between the legs as she waved goodbye and watched her friend disappear through security. She'd thought about that kiss often since, wondered whether that had been the moment when she'd realized that she was definitely a girls' girl only, or whether she'd always known and just pushed it down in order not to ruin the friendships she'd had with the straight girls around her. Most specifically her friendship with Irene.

There had been some fooling around when they were little, of course. There were the sleepover games of playing pirates, taking turns playing the abducted victim overpowered by the roguish, handsome captain, rubbing their thighs against each other's crotches through the thin fabric of their nighties, vaguely aware of the pleasure of the sensation. But as they'd grown up the games had stopped, never to be talked about. They had been replaced by swooning over this film star or that teacher, and when anything at all had happened during nights spent together it was Marianne on her own, surreptitiously touching herself, wishing her fingers were stroking the girl soundly asleep next to her. She remembered one night in particular in their late teens, after a party, when she'd gone too far to stop, already nearing orgasm and she must have whimpered because

Irene had woken up and lightly caressed her shoulder, obviously thinking her friend was having a nightmare. Marianne had climaxed under the touch and pretended the convulsions had been part of a bad dream. After that, she had avoided sharing a bed with her friend for fear of not being able to contain herself, being caught, and ultimately losing her.

Then she had lost her anyway. Irene had been accepted to one of the top performing arts schools in America and had promptly gone with *that* kiss. A good actress and a striking beauty with a lush, broad mouth and wide set dark eyes, she had been destined for the screen and had arrived on that scene with a bang shortly after her graduation. Initially, they had remained in contact, but once Marianne had started vet school and Irene had begun conquering Hollywood, it had quickly fizzled out. Marianne had never expected to see Irene in real life again. Then, a few months ago, her friend had written to her out of the blue and invited Marianne to meet her in Rome, where Irene was currently filming. Marianne hadn't thought twice about it. And now she was here, nervous and excited, with her stomach doing back flips.

The couple in front of her sauntered away from the desk and the woman staffing it eyed Marianne with professional disdain from behind her perfect make up. While she filled out the paper work, Marianne looked at herself from the receptionist's point of view. She realized that in comparison to the rest of the guests she looked cheap in her Blundstone work boots, high street black denims, and supermarket bought bright blue cashmere jumper. She had debated the color at length with herself at the time of purchase, wondering why anyone producing anything in the most sensual wool the world had to offer would ruin it by choosing such a vile color, why they would deliberately make it look knock-off and cheap, but the love for the material had won out. She had been meaning to dye it but had simply not found the time before the trip. At the end of day, practically fluorescent or not, it had been one of the few passable items of clothing that she could wear on such an expensive outing. Her job as vet in residence at a small private zoo did afford her much happiness in life but not a large paycheck, and shopping for clothes had always been way down on her list of priorities. Also, despite her issues with it, she knew the color complemented both her blue eyes and pixie-short silver-white hair perfectly. Maybe she could get away with the dressed down look after all.

She squared her shoulders, pushed out her still firm and perky breasts and smiled confidently at the receptionist who took her completed form and credit card. Irene had offered to pay for the trip but Marianne had refused point blank. Yet as soon as the receptionist saw her name on the card her entire demeanor changed abruptly and she became sickeningly friendly.

"Ah, Miss Taylor, welcome. We have reserved room 606 for you." She lowered her voice. "It is only one floor down from the penthouse. Your friend is already here. She said to let you know to come up as soon as you are settled. Here's your key." She handed Marianne a plastic card. "If you take the amber elevator, your room will be on the right. We'll take care of your luggage."

"No need, thank you," replied Marianne curtly. She lifted her small suitcase and walked toward the lift doors with her heart thumping in her chest.

"Darling! Come in, come in. Sit down." The person flowing toward her in a silk caftan of deep, dark red bore little resemblance to the girl who had boarded the plane to New York all those years ago. She was skinny to the point of translucence with hollow cheeks that made her still remarkable eyes and mouth appear even bigger than

Marianne remembered. Her obviously botoxed forehead made her look startled and lifeless, like any other person whose facial expression had been rendered impotent by toxic intervention. She walked in a cloud of light, floral perfume, which she left hanging on Marianne's jumper after the illusion of a hug had been accomplished. Even before she took the offered seat on the plush couch, Marianne's anxious anticipation of this moment had already turned to grief as she realized that Irene, her Irene, did not exist any longer and had probably been exchanged for this shell of a person a long time ago.

She wept rivers of invisible tears as the afternoon wore on, even as she smiled and was introduced to David, Irene's current husband, whose occupation in the film business eluded Marianne, and a number of other people in Irene's entourage.

To be fair, she couldn't fault Irene as a hostess. She was attentive and chatty and seemed genuinely interested in hearing about Marianne's life at the zoo and some gossip from back home. Yet all the while she remained distant, a specter playing a role, sucking energy from the room and from the life that Marianne was telling her about. Half listening, not really engaging. By dinner time, Marianne felt drained, deflated, and ready to leave. She'd seen enough. She was also beginning to wonder why she had really been asked to come. There had been some mention of a biography in their correspondence and that it would be nice if Irene's old buddy could answer a few of the biographer's questions while in Rome, but none of the people in the room seemed poised with a pen.

Just then the door to the penthouse opened and a breeze of cold, crisp evening air swept into the room. The carrier whose clothes it clung to was a girl in her early twenties in turned-up faded blue jeans and a white men's singlet over which she'd thrown a lumberjack shirt in lieu of a jacket. Her straight black hair was short on one side and cut into a neat chin length bob on the other in the kind of asymmetrical fashion Marianne hadn't seen in three decades or so. The girl's whole style, down to the black Converse sneakers with different color laces, seemed to be a homage to the time of Marianne's school days. One look into her huge dark eyes told Marianne that if it had indeed been thirty years previously she would have fancied this newcomer to the penthouse something rotten. The girl smiled a broad, beautiful smile that illuminated the room, revealing a set of bright, slightly uneven teeth with large, almost goofy incisors.

"Sorry, I'm late." She addressed no one in particular as her eyes firmly made contact with Marianne's.

Marianne felt her pelvic muscles contract, exposing her lie—it wasn't that she *would* have fancied her, she *did*. She was beautiful and *real*. She stood out in this room of bland designs, exotic fruit bowls, and affectations like a three-dimensional object in an exhibition of oils on canvas.

"Nadja, honey, meet Marianne. Marianne, meet my daughter." Irene introduced them with an exasperated undertone that seemed to say "where have you been?"

For a moment Marianne wasn't sure whether she should stand up and shake the girl's hand or what the etiquette was, but an amused smirk twitched around the corner of the girl's mouth as she nodded in Marianne's direction.

"Nice boots," she remarked lightly and went to explore the nearest fruit bowl. The nod made Marianne feel giddy and she watched mesmerized as Nadja raided the bowl, extracting an apple from underneath the more ornamental offerings of pineapple, star fruit, and lychee. She searched for Marianne's eyes again and held her gaze while she sunk her teeth into the apple. Through the rush in her veins, Marianne was vaguely aware that Irene was still talking.

"—so Nadja will take you for dinner, if that is all right? I would have loved to come but she insists on doing all the interviews on her own. She's a clever girl, my daughter." Irene inserted a lofty laugh here. "And don't hold back when answering her questions—just be kind. Off you go, darlings."

A silent elevator journey later, they crossed the lobby and hit the streets. Marianne's head was still swimming with the proximity of the girl who'd stood so close to her in the lift that she could smell her. *Her.* Not some cream or perfume but *her*, a sweet, slightly tangy smell mixed with the apple she'd continued crunching on the way down. She'd eaten all of it, core included, and was now twirling the stalk between her fingers as they stood on the steps in front of the hotel. Rome was alive with night revelers, tourists, and cats.

"You really want to go to a restaurant?" Nadja asked.

Marianne looked around. "Are we… Don't we need to wait for someone? I mean, haven't you got a bodyguard or something?"

Nadja laughed. "Nope. Did you know Irene Wicklow had a daughter?"

Marianne shook her head in response.

"See, I don't exist." Nadja flashed her a smile. "Best thing she's ever done for me. Come on, I don't really want to sit in a stuffy restaurant. There's this brilliant food market. It's open until midnight and it sells the best antipasti. Tiny, tender octopuses, olives stuffed with almonds, slivers of virgin thigh ham, that sorta thing. We could get us a picnic and find us a nice ruin to sit in. You eat food, right? You look like you eat food." She stopped herself, looking apologetic. "Not that I'm saying you're fat. You're not. You're beautiful. What I mean is, you're slender but you don't look friggin' emaciated like that lot up there."

She looked at Marianne almost pleadingly, and Marianne found herself getting lost in those big eyes again, wanting that look, wanting to be the source of that look, wanting this girl to plead and beg with her. She snapped out of it, clearing her throat. "Sounds great."

They had to wrestle a number of cats for space in the ruin of an old bath house, but once they had staked their claim and the animals had realized the intruders were not sharing their dinner, they left them more or less alone. It was Marianne's first time in the city and its bewildering mix of architectural layers—new buildings at street level designed to look old, interspersed with many large pits of excavated antique ruins that looked timeless—fascinated and repulsed her at the same time. Their hiding place in the ruin below street level meant she looked up at the people walking by above them. She could feel Nadja's eyes resting on her.

"Odd place, isn't it?" the girl stated, picking a squid ring out of one of the many little tubs between them and sticking it on the tip of her tongue before flicking it into her mouth, chewing, and swallowing. "I always feel I can virtually taste the oppression when I'm here. Two thousand years of Church rule, you know."

It hadn't been particularly eloquent but Marianne knew exactly what the girl meant. She could feel it, too. And she knew that once upon a time under that very rule she would have been burned at the stake for the way she was staring at the breasts opposite her now, at the nipples pushing through the fabric of the singlet, erect in the cool air.

"So." Nadja sat up all businesslike. "Is it okay if I ask you some questions?"

"Ah, yes," Marianne replied, feeling caught out and ashamed. "I was distracted earlier. You're writing a book on your mother's life, is that right?"

"No, I'm not," Nadja said, with a grin.

"I thought she said…" Marianne didn't finish the sentence because suddenly the girl was leaning toward her, large eyes looking deeply into Marianne's.

Nadja's tongue licked her lips clean before she spoke again. "Yeah, that's what she thinks. That's what she *wants*. But I'm not. I was gonna, but, you know, here's the problem: as long as I don't exist I can sit here with the most beautiful woman I've ever laid eyes on, inches away from kissing her, and nobody gives a fuck, right? If I write that book, I'm suddenly Irene fucking Wicklow's daughter, wannabe writer and media interest. Like, *forever*. Fuck that." She laughed and withdrew, leaving Marianne breathing heavily and with her heart racing. Nadja leaned back on her elbows, looking up at the stars. "But I haven't said anything 'cause it's kinda fun playing along. Gotta meet all these folks who knew her when she still had, you know, substance. I hardly remember her like that. I have moments from when I was very little, from when before dad saw the light and got the hell out of that industry. He was an actor also. Clever man. Got out before it could eat him up, and bought a ranch where we breed wool pigs. Ever had wool pig? Delicious. So, tell me, you were my mum's *experimental* friend, right?"

Marianne blushed. "I don't know what you mean."

"Yeah you do. Don't worry, every straight woman's got one." Nadja grinned. "I think."

Marianne swallowed hard. "How did you know?"

Nadja let her head loll sideways to look at Marianne askance with a smirk curling up the corners of her mouth. "Easy. I interview sixteen people for this imaginary book of hers. You're the only one where she takes me aside beforehand and tells me to keep my hands off. You do the math." The smirk transformed into a big, luscious smile and she turned her body to move in on Marianne once more, raising an amused eyebrow. "Seems she knows my type. And I'm guessing she knows yours, too."

Her lips came down on Marianne's—soft, large, and hungry. For a split second, Marianne wrestled with herself then gave up and opened her mouth meeting the tongue that was darting in between her lips with her own, entwining with it, letting it come in deeper and ravish her. She could feel her juices beginning to flow, a straight line of fire from her tongue, down her throat, through her chest and spreading tentacles from her heart into her belly. When she came up for air she turned the tables, taking Nadja by the back of her neck, bending her backward and sticking her tongue deep into the girl's throat. Nadja groaned with pleasure under the onslaught. Marianne retracted from her mouth and began tracing kisses along her jaw line instead, pure arousal shooting through her every time Nadja moaned quietly. Marianne brought a hand up to slip in under the singlet. To her delight the girl wore no bra. The breast felt a lot fuller than the look under the singlet had promised. Marianne had expected small and firm like her own—instead she got soft and malleable, perfect to knead, the only hard bit being the erect center pressing against her palm. When her mouth came to rest on the side of Nadja's neck and she began sucking the soft jugular tissue, she let a thumb flick over the stiff nipple. Nadja groaned.

"Harder," she whispered.

Marianne let go of the neck, looked down at the beauty in her arms squirming behind closed eyes under her touch.

"Open your eyes," she demanded and the girl followed the command. Looking deeply into the other's inflated pupils, Marianne took the nipple between two fingers, and pinched it. "Like this?" she asked playfully.

Nadja bucked gently in response and a shudder went through Marianne. The girl's eyes seemed to be turning even darker than before with pure lust, and although Marianne wanted to kiss her again, what she wanted more than anything was to delve down into her juices, watching as she fingered her lightly until she came. She wanted to drown in these eyes when the climax rocked through this perfect, sweet girl. She took her hand off Nadja's breast and ran a finger along the top of the belt holding up Nadja's jeans. A whimper from the other was all she needed as invitation. She unbuckled it and let her hand wander in, cupping Nadja's silky mound in her hand. The girl pushed up hard against her palm, her eyes pleading for pressure. Marianne gave her what she desired and then, quick as a snake, she pushed her middle finger between the folds and into the well of Nadja's juices. The girl was overflowing, her wetness instantly dripping out through her curls onto Marianne's hand. All thoughts of gentle caressing abandoned, Marianne pushed three fingers up the girl's cunt and started massaging her there while rotating the ball of her hand on her nub.

"Kiss me," Nadja whispered.

Marianne complied, plundering the other's mouth while still working her rhythmically under her hand. She could feel contractions around her fingers with every twist of tongue around tongue. She withdrew from the kiss, eliciting a disappointed whimper from Nadja.

"More," she panted.

"I want to see you come," Marianne replied, locking onto Nadja's eyes, intensifying the pressure on her clit and beginning to slide her fingertips up and down the wall of Nadja's insides with increased speed.

"Look at me, baby, come for me," she whispered, hardly recognizing her own voice.

The girl bucked her hips, hurrying the fingers inside her along with every lift of her pelvis. Finally, her muscles contracted rapidly around Marianne's fingers as she climaxed soundlessly, her eyes still locked with Marianne's. Marianne knew, there and then, that for many years to come that look, those eyes, would be with her during lonely nights. That the memory of this moment would drive her wild, over and over again. She extracted her hand from the girl's crotch and rested it on her tummy for a moment, still gazing at her.

Suddenly, Nadja broke eye contact, looked over Marianne's shoulder and sat up abruptly, pushing Marianne off in the process. "We need to go."

Marianne looked around at what the girl had seen and in the same instant heard the two men Nadja had spotted, leaning against the railings above them and staring down into the ruin, shout something in Italian. It sounded rude and angry.

The two women gathered their things hectically and scrambled up the steps from the bathhouse. When they arrived at street level the men were still there, shouting at them furiously. Ignoring them, Marianne and Nadja walked off hurriedly, back toward the hotel. They didn't speak until they had almost reached the entrance.

They stopped outside at the bottom of the stairs. After a moment's somberness during which Nadja contemplated her shoes and Marianne spread the fingers that still carried the other girl's tangy scent across her mouth and nose, they began giggling simultaneously.

Nadja smiled. "That was fun."

"Hm." Marianne smiled back.

"Can I come up with you?" the girl asked almost shyly.

Marianne hesitated, then gently shook her head. "I don't think so. Remember, hands off. We shouldn't have…" Her voice trailed off, tears forming in the back of her throat. This girl was perfect. All she had ever dreamed of. She wanted her, she wanted to know her, hear her thoughts, her secrets, her lies. She wanted to look into these eyes for a long, long time to come.

Nadja nodded, still looking down.

"I know. You're right," she conceded after a moment, then looked up with a devilish glint in her eye, beckoning Marianne with one finger to lean an ear in by her mouth. "But," she whispered into it, her breath making shivers run down Marianne's spine, "you know, I can think of a hell of a lot of things to do with a pretty lady like you that don't involve any hands *at all.*"

SHELTER
JEAN ROBERTA

I didn't intend to open my door for anyone at 1:00 a.m., but I couldn't resist looking through the peep-hole to see who was there.

Cheekbones, long nose, full lips, short dark hair, direct gaze, evil grin. Unmistakably Renee Sharp.

I opened my apartment door before I could stop myself. "You can't stay here," I told her, stepping back to let her in.

She accepted my unspoken invitation. "It's good to see you too, Anna baby. I thought about you while I was away."

A year in prison hadn't deprived her of energy. What was sex like in the joint? I didn't want to think about it, but I wanted to know.

The woman was leaner than I remembered, more compact. She could take me down. I knew I should call the police, but I couldn't do it.

"You don't have to call the cops, girlfriend. I'm not here to steal your stuff or hurt you in any way. Unless..." She let her sentence hang in the air while she looked down from my eyes to the thin cotton nightshirt that barely covered my naked breasts. I could feel my nipples jiggling with my breathing, and I buttoned my cardigan from top to bottom. Renee snickered.

"You don't really want the cops to know I'm here, Anna. No one has to know you ever met me. In the morning I'll be gone like a wet dream."

"Renee–" I started.

"Friends call me Razor." She pulled five chocolate-brown Canadian hundred-dollar bills out of the frayed pocket of her denim jacket and laid them on my hall table.

Oh my god. I still wasn't sure exactly what she wanted from me, but she obviously thought I was for sale.

I was glad she had shut the door behind her, even though that meant I was trapped in my apartment with a criminal. "Razor-blade," I said. "Mack the Knife, whatever you're called now, I don't need your money. Some of us have legal jobs."

She grinned. I didn't touch the stack of bills, and neither did she. "Well, could I get a drink in this fine establishment, Anna baby?"

I knew I wouldn't be able to sleep as long as she was my guest, and I had already shown her a kind of welcome. "Tea," I said. "The bar is closed."

"Give me the regular Red Rose or whatever," she ordered. "I'm not into that herbal shit." No surprise there.

I led the way to my little kitchen, where jolly wallpaper images of vegetables dancing with salt and pepper shakers surrounded my shiny appliances. When I felt Renee's hot gaze on my back and bare legs the coziness of my rented nest made me cringe.

I poured filtered water into the kettle as Renee settled her ass on one of my kitchen chairs.

There was so much I could have said to her but I couldn't find the words. I suspected her of using silence as a weapon against me. "Excuse me," I muttered. I dashed into my bedroom to pull on a pair of jeans, as though comfortable denim on my legs could add some normalcy to the scene.

I flashed back to a scene from grade school: Miss Chatmore's Grade Five classroom. We were learning about slavery, Harriet Tubman, and the Underground Railway that led refugees to freedom in Canada. I imagined a long tunnel with trains running through it, like the Metro in Toronto, where my grandparents lived.

Small, skinny Renee wore the same faded T-shirt with the same ventilated jeans day after day. Everyone knew she lived with foster-parents and a constantly changing family of temporary brothers and sisters.

"Jason, would you turn down the lights, please?" The teacher always called on Jason for such important tasks. Renee was sitting near him at the back of the room. She sulked visibly.

An image of the night sky filled the screen at the front of the class. Miss Chatmore used a pointer. "This constellation is called the Big Dipper because it looks like a long-handled cup. Runaway slaves called it the Drinking Gourd and they looked for it when they traveled by night because it pointed the way north to Canada. Once they crossed the border, they were free."

"Hey, can we see the Big Dipper from here?" For once, Renee sounded eager.

"Hey" was not our teacher's favorite form of address. "What do we say in the classroom?"

"Miss Chatmore!" sang a chorus of good kids, including me.

She smiled. "Yes, we can see the Big Dipper at night from here." She sounded like a fairy granting a wish. "Why don't we all look for it tonight?"

Renee glowed. A few days later, she gave a class presentation on the Underground Railway and the stars that showed the way north. She told us she had seen them from her own back yard. Escape was a topic that never bored her.

In Grade Six, Renee came to school wearing makeup, and was sent to the principal's office for carrying a knife. Her name came to sound like a dirty joke, especially when boys said it.

Like the Cheshire Cat in a picture-book in my parents' library, Renee gradually stopped appearing in school until she disappeared altogether.

The kettle screamed like an old-fashioned train whistle, calling me back to my kitchen in the present. "Anna." My name in her mouth sounded much like hers in the mouths of our classmates, so many years ago. "Do you remember when we met in the club?"

My debut in the local lesbian bar had not been a brilliant coming out. Fresh from a stinging breakup with a guy who had found someone else, I agreed to go for a drink with a group of women in the trades, all buddies of my coworker Crystal in the government telephone company. I was surrounded by no-nonsense women who knew how to fix things. I wanted to seem like one of them.

I didn't think I could attract a date, male or female, if I acted like the cerebral writer-type I really was. One of Crystal's friends, a deep-voiced welder called P.G., was flirting with me, bringing me drinks and gazing into my eyes. From time to time, she glanced discreetly into my cleavage, and I almost stopped wishing I could lose ten or twenty pounds.

Then Renee was standing in front of me. "I wondered when you'd get here, Anna," she said just loudly enough to be heard by everyone at my table, over the crack of pool cues hitting balls, and the buzz of talk and laughter. "You like girls?" That was a dare.

"I'm not—" I started. But what was I? I had always played it safe, and that hadn't gotten me anywhere. "Yeah," I told her. "I like girls."

"Come with me," she said. Just like that. And I stood up and followed, not wanting to seem like a chicken. And maybe I felt as if I owed her something for all the times I had laughed at the latest gossip about her and sided with her enemies.

She brought me to the back door. "I got some good weed," she told me. "I know the guy who grows it. You want to get high?"

I was nervous, but I wasn't a complete newbie at this. "Sure," I answered.

So we stood in the fresh spring air, leaning against the building, and passed a joint back and forth while watching stars twinkling in a clear sky. "Anna," she told me. "You always seemed like you knew what you wanted, like you were going somewhere."

Well, so did she. But I couldn't say aloud where she always seemed to be headed: straight to hell, with no detours. Whenever someone opened the back door of the club, light poured out onto her spiky, indigo hair and the tattoos on her arms. One was of a snake winding around one of her biceps as if it wanted to hiss in her ear. I could smell the faint tang of her sweat.

"I got a university degree last year," I bragged, hinting that she should do something similar with her life.

Renee gave me a condescending laugh. "I dropped out of high school, baby. It don't really make much difference now. I make more money than any of our teachers. There's so many career opportunities in this town." This wisecrack tickled her so much that she bent over to let a big, rude guffaw float out into the wicked night.

I didn't dare ask which career path she had chosen.

And then she was kissing me, her hot lips on mine and her tongue sliding in between them. I didn't want to admit that I had never done this before with a woman, and I didn't want her to stop. She stroked my shoulder-length golden-brown hair (my one physical feature that seemed adequate to me), and possessively massaged my scalp. "It's like silk thread," she told me in a low voice.

Tingles flowed from my head through the rest of my body. I wondered whether she always used the same technique.

She cupped one of my breasts. "We can't do this here," I warned. I wasn't sure where I wanted to go. As it turned out, I didn't have to decide.

The door opened, and two women stepped through. "Anna, are you coming back to our table?" Crystal obviously wanted to get me away from Renee, and didn't care how Renee felt about that.

"Play a game of pool with me," P.G. chimed in.

Renee seemed amused that I was being rescued. "Go," she said to me, ignoring the other two.

My panties were wet, but I didn't want to make a scene. "I'll give you my number," I promised Renee.

"I got it," came the deadpan reply. "You don't keep that stuff private." *Social media*, I thought. *I'm not careful enough with my information.*

Back in the bar, P.G. easily beat me at pool. She must have noticed I wasn't a worthy opponent. As soon as our game ended, a blond fan applauded the winner, and P.G. swaggered over to talk to her. I drifted back to Crystal's table, where I jumped into a vehement discussion about discrimination against women in occupations that required safety gear.

For the next month, I waited in vain for a phone call, email, or text message from a dykey suitor. I told myself that if Renee or P.G. invited me out, I would politely decline. The whole point of "coming out," I thought, was to find a soul-mate.

My thirty days of suspense ended when Renee got five minutes of fame in the media plus a year in prison when she was convicted of selling stolen goods. The charge surprised me. I had assumed she was selling weed to lesbians, since the government had loosened the law, and the police seemed more interested in chasing harder drugs.

I imagined Renee as a Godmother of organized crime. But in that case, I thought, she probably wouldn't have been caught. I wondered if she were involved in the sex trade, either as a call girl or a pimp.

Now here I was, sipping tea with her in my kitchen in the dead of night. "You don't dye your hair, do you?" she asked. I didn't see where this question was leading.

"No. I like it the way it is."

"D'you have any tattoos or piercings, girl?"

"No." The possibility that she was planning to search my whole body to verify my answer sent a pang straight to my already-awakened clit.

"You're really straight, aren't you?" Renee was smirking.

"I have a girlfriend now." This was somewhat true, though our relationship was more of a friendship with benefits than anything else. Nicole often talked about her ex, a bass-player in an all-female rock band. I suspected that their volatile, beer-soaked affair was not completely over.

"I didn't mean like that. I know you like girls, Anna." Was my physical reaction to her that obvious?

But she clearly thought I was naive. She wasn't planning to tell me why she needed to hide out in my apartment. The thought flashed into my mind that trained police officers might not be the most dangerous people who wanted to find her.

"Razor," I called her. It was what she wanted to be called, and it didn't cost me anything to say it. "What kind of trouble are you in? You must have done something."

She stood up and took off her jacket, as though preparing for action. "Here's the thing, babe." She walked around the table and held me by both hands. "You don't know—well, I'll just say it wouldn't be good

37

for you to know. Knowing too much means getting involved. Be glad you're out of it."

It wasn't the answer I wanted, but I responded by unbuttoning my cardigan. I was willing to take a risk.

"Anna," she sighed on an exhale as she smoothly pulled me to my feet. My breasts were mashed against hers, with only my nightshirt and her T-shirt between us. I noted that her wardrobe hadn't changed much since she was a child. "I've wanted you for years. Now I'm going to do something about it."

Then her insistent mouth was on mine, and I could smell weed in her hot, dark hair. I wasn't sure if I could trust my senses, or if I was just remembering that magical kiss we shared outside the club, before she went away.

We came up for air. "You've got curves in all the right places," she told me. "Don't believe anyone who says you have to lose weight." At the moment, I felt as if I could melt into a puddle.

"Baby girl, I'm not a rapist. Tell me you want me, or I'll let you go."

"I want you, Ren—Razor. This is crazy, but I don't want you to stop."

I saw the fierce gleam in her eyes, and a lightning-bolt of fear flashed up from my cunt. Or perhaps it was a pang of need. I wanted her to fuck her recklessness into me, and I wanted her to give me her pain along with it, since I had never given her any comfort before.

Why shouldn't I get fucked good, for once? I asked myself in the syntax of the streets. Extreme sports and dangerous occupations were not my thing, and I knew they never would be, but I wanted to live on the edge for one razor-sharp night, and feel such intense pleasure that all my most sensitive parts would light up like a constellation of stars.

I reminded myself that I also wanted to find out how Renee wanted to be touched, and what moves could crack her shell.

"You're a fashion statement," she sniggered, "but I want to see what I'm getting." Like a mother, she pulled the sleeves of my cardigan down my arms, and dropped it on my kitchen floor. My nightshirt cut off my vision as it was pulled up over my head.

I stood naked above the waist, and I knew without looking that my nipples were very red and very hard, like fruit waiting to be plucked. I squeezed my thighs together, and squeezed my cunt-muscles. All this unaccustomed exercise made things worse, or better.

Renee unbuttoned my jeans, and brought my hands to the waistband to show what she wanted me to do. I obediently pushed the denim down my legs, and stepped free. I wasn't wearing panties, so my brown bush was exposed to her gaze. I was completely vulnerable, and I knew that no sensible woman would choose to be in this predicament, but I felt as joyful as a child.

"You next," I told her. She grinned, and pulled off her T-shirt, and sports bra, then slid out of her jeans and panties together. Her clothes were added to mine. Somehow the stark-naked Renee still looked capable of defending herself. She had a certain deer-like grace, and her tattoos and piercings made her look like a fantasy character. Besides the snake on one arm, she had a Celtic bracelet around the other, and a pierced belly-button that seemed to hold a ball-bearing for mechanical emergencies. There was a red rose on her small left breast, a butterfly on the opposite thigh, and a green marijuana leaf on one ankle. And then there were blurry blue prison tattoos in various places.

I didn't have much time to study her anatomy. Renee pressed herself against my back, and reached around to squeeze, pinch and torment both my nipples at once. I moaned, and she laughed. "D'you have any toys, girlfriend?"

"A silicone dildo," I bragged, "never used. And a butt-plug." I had gone to a home sex-toy party with Nicole.

"No nipple-clips?" She sounded disappointed. "Your tits could really use them. You need to write a shopping-list of supplies. I hope you've got lube, or I'll have to get the butter out of your fridge."

"I have lube," I told her as well as I could while she was mauling my breasts. They had never received this much attention before, and I could feel them swelling.

I thought Renee would order me to bring her everything in my apartment that could possibly be used as a sex-toy or instrument of torture, but instead, she pushed me to the edge of my kitchen table, swept the teacups aside, and pushed me forward until my hot breasts were pressed against the cool plastic of my tablecloth. I could feel her crotch against my ass-cheeks, and then one of her determined fingers slid down my crack to my anus, and tickled it. I couldn't help wiggling.

"I bet you've never been ass-fucked." It wasn't a question.

"No," I mumbled.

A wicked laugh accompanied her exploring finger as it went down, seeking out my messy wet lips, and the alert clit that was now easy to find. She entered my cave with one finger that circled my ticklish flesh, and added another finger, and another. Her fingers filled me, but she was still in the exploring phase.

"D'you wanna get fisted?"

"Not yet," I blurted. I was afraid, but curious.

Renee laughed as her united fingers pushed in deep, then withdrew. My cunt responded, and I pushed back. Together, we worked up a good fucking rhythm. I groaned shamelessly, but I knew I wouldn't be able to come if I couldn't touch myself. Meanwhile, she would grow bored, if not tired.

"I want you to come for me," she said, and that did it. My whole cunt erupted like firecrackers in the night sky. I squeezed and squeezed around her fingers.

"Good girl!" she snickered. "You're so wet. You'd be popular on the street." I hoped she was joking.

I felt lightheaded when I straightened up and looked at her. I was about to wrap my arms around her when she slapped my ass, not lightly. "Hey? Would you like to turn tricks for me? You could make money, save up, buy your own house."

This proposal was too much for me to digest in my current state. "Make money from guys?" I asked. "I doubt it."

"Hey," she said again, and repeated the slap on my ass. "I know more about the business than you, and guys would eat you up. If you could learn to give good blow jobs, you could make a fortune." She slapped me again, and this time, the sting was sharper. "You like this too, don't you?"

"Yes," I admitted. I felt I had nothing left to lose.

"Come in here." She pulled me by the hand into my own front room, where she seated herself on the armless chair that matched my grey velvet chesterfield. "Bend over my lap like this, bad girl," she told me, placing me in position.

Whap! "You need this, don't you?" A few minutes before, I would never have guessed that I needed any such thing, but the sparks of pain on my skin sent ripples all through my ass and my cunt, and I didn't want the feelings to fade until I had reached my limit.

Whap! "What do you need, Anna?"

"A spanking," I answered. "This."

She spanked me until I whimpered. "Ow," I whined, hating my wimpiness, but not wanting any more pain. "That hurts." My ass felt blistered.

"Okay, that's enough for now. You did well for your first time, baby." First time? Was she planning more lessons? And would I take them? I decided to ponder this later.

"I think you need the dildo now, don't you?" This event was turning out to be a carnival of sex.

"It's in my nightstand," I told her. "Come into my bedroom."

And so Renee laid me on my back on the quilt that my parents gave me for Christmas, and I spread my legs while she buckled the harness that held the dildo in place at her crotch. She looked bizarrely androgynous, but I didn't mind.

"Do you want me to be a man?" she asked. "A stalker dude that breaks into your place to mess with you while you're sleeping?"

"No," I told her honestly. "I want you to be yourself. Razor."

She guided the head of the artificial cock into my cunt with care, but when she was in all the way, she began to pump with enthusiasm. She rode me hard, and I bucked and moaned. Just when I thought I wouldn't be able to reach a climax, she managed to tickle my clit, and that did it. "Oh!" I yelled, not caring who might hear me.

Renee looked smug as she took off my dildo, which I would always associate with her from that night forward. "I could use it on you," I suggested.

A wince like a cold breeze passed over her face. "No, girlfriend, that's not my thing. How good are you at the oral arts?"

"I'll show you," I bragged.

My guest stretched herself out on my quilt, then sat up with a grunt of annoyance. "Wet spot." I ran to the bathroom to bring a dry towel to spread under her.

Renee spread her knees apart, then brought them together, teasing me. I held her thighs, and noticed how firm they were compared to mine. I lowered my head between them, and inhaled the aroma of her crotch. In the dim light, I could imagine steam rising from her dark, matted bush.

With a stiff tongue, I licked her inner lips and her quivering clit. I sucked it into my mouth and nibbled it, very gently, with my teeth.

"Easy there, cowgirl."

I raised my head. "I'm not going to hurt you. Unless you ask."

Her taste was rich and salty. I licked, sucked, and poked with a pointed tongue, and at length, I got the reaction I was hoping for. "That's it!" She pushed her clit rhythmically deeper into my mouth, and I took that as a sign that I should persist with my sucking. When she exploded, I felt it immediately.

We lay in each other's arms, sautéed in our distinct female fluids. "That was a good start," she told me. "Round One. There's so much more I want to do with you."

The prospect of a night without sleep to be followed by a day in the office was not what alarmed me most. "I need to know," I said, "who's looking for you."

"Don't worry about it, Anna."

"Razor, I'm not an idiot. You told me I don't keep my information private enough. The cops could track you here anyway, but I don't think they're the only ones on your tail."

"Smart girl." Her words of praise sent chills up my spine. I guessed that she had stolen something from the Warriors, as they were known before they became a chapter in a much bigger, older, and deadlier gang that ran illegal businesses in every city in North America. She might have "stolen" some biker's girlfriend, since I was sure bikers thought of women as property.

Renee wasn't stupid; I knew that. She just didn't think ahead because she had always expected her life to be nasty, brutish and short, with occasional starbursts of pleasure. Her future had been described to her when she was too young to think of other options, and she had never seriously questioned her fate.

I could foresee the item in the newspaper: *"Anna Marie Belleville, age 24, shot execution-style in her apartment Wednesday morning at 6:00 a.m. Police are investigating."* There would be no leads. Alternatively, Renee and I could be found together, naked and dead. Speculation would run wild: had it been a Romeo-and-Juliet type of murder-suicide? Had we both run afoul of a crazy person with a grudge? Either way, the gang would be beyond suspicion, or at least beyond arrest.

"Are the Warriors looking for you?"

"They're not the Warriors any more, but yeah, probably. Those fuckers couldn't find their own asses." She laughed.

She was wrong. I couldn't have been surer of that. "Razor, you're not safe here. You have to leave right away."

Anger hardened her face. "Anna, you're scared of your own shadow. You're still the same spoiled baby girl you were in school."

Okay, I thought. *Fair enough, but my wimpy ways will keep me alive longer than your addiction to trouble.* "I don't care what you think of me," I said aloud. "Something is going down. You can't stay here because it isn't safe for either of us. You have to leave."

I jumped out of bed and rushed into my kitchen, where I picked up my random ensemble of nightshirt, cardigan, and jeans, and pulled them on. Renee followed me, radiating electricity.

"Fine." She angrily pulled on her clothes. "I need a cigarette anyway, and I bet you don't want anyone to smoke in here."

"Right," I agreed. "I wonder if it would mean anything to you if I say I want you to live a long, healthy life?"

"Fuck you, Anna." Her voice was dangerously quiet.

"You did. I appreciate it." I couldn't save her, and apparently she couldn't save herself.

"You know what?" she demanded. "I don't envy you. You're living in your own cage."

So are we all, I thought.

Renee and I shared a bruising kiss after I grabbed her for a farewell hug. "I won't come back here," she told me.

"I know. I hope you remember what I said."

She softened for an instant. "Have some good times for me, babe." Renee opened my door, stepped forward, and closed it behind her. I made sure the door was locked.

That was the last time I saw her. For the next few nights, I dozed with a butcher knife under my pillow. Footsteps stomped through the hallway of my building, fists pounded my door, fingers pushed my buzzer, and masculine voices ordered me to open up. Each time, I stayed in bed and tried not to breathe until the sounds went away.

I never told anyone about that night, not even Nicole. Two weeks later, I could sleep through the night without interruptions, and I could get through a day of work without feeling like a coffee-guzzling zombie.

I haven't heard any news about Renee for several months. On clear nights, I can see the stars through my picture window, and they always give me hope.

UNGODLY OURS
ALLISON WONDERLAND

Lesbians 1:6

"Is it okay for Christians to listen to that 'Jew Day-O' song from *Beetlejuice*? Or is that, like, against your religion or something?"

"Judeo," Mr. Ferguson says, moving a giant spoon around a pot of pasta. Then he spells it out for us, and laughs a lot between letters. "You like that song, don't you, Nadine?"

My head goes up and down like a dashboard Jesus.

"Well, it drives me bananas," Mr. Ferguson shares, setting two bowls onto the table. He chimp-grins at his daughter.

Rebecca giggles then gasps, her mouth stretched open like that fish symbol us Lord lovers love. She gapes at the telephone-shaped pasta in her dish. "We can't eat elbow noodles in the kitchen. We have to keep our elbows off the table, remember?"

"Don't get saucy with me, young lady," Mr. Ferguson teases, ruffling Rebecca's hair. It is bright blond, almost yellow, like Funshine Bear, which I'm not allowed to play with anymore because Daddy decided it's demonic, whatever that means. "You can eat in the family room, but please don't monkey around."

Rebecca scoops up our bowls. "Yes, sir," she says, and I wonder if it sounds that strange when I say it to my father. "Come on, Nadine, follow me."

"My daddy says always let the Lord lead," I mumble, following Rebecca into the family room.

"My daddy says everyone has to take turns, so I'll take my turn at leading today and the Lord can take a load off."

I should probably say something in His defense, to show I'm faithful and committed and all that good stuff, but to be honest, I'm... well, I'm... I'm bored with the Lord, okay?

There, I said it. Don't worry—it's not a sin yet. Satan's the bad guy here. He's the one who put that thought in my noodle. But if I dwell on it, if I let Satan stay there, then it's a sin. So I have to evict him pronto.

"So, Rebecca, do you accept God the Father as your Lord and Master?"

Rebecca stops chewing and stares at me. "I have a father," she reminds me. "Are you saying it's okay for me to have two dads?"

She sounds shocked. Also like she thinks that what I said is really neat, even though that's not what I think I said. "I don't... think so."

Rebecca doesn't have two dads. She's got one. As for mommies, she's got none. That's why she and her dad were at church once upon a time—he thought when Rebecca got old enough to understand what happened to her mother, God would do an awesome job of making her feel better.

But Rebecca said God's imaginary and she's too old for imaginary friends and God makes a lousy one anyway because He never answered her prayers and is the worst listener ever. I told her God listens with His heart, not His ears, but she didn't want to hear it.

After a while, Rebecca and her daddy quit going to church. I thought my parents wouldn't let us be friends anymore, but they said I shouldn't give up on her, that she needs God's guidance now more than—

"Ever listen to someone when they're talking to you? Hello in there!" Rebecca knocks on my head like she thinks it's a door. "Do you wanna watch a movie? Pick: *My Girl* or *Teenage Mutant Ninja Turtles*."

That gives me the giggles.

"What?"

"When that *Mutant* movie came out, my parents wouldn't let us see it, and when I asked my brother Nelson why, he said it's because our family cares more about Fertile Power than Turtle Power."

"What does fertile mean?"

"He said it's like having an active imagination, except you don't use your brain."

Rebecca huffs. "I like using my brain. You do too, okay?"

"Okay."

Rebecca smiles. She's got a gap in hers, in the same place I do. I smile back. We're sitting on the cherry wood floor, our legs twisted into soft pretzels and our knees touching, like the pretzels were placed too close together when they went into the oven and so the dough got stuck together.

She moves away for a minute, to put the video in. She picks the one about the girl whose mother died. I don't mind. I just have to hold her hand a lot during it, that's all, which is fine because her hands aren't boring like mine. Like right now, the left one's got a dinosaur band-aid on the back of it, there's purple paint on her nails, and she's wearing a plastic pink spider on her finger.

It's got long, creepy legs that tickle when we get to the part of the movie where the boy says grownups have to get married and then he and the girl smooch together. Later, he dies, so I guess he doesn't have to get married after all. I hope I don't have to die to get out of getting married. I close my eyes and pray that God never gives me the kinds of wrong feelings for boys that the homosexual people have.

When I make myself see again, I see Rebecca looking straight at me, so I look straight back. Her eyes are brown like a rocking horse and she has pretty lashes like on a plastic pony. "Do you know what it means to be fruitful and multiply?" she asks suddenly and before I can even think or blink, she says, "It means eat an apple a day and do your times tables."

"Got it."

When the movie is over, Rebecca pushes the coffee table forward and says, "Let's act out a story from the Bible."

This is not weird. There are lots of Bible stories that Rebecca likes: Noah's Ark, the Good Samaritan, Joseph and his jealous brothers. But we haven't done any of those in a while, so I know exactly which one she's going to pick.

"Let's be Ruth and Naomi."

The Ruth and Naomi story is about two women who take care of each other after their husbands croak. The story is sort of like that hymn, "Wherever He Leads, I'll Go," except in their case, it's wherever Naomi leads, Ruth'll go. Ruth even told her so, because they are the best of friends.

"I'll be Ruth," Rebecca says. She is always Ruth. "Nadine, you'll be Naomi."

We start the story, skipping over the bad parts to get to the good ones, like when Ruth is making all these promises to stay with Naomi forever—or at least until they're R.I.P.-ing.

Rebecca grabs my arm and kisses it all over the place, like the boy and girl do in the movie to practice their kissing, except they practice on themselves and not on each other. Her lips make silly noises and feel funny.

"Naomi, my darling, would you mind if I spent the rest of my life with you?"

I sigh really loudly, like this is gonna be the biggest sacrifice ever. "If you must."

"My prayers have been answered!" Rebecca gushes, clinging to me like goopy green Turtle ooze.

I cling back.

I can't stop smiling.

Even after we're done oozing.

Even after we say, "The End."

Even after I go home.

Mommy asks, "What are you smiling about?"

I say nothing.

But then, because us kids are supposed to speak when spoken to, I say, "Nothing."

I am lying. I just don't know how or why.

I say sorry to God anyway.

He'll forgive me.

God forgives all grinners.

Lesbians 2:12

Mom is big-bellied again. Dad says our family is getting another blessing, but I'm pretty positive the only thing inside Mom's uterus is a baby.

Speaking of which, I just started my... menses.

My period and I are not exactly on the best of terms and probably won't be for a while, if ever. You could say there's bad blood between us. You could also say—and practically everybody does—that blood is thicker than water, which means one day I'll have to stop thinking of eggs as just something to put ketchup on.

Because now that I'm a menstruating woman, I can be fruitful and multiply, the very definition of womanhood.

Oh, man.

Menses.

Menstruation.

Why is everything always about men?

We praise Him, pray to Him, sing hymns to Him. He even has birth control over us, because God forbid a *wo*man should have control over the number of babies she gives birth to.

Sorry, I'm sorry, it's just... Maybe my parents are right. Maybe Rebecca has been a bad influence on me. I mean, ignorance is bliss, right? And now that I'm not all that ignorant, I'm also not all that blissful.

See, my parents view the world as Bible verses us versus them. Them being people who don't share our values. The Fergusons are them people, which is why Mom and Dad think I should spend less time with Rebecca, now that I've reached a delicate age. For one thing, my folks have become terribly troubled that the Fergusons are, as Rebecca put it, churchgoing going gone. They're concerned about her spiritual wellbeing, and also her... sec appeal. Sec as in secular, and, well, she's liberated me, *not* corrupted me, although I guess it's a lot like love and marriage: you can't have one without the other.

That goes for Rebecca and me, too. We're like... We're like Ruth and Naomi. We can't be split up. We won't. Not by anybody but God, and if God disapproves of Rebecca, then He'll remove her from my life. But He won't. He wouldn't. God would never do something so unbelievably unmerciful.

But my father is not God. So I make a wise appeal, being careful to give my parents gratitude and not attitude. I acknowledge their concerns, remind them that I respect their wishes and their authority, and assure them that I am still working on Rebecca, still sharing God's Word and God's love and my love. For God. I explain that if I give up on her, that's like giving up on Him, and not just on Him but also on one of His blessings, because Rebecca's a child of God just as much as me, isn't she?

I bring over Bibles. I don't expect her to read them—I can teach her all the Scripture she can stand—but we need to keep up appearances. Besides, Rebecca has a good book of her own. A ton, in fact. Right now, she's enjoying *The Lord of the Rings*.

And right now, I'm enjoying the rings of the Lord.

It's been a whopping ten seconds since Dad slipped the purity ring onto the ring finger of my left hand, the non-dominant one, and I wonder if he would've put it on the right one instead if my left hand *was* the dominant one, although no part of me is supposed to be dominant at all, so I guess that's a perfectly pointless thing to ponder.

"Nadine," Dad says, and it sounds like he's reprimanding me rather than addressing me. "This ring represents your decision to remain pure of heart, mind, and body while you wait for the man God has chosen for you. You want to share these things with Him and only Him."

Dad may have meant the lowercase, mere mortal *him*, but I doubt there's much of a difference.

"The ring also," he continues, "signifies your desire to involve Mom and Dad in your decision of a husband."

Decisions, decisions.

Too bad none of 'em are mine.

"If marriage is in God's plan for you," Mom chimes in, and I love how she starts things off on a high note instead of a high and mighty one, "you need to know what sort of qualities you're looking for in a life partner."

Life partner? I could live with a life partner. If that's what God wants and all.

Mom takes my free hand. "You'll probably start to experience... feelings for boys, physical feelings." She sounds uncomfortable, and also sort of unprepared, which is silly, because I know she's had this exact same conversation with my four older sisters.

Dad clears his throat. "When you begin to experience these physical feelings for boys—" and he says this as if it's something to look forward to "—there's no need to be afraid or ashamed." He taps my ring. "Just don't act on them," Dad adds with a chuckle, but of course this is no laughing matter. "Wait for the one God has in mind for you."

Rebecca.

God certainly didn't wait to put that in my head and poke it—all around, in every last lobe, right down to the brainstem, which is responsible for keeping me conscious, although not much consciousness is stemming from it at the moment.

I've been praying for the last six years that He will never give me feelings, physical or otherwise, for boys.

My parents will spend the next six years praying that He will.

I wonder if He plans on telling them that He picked my prayers over theirs.

God, I love the Lord.

"So let me get this straight: your dad put the ring on your finger right there in the restaurant, in front of everyone? I wonder if anybody lost their lunch." Rebecca shrieks with laughter.

I don't shriek the same. "Oh my gosh, what if someone thinks I got engaged to my father?"

"You kinda did," Rebecca replies, nibbling thoughtfully on her lemon bar. "I mean, he's gonna be involved every step of the way, and he has the final say. Pretty soon he'll be dragging your sorry butt down that aisle and pretty soon after that you'll be counting your blessings."

My tummy hurts. Rebecca hands me Cheer Bear. I rub its rainbow. "I'm supposed to make a list of everything I want in a guy."

"Oh, yeah, your funda-men-ta list," she says, like the words hurt her mouth. "Do you want one?"

"A fundamentalist?"

"A guy," she clarifies. "A husband."

"Husband?" It sounds sour on my tongue. I'd blame this on the lemon bar, but that would be wrong.

"I'll bet it's fun being a husband in your religion," Rebecca remarks. "Not that I want to be a boy or anything, but I mean you get to get out of the house, get a job, never get pregnant, get taken care of—if you get my drift—whenever you want."

I look at her. I see something pure and simple in her eyes, outshining several of the Seven Deadlies that are presently living in sin inside her eyeballs. I've never seen them before. They're not creepy like I thought they'd be. I like the way they look.

I like the way she looks.

"Don't worry," I say. "It's not in God's plan for me. He said so himself."

Rebecca looks skeptical, but not judgmental. It shouldn't matter if she did. I'm not supposed to care what other people think of me. The only opinion that matters is God's. Plus my parents'. And my siblings'. But I care what Rebecca thinks of me. If I shouldn't, then I wouldn't.

And I certainly wouldn't tell her what God told me, how He wants me to share my heart with her.

But... But what if I shouldn't?

What if her heart isn't in the right place?

Rebecca is not exactly God's biggest fan. Maybe the feeling is mutual. I doubt it, but I can't rule out that possibility completely. There are lots of ways to read the Bible. Some right, some wrong. What if the way I'm reading Rebecca is the wrong way and I end up stupidly giving my heart away, the way Dad wants to give me away to some man someday?

Oh! Speaking of giving things away… "I got you something. We went to the church rummage sale last week and I thought these were kinda cool." I present her with a bundle of books. They're from a series for teen girls called Cedar River Daydreams.

Rebecca looks through the books: *Unheard Voices*, *More Than Friends*, *A Special Kind of Love*.

She starts giggling. I'm not sure what's so funny, but I like the sound of her laugh. It's like milk-and-cookies and fuzzy bunny slippers all rolled into one. I start giggling also, just so she'll keep making that sound.

Take delight in the Lord, God reminds me, *and He will give you the desires of your heart.*

"I got you something too," Rebecca says. Slowly and shyly, she reaches into the front pocket of her pants.

Then she reaches for my hand. Hers holds mine as she presses something into my sweaty palm. A silver circle sits in the center of the sweat.

I gaze at it, in all its glorious simplicity, as if it's the keys of the kingdom of heaven. "What is it?"

"It's a ring, Nadine."

"What kind of ring?"

"I don't know. Boxing. Circus. Around the rosie. Friendship, purity, take your pick."

"I pick purity." I look to Rebecca for affirmation. "Is that right?"

She nods. In her eyes I see God's light and might and love.

I have to keep my parents' purity, so I put Rebecca's on my right hand.

"Dad took me to get it," she shares. "It must've been a religious experience for him, because he kept saying 'Heaven help us' and 'Lord have mercy.'" She blushes, fiddling with her fingers. "Which one do you like better?" she asks, and she seems anxious about how I will answer.

I take a good look.

One is silver, the other is gold.

It's easy to tell them apart.

"Your ring runs circles around their ring."

Mom and Dad will be pleased—not that I said that, although *I won't tell them if You won't, God.* They'll be pleased because now I am twice as pure as I was this afternoon.

I don't think I can get much purer than that.

But then Rebecca kisses me.

Hark! the herald angels sing, and in that divine spark—that lovely, brief, lemony lip lock, God and sinners are reconciled.

Rebecca gasps.

I grin.

Cheer Bear's rainbow looks especially bright tonight.

Rebecca moves her smile over to my ear. In soft, sticky words, she says, "Wait 'til the Lord gets a load of this!"

"He already saw," I tell her. "He sees everything."

Rebecca shrugs and hugs me, her heart fearfully and wonderfully close to mine.

Lesbians 3:18

"Mom and I have something we'd like to discuss with you."

You snitched, didn't You? I glower at God. *I begged You not to tell. I even promised You my firstborn.*

I scramble to get my jumbled thoughts in order. I haven't been sinning. I haven't even been rebelling. I've just been... resisting. Gently, passively, secretly. Submissive in practice, dismissive in theory.

When Rebecca comes over, my parents and siblings hold us accountable for our purity, even though they have no idea that that's what they're doing. It's acceptable for girls to show each other physical affection, but Rebecca and I barely brush arms and we absolutely never kiss, not even on the cheek. When we say goodbye, we don't frontal-hug, because that would make our breasts touch. Instead we side-hug, arms around each other's shoulders, a perfect imitation of Thing 1 and Thing 2.

At all times we are careful and prayerful.

So how did Mom and Dad discover that I am disobedient?

Imperfect.

Satanic.

They will hate the sinner, not the sin.

I will be excommunicated, exorcised, and excised from my family like bad words on TV or a filthy passage in a book.

Unless I tell them the God's honest truth.

The truth is He's got designs on us, and I don't mean that disrespectfully. I mean we don't get to decide how we're designed. We only get to decide how to respond to God's design, and I choose to respond by accepting the way He created me: in His image.

Our Savior is not unsavory. So, by association, I am not guilty. Jesus already died for my sins. It's no longer His cross to bear. Just because I've fallen for a woman doesn't make me a fallen woman. It's not like I've bared my body or shared it with some man. I haven't even shared it with her.

Mom and Dad have taught me well and I will show them how much their dutiful daughter has learned, so help me God.

Seriously, God—I need you. So help me. Please.

My father smiles, but it's not imperious or deleterious. It's… impish, gleeful even. Mom looks more subdued, if not a little nauseated.

Dad says, "A young man from our congregation has expressed an interest in you."

I try to exhale in relief, but my breath gets lost somewhere between my lungs and my mouth. Dad tells me the guy's name and assures me of his commendable character, missionary mindset, and other generically godly qualities.

Mom squeezes my hand, the one that's wearing Rebecca's ring. "Tell us what's in your heart."

Love.

For the one God has already chosen as my life partner.

I sense the hard line of my mouth shifting into a smile.

"Man plans and God laughs," I reply, feeling a funny kind of calm. "And right now, God is laughing at your man plans for me."

"You can lead a lamb to slaughter, but you can't make him think," Rebecca remarks, and she's glowing, as if she's been waiting her whole life to say that.

"I certainly don't intend to be their sacrificial lamb," I grumble, still feeling defensive, even though I know Rebecca is on my side.

Now more than ever, I realize, as her thigh, naked beyond her shorts, leans against my skirted one. Sometimes, Rebecca wears what's called immodest clothing, meaning she dresses like a regular person. If the guys in my family were here, they'd be mistaken for a tribe of See No Evil monkeys. And even with these primitive precautions, Rebecca could still be held responsible for goading their… gonads. I'm a girl, so the sight of her legs or arms or feminine charms is assumed to have absolutely no effect on me.

Well, considering that lately I've spent more time craving her than saving her, I'd say it's having an absolutely awesome effect on me.

"This won't affect our relationship, will it?" Rebecca is asking, and I wonder what else she said while I was off in ooh-la-la land.

"What won't?"

Rebecca rolls her eyes and nudges my knee with hers. "Whatever happens with your family," she clarifies. "If your mother or father or Father God or whoever doesn't... I don't know, see the light, you've still got my father. My dad loves you, Nadine. You're his little Jesus geek."

I smile. "Thanks. God will protect me, though. My parents will have a heart-to-heart with Him and He'll give them a good talking-to and set 'em straight."

Rebecca nods, but really she's shaking her head.

We gaze at each other for a while, and I do everything in my power to keep my eyes from wandering like Moses all over her... biblical proportions.

Until I was twelve, I thought only boys experienced sensual desires. But these physical feelings have matured a lot these past six years.

I want to know her.

No.

We're not married.

We're not allowed to have carnal knowledge of each other until we've been joined in holy matrimony, as God is my witness. I accepted two purity rings, for Christ's sake.

Pure means homogenous.

Homo for short.

Same.

Homo.

Sexual.

My purity is intact.

Exact.

Mine.

Jesus loves me.

I accept the things I cannot change.

Wherever He or she leads, I'll follow.

"But we're not married!" I insist, a protest without preface.

Rebecca's smile is tender. She can't read my mind, but she can read my heart. It's a God-given talent.

"We've taken the be-all end-all 'til death do us part vow as Ruth and Naomi," Rebecca reminds me, as she laces her fingers through the spaces in mine.

"We were kids. We were playing."

"We were preparing. Ruth and Naomi: To Be Continued."

My heart bops around inside my chest like a Bernoulli ball. *Ruth and Naomi, sittin' in a tree, s-i-n n...* "I wonder if we could... if we should... Should we? Continue?"

Rebecca's grin curls into her cheeks. Then she places her lips on mine and keeps them there until my heart becomes tranquil and damnation gives way to salivation. Um, salvation.

God, it's great your eyes are everywhere, but could you close them now, please? There's no need to watch over me every minute.

We kiss, sweetly and neatly, until our lips stick together like conjoined cherry popsicles.

I immerse my hands in her glorious blond hair, careful not to get my rings caught in her tresses.

While we're kissing, my clothes go missing. I don't mind. The Lord doesn't either, I'm sure, since I've disobeyed His demands for purebred threads.

"Do undo others," Rebecca suggests, guiding my fingers to the receiving line of buttons that stretches all the way down the front of her blouse.

My hand starts shaking.

By the grace of God, at the pace of a bridal march, I manage to undo the first button and all the others.

But at the hem, I hem and haw.

"Isn't there something in the Bible about an eyeful for an eyeful?" Rebecca remarks, and her words are more encouraging than a lifetime of daily devotionals.

Before long, we're… you know, we're—

"Even," Rebecca supplies. "Like Eve."

Exactly, just your garden-variety nudity. And now, with our… loins leafless, we can begin our genesis.

Atop the pile of pillows, Cheer Bear's rainbow smiles upside down at us. Amen, demon toy, go tell it on the mountain.

Over the hills and everywhere, my gaze goes. Rebecca's skin is ivory, like King Solomon's throne. Her chest, pretty and prominent, reminds me of the Dome of the Rock in Jerusalem, only now I'm seeing double.

It's a whole new Holy Land.

As I touch Rebecca's breasts, I discover that they are sufficiently supple, inexcusably soft, and needlessly guarding her heart.

It's safe with me.

And mine is safe with her.

It's a servant's heart, desiring to put the needs of others before my own.

It's the heart of a virtuous woman, the kind who, proverbially speaking, works willingly and zealously with her hands.

To protect my virtue, I begin exploring Rebecca's body, investigating every nuance and contour and texture like a woman on a mission. I wouldn't call it a healing mission, though. A feeling mission, maybe.

Rebecca is receptive to my touch, her spine curving, which makes her hips dip, and I follow the incline to the inside.

Here, my hand trembles and my fingers are all thumbs and instead of stroking Rebecca I'm poking her.

"Nadine," she scolds, giggling gently. "It's not a juice box."

I gaze at her glory on high and... well, not so dry, and I wonder if my blush is the same color as her... juice box.

I can do this.

The spirit is willing and the flesh is sleek.

I start anew, moving my fingers down then across, up then across, creating crucifixes in the creases. This is hardly the right hand of God, but as long as my hand does right by her, I can't go wrong.

Rebecca sighs and tries to get closer. To me, not the... pinnacle. Although that too, I suppose.

A hymn pops into my head: *Delay not, O sinner, draw near*, but I don't hear the sinner part. I hear only Rebecca's divine expression of love.

"For God's sake, Nadine, come here," my girl demands.

She is quaking, and taking me into her arms.

She is Christ the vine and I am Believer the branch.

We are joined together, the mesh of our flesh sanctioning our union and galvanizing our urges.

I press my lips to her shoulder. She smells like ginger and lemongrass and tastes like the salt of the earth.

We cling to each other, rejoicing as our love swells and bursts into a million perfect pieces.

No reassembly required.

"Good Lord, Nadine!" Rebecca cheers, her heart thwacking happily against my chest. "We just celebrated our first spiritual victory, didn't we?"

I nod and smile and let my love soar some more.

I feel blessed, serene, pristine.

"Would you mind if I spent the rest of my life with you?" I ask. It's not a proposal, but it's not a rhetorical question either, and it's definitely not a stupid question, because nothing about it feels immature or premature.

"If you must," Rebecca answers, at once casual and cautious, as if she's afraid of reading too much and too little into the question.

I reach into Rebecca's nightstand and fish out the kid-friendly Bible I gave her the day we met. I flip to the story of Ruth and Naomi and at the top of the page I consecrate our commitment with the pink-inked proclamation R + N *Forever*.

I start on a heart, then stop and pick up another pen. I hand it to Rebecca and we restart our heart, me designing the right half and she designing the left half, until the two halves form a whole.

Because I love her the same way I love Him: with my whole heart.

I see her gaze gravitate to our *Forever*, and I know she has her heart set on it too.

"I just hope the Lord's on board," Rebecca says, and kisses my arm.

"Yep," I murmur, cleaving to her. "God willing and the Jesus geek don't rise."

THE RULES
RACHEL O. ESPLANADE

I haven't been this fit in a long time. It's been a few years since the last player I had to run out of my head graduated from the team. Sarah was a bouncy forward whose friendly flirtatiousness drove me wild every practice until she finally got her Bachelor's degree in Biology, cum laude. "Cum loudly," her teammates chirped when she graduated. I didn't know that story and dared not ask. It was better to keep a distance from the girls. At any rate, Sarah was straight and naive. So naive I doubt she realized that she was flirting with me, or that I was turned on by her attentions. "You look tense, Coach. Can I give your neck a rub?" And my shoulders, and my head, and then my "pecs". She seemed to be all bounce, bounce, smile.

The increasingly stern looks from the head coach, the real Coach, when I accepted these offers eventually made me realize that I was getting unacceptably close to the girls. I had already stopped meeting them for beers after the game in order to keep that professional distance. I had to abide by The Rules Coach had laid out for me, and in particular her golden rule of coach-player relationships: no fraternizing. Knowing that Coach was keeping a watchful eye on me and my youthful hormones, I decided to literally run young Sarah out of my head

As I am trying to do now, to my thoughts of you.

Twenty years later, and I'm the head coach now. I know why I shouldn't even entertain tantalizing thoughts of inviting you over to my place. Of flirting with you, then kissing you. Of taking you with my hands, my mouth, my cocks. Of licking you until your hard, muscular thighs squeeze tightly against my ears. There's an entire coaching career of reasons why I shouldn't so much as hint to you what I want. It's more than keeping my career free of scandal; it's also about the many, many reasons why it would be best for you if we didn't hang out together, let alone fuck and cum.

So I'm running. I trip a little on one step going up. It's misty this evening and the concrete is damp. It's spring and the end of the exam period. Our last indoor field hockey tournament was over a month ago and our last practice before the summer break was last week. This time of year is always bittersweet for me, no matter how successful the season has been, with so many permanent goodbyes. Soon you will be gone out of my life and somehow, despite the anxiety I feel in your presence, I can't quite feel relief.

As I run up and down the Molson Stadium stairs, I take solace in the knowledge that stair sprints have kept me abiding by The Rules in the past. I hope to keep my libido in check for another week. I trust that sprinting up then jogging down the north side bleachers, occasionally emitting a soft "no" to myself, will eventually fatigue me out of my horniness. I'm doing five ascents this session, fifteen punishing flights in each repetition. I pant desperately up and down, trying to eradicate thoughts of touching, of kissing, and licking you. Dangerous thoughts. Thoughts that a head coach certainly should not have about a player. If after five repetitions of panting punishment, I still cannot get your curves out of my head, I will take a cold shower in the locker room. I have 24/7 access. There are advantages to being Coach.

I reach the top step for the final time and turn around, panting, to take in the view of Montreal as the light slowly seeps out of the crisp April sky into the west. My cheeks are hot from the effort but I can't help but feel they are still blushing from last night.

Three years, three whole years I've managed not to slip up, managed to not show any form of preference for you. Three years of holding back, of not letting go, of sticking to The Rules. Those fucking rules. Coaches should not have sex with players. It's too loaded, too crazy a power dynamic and unfair to the other players. I resisted the temptation of hitting on you right from try outs. You are smart, sexy, sporty-hot with some serious hockey skills. Truly a triple threat. Three years of doing the right thing but then, last night at the Annual Sports Award Gala, I had all kinds of slip-ups, where just one was too many.

You were so blissfully happy when you received your Most Valued Player award. Your mini dress displayed your beautiful full form in a classy, sexy way— the skirt stretched over your strong thighs, with the tiniest hint of the snaps at the end of the garter belt holding up your stockings. I remember being lost in the aural fantasy of the snap of garter belt straps against your skin. I wanted to snap them while my lips nipped at the hem of your skirt and my other hand glided up your thigh to find a purchase around a cheek, a fesse as you call it. Mes fesses you'd say to the other players if they ever made fun of your horrible French. Mes fesses—my ass, or, I suppose, my ass cheeks. I was sitting there, fully enraptured in my fantasy when you accepted your well-deserved award. Until you thanked me in your speech and pulled me out of my erotic reverie into an unsettling, blushing moment when I had no idea what you'd said and I felt like the biggest creep. Especially when you beamed your happy, grateful smile at me.

Later, when I held your award as you collected your things, I sensed you caught me checking out your ass, your fesses, in the mirror as you changed out of pumps into walking boots in the ladies' cloakroom. A movement at the corner of my eye informed me the gig was up— you were staring at my reflection in the mirror. But when I looked in the mirror, your eyes were focused on your boots.

Why did I check out your fesses? It was only a quick glance. Barely worth it. How old am I? Forty, not fourteen. Too old to be sneaking looks and blushing at unobtainable crushes. And you—twenty-three or twenty-four? Even if I weren't your coach, I was being creepy. What was I thinking? But that was it—I wasn't thinking. I was drinking you in, enjoying your flushed cheeks from your well-deserved moment.

A well-deserved moment for me too. One more year. One more year of keeping those boundaries solid, in high relief.

I shake my head in shame at the memory of last night. Physically spent, it's finally time for me to hit the showers. I descend the bleachers toward the tunnel to the locker room. The door is ajar when I reach it and the combination padlock lies on a bench inside. Did I leave it unlocked when I dropped off my shower bag? I stare in puzzlement at the lock until it dawns on me that you, as team captain, also know the combination. You are here. You are in the locker room.

"Hi, Coach."

"Hi." I am both excited and frightened to see you. I can feel the heat return to my cheeks as I greet you. I hope you think I am flushed from my run. "What are you doing here?"

"I'm just packing up my gear. I handed in my last paper today. Such a relief! I head back to B.C. at the end of the week." You are all smiles, aglow from finishing your semester and winning your award. You look downright edible.

"I'll let you finish and lock up then." I grab my shower bag from the locker I'd stashed it in earlier, and throw you a quick smile as I turn to leave. "You had a great season—you really deserved MVP."

"Were you running the stairs again?"

I don't look at you but stop with my hand on the door. "Yes."

"Do you often run the stairs?"

"Only when I need to clear my mind. I find it a great way to keep myself in focus."

"Focus on?"

How it's more important to keep my job than to fuck you. "On the training plan for next season."

"Aren't you sweaty?"

I nod.

"Why don't you have a shower?" You seem closer somehow. I am afraid to look.

"I'll have one at home."

"I think you should have one here."

You are closer, dangerously close. I can feel your breath on my cheek. Your hand reaches out and slides the heavy metal bolt home. We are locked inside. No one else can get in.

"You should have a shower. With me."

I am speechless.

"I saw you last night. I saw you checking me out."

I lean forward until my forehead presses against the cold metal door. I am conflicted; I want to be anywhere but here, and I want to be only here, both at once.

"Coach, I know you want me."

"I can't."

"Why not?"

"Those are The Rules."

"I'm an adult and I'm hitting on you."

"It's still not right."

You brush the hair back from my ear and bring your mouth a whisper distance from it. "I want you. I want your smile lines, and your small strong hands. I need you to fuck me."

Your husky tone places my body on alert. My heart begins to race. I close my eyes and maintain my stoic silence. My pussy starts to tingle. Oh, no.

I open my eyes and turn to take you in again. You are staring intently at me. You defiantly kick off your flip flops then take off your shirt, crumple it and fling it at me. Your sports bra, shorts, and panties swiftly follow until there is a small pile of your crumpled clothing at my feet. Except for the panties. Somehow I caught your slightly damp panties. I clutch them in my hand while I stare hungrily at your mouth and full lips which part to say, "Fuck The Rules."

With that, and seemingly satisfied that my resolve has begun to crumble, you turn away from me and saunter your heavenly self to the showers.

Once you disappear from view, I stand there for a beat until the sound of rushing water finally steals my last bit of resolve. My soaked panties and hot cheeks finally propel me into action. I start toward the showers discarding my bag and hurriedly stripping off my clothes along the way.

When I reach the shower room, you face me fully lathered. I pause on the threshold as the suds slide down your chest, your belly, and the chevron of your pubic hair. The shower jets go off and on as we stride toward each other through the motion sensors until we meet in the middle of the room. Finally you are on me, embracing me with your soapy body just before our tongues meet. I am so hungry for you. I grab your back, your thighs. I nibble on your neck, your ears. You taste so good. Suddenly, you break the kiss.

"You stink."

"I do." And with that, we giggle as we push, pull, and slide over each other to your bottle of shower gel and take turns lathering each other up between kisses.

I am ecstatic. My hands are nimble as I soap and stroke my way about your body and my sudsed-up fingers slip between your fesses. You arch your back, pushing your ass into my hand and rising onto your toes. I reach farther down and start stroking your pussy from behind. You gasp and our kissing intensifies until we slowly tumble through the wet and steam to finger each other on the tiled floor. That is when you surprise me by flipping me onto my back and plunging your face into my cunt. Your tongue is amazing as it flickers around my clit. You plunge fingers into my hole, fucking me until the want that has been building inside of me for three years crests, and my mind and body explode. You pull back, slip your fingers out and hold me as I come down. We stare at each other, and the motion sensors click off and the shower stops streaming hot water over us.

We hold each other until I realize that you are shivering.

"Let's go dry off." I rise and pull you up with me.

We walk back to the locker room holding hands. We sit on the bench and start toweling each other dry. Soon we are kissing again. My fingers find your erect clit and I start stroking it. You shiver, but not from a chill this time. "Yes, Coach. Please, Coach."

Your cunt is slick with juice, and one, then two of my fingers slip easily inside. Frantically, I fuck you with my fingers while stroking your clit with my thumb. Your cunt contracts around my fingers. You brace yourself by gripping my shoulders. "More. More!" It is easy to comply. Three, then four fingers slide in until I am pushing my hand in and out of your cunt: fingertips, fingers and nearly my whole palm.

"I want everything," you hiss urgently at me.

I fold my thumb into my palm and fuck you all the way up to the widest part of my hand while my other hand continues to stroke your clit.

You buck, arch your back, pull my hair, and push your face into mine. Your yells of "Yes, yes, yes" echo in the tiled chamber only stopping once you tense completely and push me out of your body. I hold you tight so you won't fall off the bench, softly kissing your face and your neck, and watch your face in wonder as your body twitches sporadically. Slowly you open your eyes to smile at me. You shift into my lap, and I'm happy to keep you warm. Seemingly content, you glance around the room until your eyes rest on the long grip and wide flat shaft of the stick poking out of your bag.

"Coach, will you fuck me with my stick?"

The thought of your pussy embracing the toe of the field hockey stick until the entire curved head is inside you and your clit is pressed up against the wide shaft of the handle is very enticing. But even my love of field hockey has its limits. You are a horny girl, but a wooden stick in your cunt with no condom... The stick will have to wait for another time. I glance around the room. Finally my eyes light upon the recently replenished med kit, complete with its neoprene gloves and the hefty tube of hydrogel to relieve turf burn.

"I have a better idea."

And that's how we end up with you propped against a locker room stall on a bed of towels, knees spread as you come hard, screaming and spurting, while my gloved fist twists inside of you.

It's April again. I'm daydreaming of you as I examine the photo of you I have in my office. It's the one you sent to me after you had graduated and moved back to the "wet coast". I pretend to those who visit me that I keep it on my desk as a fine example of defensive short corner positioning. It is. In the photo, you are poised, ready to explode out of the net as soon as the ball is put into play. Your delicious leg muscles are contracted under your kilt as you balance on your toes and hockey stick. Your intense eyes stare defiantly out of the frame. The tension in your legs, that fierce look, take me back to our sweet moments in the locker room and the rest of the week we had together before you went home. Your right toe, slightly over the goal line where it shouldn't be, reminds me of your husky voice in that moment when you decided that we needed to Fuck The Rules.

THE FURTHER ADVENTURES OF MISS SCARLET

EMILY L. BYRNE

Kendra could almost feel someone's eyes burning a hole in the back of her head. She didn't even need to turn around to confirm the feeling, thanks to the mirror over the bar. If it had been any other bar, she would have been more surprised. But Riley's was a cop bar and it attracted a specific clientele, mostly law enforcement and their families and friends. Plus the occasional groupie.

Whatever this woman was, she wasn't law enforcement, at least not any kind that Kendra had seen before. Or could imagine. She was beautiful: heart-shaped face, arched thin eyebrows over wide dark eyes, bright red kissable lips. Her red dress set off her curves, accentuating her small, full breasts and curved hips, even sitting down. And what was she looking at? A big African American butch with dreads, a broken nose and shoulders like a linebacker's. For a minute, Kendra wished with everything she had that she was cuter, and bit back a sigh.

But that moment passed; she was cute enough to stare at, so that was as cute as she needed to be. At least for now. She could turn her attention to wishing she was less shy around pretty ladies instead. That wish settled down into her crotch with a dull, aching thud of thwarted desire. It had been way too long, and she was uncertain and out of practice.

She was entertaining herself by covertly studying the other woman's reflection, trying to figure out if she'd run across her before and could use that as a conversation starter, when her partner nudged her. "Got yourself a badge bunny, Ken? Not too shabby." James grinned as she turned and wrinkled her nose at him. He took a swig of his beer and glanced around the rest of the bar as if her potential romantic drama held no more interest for him.

It probably didn't. James would finish his beer and head home to his wife and kids, just as he did every Thursday night. In the times between his one weekly night out and his biweekly card games, he mowed his lawn, played with his kids, and stayed home as much as he could. And worked with Kendra to solve homicides the rest of the time.

Although, come to think of it, that last part was more than enough drama for Kendra, too. She found her eyes wandering back to the mirror anyway. The woman had disappeared and she stifled a sigh. There had been something intriguing, challenging even, in the other woman's stare. It had been a while since anyone had challenged Detective Kendra McClain, and she hadn't realized how much she'd missed it until now.

Disappointed, she called it a night, said goodbye to James and the others, and left the bar. She let her steps take her toward the subway while her mind wandered back to the woman in red. She had a weird sense that she'd seen that same woman, or someone who looked like her, before.

The fact that she couldn't place her bothered Kendra. It wasn't as if she knew that many beautiful women of Asian descent. She didn't, she realized with a heavy sigh, know very many beautiful women, period. Not that beautiful, anyway. And certainly not any who would stare at her like that.

For a wild moment, she imagined the other woman in her bed, tan skin silky under her hands, the woman's long black hair cascading over both of them like a veil. Her wet, warm flesh parting around Kendra's hand. The detective bit her lip, her skin on fire, her body one giant, quivering nerve ending that ached with longing.

Clearly, it had been way too long.

Kendra drew a shaky breath and walked down the subway stairs, grateful for the cool night air on her cheeks and the fact that the stairs were deserted at this hour. If she was blushing, at least there'd be no one around to see it. She smiled, laughing at herself as she entered the dimly lit corridor that led to the ticket booth.

Then her instincts took over. Something was wrong. She caught a flash of red at the end of the corridor. Then someone either turned or ducked back around the corner, as if they were hiding from her. Kendra moved her hand closer to the gun in her jacket and kept walking, all senses alert and focused. A quick glance at the booth told her it was unoccupied so she'd need her pass to get through the gate to the platform. And there'd be no one to call for backup if she needed it.

She paused for a moment. Maybe she should backtrack and go to another entrance. More trouble was no way to end an already stressful week. She could always call the Transit Police when she got back up the stairs. That was when another flash of red caught her eye. This time, though, she could see that it looked like a red dress. A familiar red dress.

Kendra frowned; this was one coincidence too many. What if this woman, whoever she was, wasn't alone? She might be walking into a trap. It might not even be the woman from the bar. But her curiosity, leavened with a bit of residual lust, overrode her common sense. Instead of turning back, she loped forward, dashing around the corner to catch whoever was waiting for her by surprise.

But the station looked empty from where she was standing. She cursed quietly and pulled out her pass. A train rumbled in the distance and for a moment, she wondered if she was letting her imagination run away with her, fantasizing about a strange woman in her bed, then stalking her for good measure.

She stepped onto the platform and looked around. The woman from the bar was sitting on a bench, seemingly engrossed in an e-reader. She slowly crossed one long, lithe leg over the other, displaying them to full advantage in the latest fashion in stilettos. She shifted on the bench just a hair, giving her back a tiny arch. The movement was clearly an invitation and Kendra bit back a grin as she went over to sit next to her.

The other woman ignored her, but she twisted one lock of hair around her finger and Kendra could see her white teeth chewing her scarlet lower lip. Something about the way she did it went straight to Kendra's crotch. If she licked those lips, the detective knew that she was doomed.

"Didn't I see you at Riley's Pub tonight?" Kendra tried to make her tone sound innocent, as if every inch of her body wasn't stirring to a slow, fierce arousal.

The other woman tilted her face up to look at Kendra and the detective had the nervous urge to straighten her dreads and check her teeth for scraps of food. The woman in red was every bit as beautiful as her reflection in the bar mirror: dark eyes above high cheekbones, kissably full lips, low-cut dress showing more than a hint of cleavage.

Her expression was anything but welcoming, though, and that detached, even icy, look triggered a memory in the back of Kendra's mind. She knew where she'd seen that face before, knew that it was something to do with another department's case. But which one? Not a homicide. That much, at least, she was sure of. Hopefully.

"Yes, Detective. You did see me at Riley's." The woman's voice was a purr, stroking its way up Kendra's thighs. "I'm glad you found me so... memorable." Her lips curled in a smile that didn't work its way up to her eyes.

Kendra's brain murmured words like "drama" and "trouble" and "potential criminal" while her pussy sang a different song entirely. "You certainly seemed to want me to notice you. What's your name?"

The smile widened, brilliant lipstick parting over bright white teeth. "You can call me Scarlet; Miss Scarlet, if we're going to be formal." She tucked the e-reader away in a small black bag that matched her heels, but she didn't take her gaze away from Kendra's face.

"Are we playing *Clue*? I'm not sure I want to be Colonel Mustard in the library, with or without a candlestick." Kendra grimaced. She glanced down, this time looking beyond Scarlet's body to her accessories. James always said that you could read a lot about a woman by the kind of jewelry she wore and how she put together her outfits. Kendra usually blew that off as his one concession to metrosexuality, but she was willing to make an exception tonight.

Everything matched, not a hair out of place, not a chipped nail or a makeup smudge. Everything this woman wore was assembled with such care and thoroughness that she might have been playing a part on stage. With one exception: one of her rings was a giant, gaudy bit of bling that didn't match her industrial-style silver earrings, necklace, and watch. The ring was a mass of ornate curlicues around a faceted glass stone that was far too large and shiny to be a real diamond.

"Nice ring," Kendra drawled as the station signal beeped to let them know that their train was coming in.

"Like it?" Scarlet smiled at her upraised hand. "I—" The noise of the onrushing train cut her off. But for one crazy moment, Kendra could have sworn that she said, "I stole two others nearly the same size in Monte Carlo last year."

"What?" Kendra looked at Scarlet as closely as she could as she trailed the other woman onto the train. She reached for her phone, wondering if she could do a quick search on jewel thefts in Monte Carlo without arousing too much suspicion. But they were alone in the train car and headed into a tunnel, so there would be no signal even if she tried to claim a text message.

They were sitting down and Scarlet was resting her hand on Kendra's arm, caressing it, stroking it until Kendra, watching it, thought she might go up in flames. "You're so very strong, Detective. I do like a nice strong girl." Scarlet looked up at her through thick black lashes, her gaze an invitation.

A tiny bit of Kendra's remaining common sense prompted her to ask, "How did you know I'm a detective? Maybe I'm just out of uniform." Scarlet's hand was on her thigh now, and common sense was becoming very hard to come by. Self-control was going to be next. Kendra hoped that she wasn't actually panting.

Scarlet smiled at her. "I saw you on TV when the mayor commended you and your partner. I pay a lot of attention to the police force. You could say that they're terribly important to me. And you were such a stud up there on the podium that I couldn't resist tracking you down. Do I scare you, Detective? I wouldn't want you to have to use those cuffs on me." She watched Kendra through lowered eyelashes, her expression school-girl demure and about as real.

It was an invitation that Kendra couldn't ignore. She reached over, tilted the other woman's chin up and kissed her. Then Scarlet's hand was wrapped around her neck and buried in her hair and Scarlet's tongue was in her mouth. She tasted like piña coladas, expensive lipstick, and lust and Kendra responded to all three, picking her up and swinging her onto her lap so that the other woman knelt on the seat with her thighs on either side of the detective's. Scarlet wriggled up close to Kendra, pressing her lithe body against the detective's and shoving one of Kendra's hands up under her skirt.

Kendra bit back a moan and a moment of panic. Transit police or more passengers could enter the car at any moment. This was nuts. She didn't know this woman, even suspected her of being a criminal. This had to stop... but her hand had developed a will of its own and was stroking Scarlet's thigh. Her smooth silky thigh above her lacy garter belt. Kendra deliberately stopped her hand just shy of Scarlet's panties, ignoring the other woman's efforts to pull her hand farther up.

Instead, she broke their kiss, running her tongue down Scarlet's neck and gently nipping her shoulder. Part of her brain noted they were pulling into a station, and she adjusted their positions a little so that what they had been on the brink of doing was slightly less obvious. Scarlet's mouth was at her ear, her teeth nibbling her earlobe.

Her voice in Kendra's ear whispered urgently, "Oh c'mon, Detective! If someone gets on, let's give them a show. I like an audience for my performances. Don't you?"

She shifted her body on top of Kendra's and ground her hips against the detective's. The wave of pure desire that swept over Kendra made it hard to talk, to tell this woman that, no, she never made love with an audience. The thought of doing it was revolting and gross. And unbelievably hot.

Then Scarlet's hand was under her jacket, kneading her breast and tugging her nipple into an excruciating point and who needed to think right now?

With a growl, she buried her face in Scarlet's cleavage, biting and licking every bit of bare skin she could reach from that angle. Scarlet yanked one of her small breasts free of her bra's lacy cups, holding it up with her fingertips so that Kendra could engulf it with her mouth, sucking and nibbling until she could feel the other woman's groan start at her toes and work its way up.

She gave up her struggle to hold her hand still, instead letting it slide up Scarlet's thigh to her soaking wet panties. She ran her fingers over them, gratified at the abrupt tilt of the other woman's hips that followed her movements.

"Inside me, Detective. C'mon, baby. You going to make me beg?" Scarlet murmured the words in her ear, her voice caressing enough to call up a full body shiver.

It would be tempting to see what this woman could do if she was really begging for it. Kendra grinned into the sharp point of the nipple that she held lightly between her front teeth. But then, turn about might be fair play. Kendra twitched a little at the thought of what she'd be willing to do to get this woman to say "Yes" to her. And act on it.

She sent her fingers up and around Scarlet's panties, until she could bury them into the wet welcome that awaited her on the other side of the satin barrier. Scarlet moaned and humped her hand, rocking forward to take in as much of Kendra's hand as she could. It was so sweet, this beautiful woman's desire, so novel and lovely, that it was almost enough to shut off the detective part of Kendra's brain.

But not quite. On autopilot, her brain ran through everything she'd done and seen at the station recently, cataloging and searching her memories as she was trained to do, looking for the one that would tell her why Scarlet looked familiar.

What came back was a photo on a case file that she'd seen some colleagues passing around at a meeting. "Interpol says she's one of the best they've ever seen. And my buddy says she's hotter than hell, even better than her picture. The cops in Macao and Monte Carlo and everywhere else on the effin' planet are looking for her. Maybe we'll get lucky and she'll come here next." The conversation had trailed off into chest-thumping commentary about what they'd like to do with a gorgeous female jewel thief and Kendra had tuned them out. It wouldn't be her case unless the woman killed someone so what did she care?

The tensing of Scarlet's thighs overrode her train of thought as she brought the other woman to orgasm right there on the train, just as it entered a new station. Head tilted back, red lips parted in a series of moans and cries, Scarlet had given herself up to the moment, and she wanted that moment to last. Maybe she was wrong about who this woman was. After all, why would a world-class jewel thief go slumming at Riley's to pick up a detective?

Then Scarlet's lips fastened on hers, her tongue so urgent that wrestling with it, added to the press of Scarlet's body on hers, was enough to drive any other thoughts from her head. She barely noticed that they weren't alone in the car anymore. She finally opened one eyelid, just a slit, and verified that the couple who'd gotten on was sitting far enough away not to pose an immediate threat. Kendra was willing to take that for now.

Or at least she was until Scarlet began wedging her hand down her pants.

"We've got an audience," Kendra growled, breaking off the kiss and moving to intercept those enticingly long fingers, now suddenly ringless. *Where did it go? It might be evidence.*

"Let them watch. We'll show them how it's done," Scarlet whispered and ran her tongue down Kendra's neck. "You've got a gun to hold them off if they want to participate. I don't like sharing." Scarlet gave her a satiated half-smile, like a happy cat's, and tweaked her nipple, pulling a suffocated moan from Kendra's closed lips. "I'll keep an eye on them. Let me finish what we started, Detective. Trust me."

Kendra's instincts woke up. Could she really trust this woman? How far? She hoped the couple were just voyeurs and wouldn't think of shooting a video on a cell phone that would end up on YouTube...

Scarlet took advantage of the lapse in Kendra's attention to shove her hand down Kendra's pants and Kendra felt her hips rock forward to make more room for her, her body responding as if it belonged to someone else. Scarlet, perhaps. Not that she'd be able to relax enough to come, not here and now. She was certain of that much.

But Scarlet's fingers said something entirely different as they slid into her and one finger found her clit. Kendra jumped a little at the shock of the sudden, longed for, contact and Scarlet leaned down to kiss her again, her exposed breast rubbing against Kendra's until the detective wondered if she could slip her t-shirt off under her jacket. She wanted to be naked with this woman so badly that she wasn't sure that the location mattered any more.

"Just me. Just my hand and your pussy. That's all that matters. Give me what you want to give so badly," Scarlet crooned as she covered her face with little kisses. "I can feel how much you want to come for me, baby. Let me get you there." The pressure of her fingers increased, sending a spark of pure fire through Kendra, circling and pushing in just the right amount.

Kendra's brain disintegrated into a jumbled mass of fantasies, all of them about this gorgeous woman and all the things she wanted to do with her. But the weight of hungry eyes was making her anxious. Well, that and the possibility that Interpol was looking for her companion. What was a good detective to do?

She risked a quick glance down the car. The straight couple was watching them, but their hands were so busy that they'd have other things to occupy them soon. Part of her cringed at providing a free show for them.

"Just us, baby. They're just trying to have as much fun as we are. Show them how it's done," Scarlet's voice cut across her thoughts and fears as she kissed her eyelids closed, shutting out their watchers.

She could feel Scarlet's hips thrust against hers, feel the urgency in her breathing and the rapid pounding of her heart. She let it carry her away, shutting out everything except this woman and her maddening, exciting touch. Her thighs locked instinctively and tightened until all of her being centered on that single point of fire being coaxed into unbearable sensitivity. A moment, a breath, and someone was shouting, the sound muted by the train screeching around a corner.

When Kendra came back to earth, Scarlet was grinning at her and kissing her fingers, a sight that sent a stab of soft fire through the detective. "My, my. I knew you'd be hot, baby." Scarlet leaned over and kissed her hard as she tucked herself back into her bra and pulled her dress closed.

"Come home with me," Kendra murmured as Scarlet finished rearranging her clothes. "I'm even more fun horizontal. Or vertical, if you prefer."

Scarlet swung off her as the guy from the other end of the car approached. "We were wondering if... you two were, um, bi-curious?" He stopped a few feet away, as if he expected to get punched if he got too close. It was a good idea on his part; Kendra was considering the option, hard.

Scarlet gave him a twisted grin. "Not tonight. Or probably any night thereafter. I think your lady's got enough to fuel her imagination for quite awhile to come as it is." She waved him off and he turned and went back to his date, keeping any growling he wanted to do about his dismissal to himself.

"That happen every time you have sex on a train?" Kendra glanced sidelong at Scarlet, her mood turning dark as her brain warred with her body. At the very least, she needed a closer look at the ring. A memory of a certain sparkle crossed her mind and she couldn't shed the suspicion that she'd heard Scarlet correctly back at the station.

"Haven't done this before. Not in this city at least. But I always like to try something new in a new town. Souvenirs are some of the best parts of any trip, aren't they, Detective?" Scarlet's smile had turned wistful.

Then she gave Kendra a speculative look, and rose slowly, tugging at her dress to straighten it out. She glanced up as if to see what station they were pulling into and Kendra glanced over her own shoulder. Only two more stops to her apartment. She wondered what, if anything, she could say to get Scarlet back there. Though maybe exposing a suspected thief to her meager possessions wasn't the best idea.

But she couldn't let her get away, no matter what. She gathered herself to reach for Scarlet as the doors opened.

There was a familiar flash of red on the platform and Kendra realized her pants weren't fastened any more. She grabbed them with a curse as the doors closed. Scarlet stood on the platform and blew her a kiss. She tapped her shoulder as the train pulled out of the station and after a moment, Kendra realized that she was supposed to check her jacket pocket. There was something hard in it, something that hadn't been there at the beginning of this crazy night.

The ring was heavy and solid in her hand, the stone sparkling in a way that confirmed her suspicions. She gingerly placed it on the subway window glass and used it to make a tiny scratch. *Shit.* Was it a memento? Or was the other woman trying to frame her? But that didn't make sense. All she had to do was to turn it in and say she'd found it on the subway and wondered if there was a report out on it.

She pocketed the ring and contemplated taking a cab back to the previous stop. But Scarlet would be long gone by then. She knew that in her gut. Her aching, empty gut. Kendra rested her head against the cold glass and watched the dark walls of the tunnel blur past until the train pulled into her stop.

It was only when she was trudging up the stairs to the street that she realized Scarlet had been telling her that she'd be sticking around for a little while. Maybe the ring was a goodwill gesture as well as a souvenir. Maybe Scarlet would come looking for her again.

Or maybe she needed to concentrate on being a cop and take a closer look at the other woman's file to see what she could find out. One way or another, she hadn't seen the last of Miss Scarlet.

She held her fingers up to her nose and inhaled the other woman's scent, grinning despite herself. Detective Kendra McClain liked a challenge and it looked like she was in luck. Kendra whistled as she headed home, checking for a flash of red dress around every corner.

SUNSET, SUNRISE
SACCHI GREEN

Oh, damn, I had it bad this time. And no way in hell would the truck that hit me pull over to take me for a ride.

But I'll never be old enough to know better. "I'll take table six," I hissed at Audrey as she passed my office door. "Don't worry, you'll get the tip. And it'll be a good one."

So much for avoiding temptation this summer. No Provincetown beaches and clubs and babydykes on training wheels; with my life at long last cleared of distractions, I needed to focus on my Wellfleet studio and the restaurant bookkeeping job that pays the bills. But if trouble had come looking for me, how could I look away?

Not that Trouble, with a definite capital T, was actually looking my way. The big salt-and-pepper butch had eyes (and hands—such broad, strong hands!) only for the gorgeous young redhead who made voluptuous seem like a four-letter word.

Audrey sized up the situation fast. "So what else do I get?"

"All right," I muttered, "come around tomorrow night." Audrey might be more intriguing if her interests weren't strictly confined to getting her posterior paddled. I always make her earn it.

At table six I stood by the young lady's shoulder, gazing deliberately down into the lush cleavage revealed by clinging azure silk. Then I glanced at her companion, hoping for a reaction. It didn't even much matter what kind.

Clear hazel eyes in a sun-ruddy face surveyed me with a hint of amusement, and recognition.

"Good evening, I'm Rory," I said demurely. "I'll be serving you tonight."

The corners of her mouth twitched. (Her? Sir, on occasion, without doubt; definitely a Daddy; but yes, in my own private lexicon, Her.)

"Hi Rory," she said. "You must be moonlighting. Didn't we last see you covered in mud?"

"Close enough," I acknowledged. "Art feeds the soul, but that's about all."

I'd been smeared with clay when they'd wandered through the collective gallery that afternoon and glanced into my studio, obviously looking for a corner just secluded enough to pretend no one could see them making out. The butch had resisted the kid's tug on her muscle-T long enough to look appreciatively at my nudes in porcelain and stone. "Go ahead," I'd said, as her hand hovered over the rounded marble ass of a full-bodied figure crouching on all fours. "Go on, it's meant to be irresistible."

The carnal magnetism of her grin hit me like pounding surf. When her big finger stroked the smooth buttocks and probed down between the tempting thighs my crotch got wet enough to dampen the clay dust layering my jeans.

"Must have been quite some model," she said appreciatively, ignoring the pout of jealousy quivering on her girl's full red lips.

"So's yours," I said, looking boldly over the delectable young flesh my sculptures could only symbolize. This got me a sultry look through the girl's long lashes, a reassessment of my weathered androgyny, but Daddy just laughed and steered her back into the hallway.

My imagination seethed with visions of those large hands kneading and squeezing tender breasts and belly and thighs. The girl's shorts had been brief enough to reveal rosy traces of the proprietary bar-code Daddy's hand had imprinted on her naughty ass, with possible assistance from the back of a hairbrush. They must be staying somewhere close enough to have indulged in a bit of after-lunch action before taking a stroll through the galleries.

When they'd gone, I stepped out into the hall for a moment just to immerse myself in the space that large, solid body had occupied. I could feel her primal energy flowing through me. My hands tingled with the remembrance of contours never actually touched.

Cadillac Mountain granite from Maine, speckled pink and gray, I thought, sketching furiously in my mind. But something deeper than thought flooded me with a longing to feel her generous flesh against mine. I would run my tongue from lips to jaw to throat and down between her breasts, licking sea salt and sweat from her skin, hearing in her low moans, as I probed and explored, the swelling of the tide I hungered desperately to taste.

Well. Another case of lust at first sight, with no expectation of repeat sightings. Better off that way. I'd still scanned the crowds on the sidewalks and at the beach for the rest of the day, but saw no imposing figure with granite-gray hair, moving with just that confident set of head and shoulders and hips that had imprinted itself on me. Not until right now, tonight, in this four-star, white-linen-and-crystal-goblet restaurant.

I knew better than to disturb the elegant ambiance, but I couldn't resist a bit of subtle meddling. Just for the diversion. "Would you like to order appetizers while you consider the entrees? The Wellfleet Oysters on the Half

Shell are especially plump and juicy tonight, and the Ceviche of Chatham Bay Scallops is, as always, superb."

"Excellent," Daddy said firmly, laying a casual hand over the girl's smaller one. "We'll have one of each, and share."

The girl looked suspiciously at the menu. "At least those snails last night were cooked," she muttered, then stifled a gasp as Daddy's hand tightened on her wrist. My hunch had been correct. Raw seafood was way outside the youngster's comfort zone.

"The lime juice in the ceviche has the same effect as cooking," I told her smoothly, and, to do her credit, she murmured faintly that it sounded very nice.

I couldn't dislike her, in spite of her youth, her sensuous beauty, all she was that was just what Daddy wanted. The role-playing itself evoked only a lingering nostalgia; I'd been on both sides of the equation, at one time or another. My hunger now was for an intensity driven by a common weight of years, of life, of howling pleasure into the teeth of mortality. All right, what I really needed was to get laid by someone who could give me what I wanted, and could handle what I wanted to give.

Not that there was any chance I'd get it. Or wanted to. The last thing I needed was for someone to make me melt inside the shell I'd finally managed to build around myself. I was just playing a harmless game as I served them attentively. A dropped oyster fork was promptly replaced next to the girl's scarlet-tipped, manicured hand—with a private reflection that from the length of the nails I knew what Daddy wasn't getting, presumably by choice. An errant napkin was retrieved and allowed to drift briefly against the naked swell of breasts above the blue silk décolletage before it was restored to her lap.

Daddy saw me watching for her reaction. Did she know that with every glance at the girl I pictured an older, stronger body pressed against her, large hands pressing and tightening on full breasts, smooth shoulders, dampening thighs? Or was I staring too hungrily at her firm lips when she brushed her napkin across them? Her eyes held mine as her fingers deliberately relaxed and let the linen slide down over shirt and tie to her wide lap, and then to the floor.

I bent swiftly to pick it up, stroking her hip in passing, then stood behind her with my breasts nudging against her back as I leaned forward to spread the white cloth across her thighs. She turned to thank me, leaning her shoulder into me, and I saw in her upturned face that she felt the current of sensuality, knew perfectly well what I was up to, and was amused.

I started to move away for a fresh carafe of coffee. "Rory, just a minute," Daddy said. "Are there any evening activities around here you'd especially recommend to visitors?"

"Aren't we going to Provincetown to the clubs?" the girl blurted out before subsiding under a stern look.

I listed a few theatrical and musical events of a sedate and worthy nature, then told the truth as I saw it. "On a summer night like this, there's nothing more beautiful than watching the sunset from the beach on Chequesset Neck. If you're here tomorrow you should try it. It's already too late now." I nodded toward the view from the front window where the sky's afterglow still tinted the rivulets winding through the marsh with a russet sheen.

"All right, it's the bright lights of P'town tonight," she told the anxious girl. "Maybe we'll catch the sunset tomorrow and then make an early night of it before the long drive home."

Only here for the weekend, I thought. Figures. So much for looking for trouble.

And then Trouble turned again in her seat and looked up at me. "Do you ever get time off to watch the sunset, Rory?" she asked.

"Once in a while. But even on my nights off I usually work in my studio. I'll be there late tonight, sketching out a project that's begun to obsess me." I looked from the hands resting on her broad thighs slowly up along her body to her face. If the sun hadn't already reddened her skin I'd have suspected that she was blushing.

"Maybe you could draw me a map to this sunset beach," she said. "Just in case." She turned to the girl. "Juliana, you run along to the ladies' room. I'll be with you in a minute."

I stepped close and pressed against her side. Her head was level with my breasts as I leaned over the table; my nipples tightened at the thought that her warm breath would brush them if she turned toward me.

Since linen napkins were out of bounds as scrap paper, I drew a map on a page from my order book. When I started to embellish it with a sketch of the sun setting over Boston across the Bay, her large hand grasped mine and moved it, pen and all, to the lower edge of the paper.

"So your studio would be about here?" she murmured.

I moved both our hands across the tablecloth a few inches. "Here," I said, nudging the saltshaker. "Where you saw me earlier." And then Juliana was beside us, the check was settled, and they were gone.

The night was warm even at 2 a.m. I stood outside my studio flexing stiff shoulders and fingers and watching the high, white moon sail above the salt marsh. Sketches sprawled across my drawing board; hands, the set of a head, the turn of broad back and shoulders.

A car turned into the deserted street... approached... slowed... I didn't look around, didn't let myself hope, didn't move.

"Still obsessed by that project?" she asked, her breath warm against my ear.

"It's coming along." I turned toward her. "When I find just the right piece of granite, I'll know what to strip away to get at what I want."

"Wait a minute, you're not going to cut anything off, are you?" Shirt and tie had been left behind, along with the presumably sleeping girl whose musk still clung to Daddy. A good kid, really, as youngsters go these days. Trying hard to please. She didn't deserve to be hurt...

I grasped the ribbed undershirt and tugged it upward.

"Not unless it won't go willingly," I said, and yanked it off over her cropped hair. My mouth pressed fiercely over hers to hold back whatever she might try to say. I got her belt unbuckled and my fingers inside her damp boxer shorts before she counterattacked, grabbing both my wrists in one big hand and stretching them up high while the other hand unbuttoned my shirt.

"Don't forget I'm an expert with a chisel," I panted, and ducked my head to set my teeth where neck met shoulder. She tasted of sweat and smoke and sea air. I scraped down across her chest to the swell of a breast, left a suction mark on its inner curve, and moved along to an insistent nipple. No more resistance, just her groans and sharper cries as I chewed her flesh to soreness, and my own gasps at the harsh clutch of her hands on my back and buttocks.

I lifted my head to blurt, "Inside!"

"How deep?" she shot back, gripping my crotch so hard I yipped like a pup.

"Whatever you can handle," I managed to get out. "But in there," jerking my head toward the interior of my studio.

We tumbled onto the futon in the corner. I'd left lube and gloves handy beside it, just in case.

She won the race to strip away what remained of each other's clothing, yanking my sweatpants off in one sweeping motion and swatting my ass hard before I rolled over and got my fingers hooked into her loosened belt. I slid to my knees on the floor and tugged, and she had to cooperate or be hobbled. As soon as her boxer shorts cleared her knees I had my head between her strong thighs, forcing them apart, pushing toward her pungent heat; she could have crushed me, but when I nipped at the tender skin near her crotch she leaned back with a gusty sigh and opened to me.

Her coppery bush was still untouched by gray. I licked my way across her full lips and whipped at her straining clit with my tongue, hard and fast, until her hips arched high and her moans quickened.

I needed a deeper taste. My fingers took over externally, letting my tongue probe into her hot, slippery cunt until her groans and curses demanded more, and I reversed again, giving her two fingers, three, easing in my whole fist. Her muscles clenched around it, and her full-throated, jubilant cry rang through her flesh into mine.

I'd barely retrieved my hand when she rolled onto me, shoving her thigh between my legs, working my nipples savagely while I bucked against her greater bulk. "Inside!" I demanded again. "Deep." Her large finger moved skillfully into me. "More. All of it. " I begged. "I can handle it, damnit, give it to me." Through my haze of need I saw her doubt, until I took in her whole large hand, gradually at first, and with increasing urgency—and then I couldn't see any thing at all, gripped by rolling waves of intensity.

I'd been wrong about the sunset. Dawn over her shoulder as we lay entangled was the most beautiful sight I'd ever seen. And the saddest.

Wordlessly I memorized her taste, my lips and tongue and teeth tracing the contours of her throat and collarbone. She drew in a deep breath, her chest rising beneath my mouth, but there was nothing to be said.

While she dressed, I slipped last night's sketches into a folder and handed it to her before she left. "For Juliana," I'd scrawled across it. Maybe she'd pass them along to the girl, maybe not.

I kept what was mine alone. There were more sketches, stored in my imagination, in my fingertips; views of her lover that Juliana would never see, on the page or in the flesh.

As the car dwindled along the deserted street I wrenched my mind away from what couldn't be, and toward the quest for just the right piece of solid granite.

THE CLINTON COUNTY HORSE THIEF SOCIETY
AXA LEE

The call comes in by the post rider. Inside, my stomach flutters and tightens. I work to control my breathing. I keep my face blank, hidden beneath the brim of my hat until I can look up at him and nod once in acknowledgement. It might not be her, I reason. It might be someone else. But as I swallow past the urgent lump in my throat, I admit to myself that there's really no one else that it could be.

I set down my hoe, stand and stretch my back. The kinks pop as I straighten. I whistle Little Joe, the black pinto, up out of the lower pasture, and trudge up to the house for a change of clothes, some water and victuals, and my pistols.

I tell Momma I'll be back when I can.

"How long this time?"

I shrug, toying with a button on my sleeve, not meeting her gaze. "No way to be sure."

"I wish you wouldn't go."

But since Pa died, the only one to go is me.

"Take care of your momma," he said. "Take care of the horses." Like him, I don't much like thievery, especially of a man's horses. That's why, when these calls come, there's the conflict in my belly, like two cats sparring in a sack.

"At least let me do your hair."

Momma is obsessed with my hair, the big brunette curling mass of it. She loves to brush its thickness, even though it breaks the comb's teeth, trying to tame it back into something worthwhile. I usually just tie it up, stuff it up under my hat, and let it idle.

"Hair is a woman's crowning glory," Momma is wont to say.

I sigh, knowing Joe is waiting for me at the barn. My belly rolls and I try not to fiddle with my clothes, betraying my nerves. I'm eager to be gone, can already feel the horse joggling beneath me, the chomp of bit and earthy scent of well-used leather. But Momma looks at me with such raw need, twisting the damp blue and white checked dishtowel almost to pieces between her thin, ragged hands that I submit.

She guides me to sit on a high kitchen stool before her, runs her fingers through my hair to shake out the tangles. She clucks her tongue over the riotous mess. She makes quick work of it, untangling snarls and smoothing back wisps, so that when she's done, my scalp is pulled tight. I'll be glad of this in the days to come, when I won't have time to stop and mess about with my hair, for all that I'm losing precious minutes now.

"You'll bring them back with you this time," Momma says as she braids. "And even if you only bring the horses again, your pa would still be proud."

The cats in my belly hiss and claw.

Pa headed the local group of horse thief catchers and with all the young men still gone in the war, it's now up to me to track down the thieves. Problem is, I'm getting a bit of a reputation. I always come back with the horse, but never the thief. People are starting to talk. If I don't come back with something to show this time I'm afraid they'll start thinking I'm stealing horses for attention. The Gazette ran a story about a woman over in Onondaga county who did that last year.

I stand, running my fingers over the braid. It's tight as weave and just as strong.

"Thanks, Momma," I say, and on impulse, I hug her.

Little Joe jerks beneath me, tossing his head, feeling his oats, as we clomp out of the driveway. I have to set my heels to him, to get his attention.

"You stop that now," I say. "We got a long ride, you just simmer on now."

He snorts, stamps, and sets off at a jaunty, bone-jarring pace that I know will cease after a mile or two. Joe is the type of horse who needs the vinegar worked out of him every day, else he's a pistol. Once he's rode down though you won't find a sweeter, pluckier pony.

We ride across country, making good time. Secretly, I'm glad for a break, glad to be off the homeplace for a few days, breathe some new air, see some country. It's been back-breaking labor getting the garden in and fields tilled and planted when we're so short-handed. Let alone riding the colts I take in from neighbors to train to saddle. The horses are easy; it's the people that are hard. Some of them need a switch taken to 'em, the way they treat their horses. Now I understand what Pa meant when he said people needed broke more than the horses ever did.

The trees and grass are green and new, the mud still has ice crusts in the shady places, and the critters—the squirrels, possum, raccoon, and such—remain lean after such a long, hard winter. I close my eyes, turn my face up at the sun, and I see her face. My belly twists again.

The horse and I splash through a stream, startling a doe and twin fawns, who throw up their heads and vanish with flashes of white tails. Joe splashes first one foot then the other in the knee-deep water. I snort at him, then laugh out loud, feeling free and wild for the first time in months. He tosses his head, twisting back to look at me, snorting as if laughing.

No one can ever say horses lack a sense of humor.

We ride out of the stream bed and up into the rolling country.

Since Pa died, times have been hard. We lost one of the boys to scarlatina, another to the war. There's only Momma and me to run the place, and the hired hand, so I feel badly, leaving them with so much work to be done. But this is important work too, and as such I ignore the cats wrestling inside me and study the ground and trees and shrubs for signs. There's a language, of broken branches and scatterings of rocks, which horse thieves use among themselves. It's possible, Pa taught me, to track them not by their prints but by their own language. They used to tap the telegraph lines, Pa said. They'd learn the imprint that the operators used and impersonate them on the lines, to throw off pursuit by law enforcement. But moss and twigs never lie, Pa said, not if you're clever in reading them.

Joe and I stop for the night. It feels like we've hardly been riding at all since we didn't start off until the afternoon. We make a fire, I rub him down, and we set a can of beans over the fire to warm. I fetch water from a stream nearby and set some coffee on. I don't really want it, but I want something warm before the chill of the evening sets in. I lay the bedroll out over the horse blanket, smoothing the top with a lingering touch of my hand.

Joe grazes on his picket while we watch the sun go down, all orange and red. I think of the boys in the trenches in France. I think of all those lost to the influenza last year and press my mouth together, hoping to whoever might care enough to listen that last year was the worst and that this year will be better. Momma deserves for this year to be better.

The fire has almost burned out when I hear something moving beyond the ring of firelight. I reach for my pistols as a precaution, but since Joe just looks out, swivels his ears, and returns to grazing the area where I've picketed him, I already know who's there.

"You didn't stray far," I say.

She swings down off her mount. "I like your hair," she replies.

I stand up and put the pistols away, making her a plate of beans and hardtack while she pickets her horse next to mine. She loosens the cinch, but doesn't unsaddle it. I dump the half-drunk cup of coffee I've been sipping onto the embers and pour her fresh into the same mug. I try not to look at the horse, but I can't help it. It's a sorrel this time, three white socks, white blaze. It's Llewellyn's horse, I think, but can't be sure in this light. She hasn't taken time to dye it yet, if it looks even vaguely recognizable. She prides herself on how well she can disguise a horse.

"I can steal a horse in the morning and sell it back to the owner in the evening as a wholly different animal," she boasted once. We'd been up in the hills then. I remember sleeping on a horse blanket with a rock in my back. She and I raced down on horseback to the lake below, charging the horses straight into the water that splashed up in a stinging spray, then we fell into it, rolling in the water like seals.

She drops her pack beside mine and makes a long "Ahhhhh....!" of contentedness when she sees the plate and mug I've set on an upturned log for her. She smiles at me and cocks her head to one side, crooking a finger at me.

"Give us a kiss, love," she says.

I go to her, tugged into her orbit like a bird on a string. She only has to gesture and I move to her will.

Her lips are soft against mine. Too soft, perfectly soft. Not like Tommy Houghston's, when he tried to steal a kiss out behind the barn that time. I shoved him into the manure pile and ran off. When Momma heard about it from Mrs. Greene, she scolded me.

"You'll never catch a husband like that," she said, "being as you are."

She meant about being a girl who worked like a man, who rode down colts and knew the ins of fixing tractors or mending fence, not about being a girl who liked kissing girls more than she liked kissing boys. Momma didn't know anything about that. No one did.

Except Beryl.

Beryl Hayes. Beautiful. Wanted. Horse thief. Who preferred the nickname Belle, after the famous horse thief Belle Starr. And I was the one sent to bring her to justice. The problem was I didn't much feel like bringing her to justice while she was diddling on my lady bits.

Luckily, she wasn't doing that now, but instead after kissing me hello, had fallen on the plate like a starving pig, scraping up the beans with the hard biscuit, her chin an inch from the plate.

"I rode twenty miles today," she says, "or thereabouts. Thought my belly would worm its way out of m'backbone."

"Is that Llewellyn's horse?"

Belle shrugs. "Doubt it. I walked out of the livery with it."

She's lying. And I know it. But as always, I try to pretend that what she says is the truth.

"You've got the balls of a brass monkey."

Belle snorts with laughter. "That's me. Brass balls, and the only honest horse thief in the state."

"You know why," I say.

She's still laughing, but she eyes me with flint in her gaze. It's an old argument between us. She'd like me to let her take the horses on, is resentful that I insist on returning them. "I know it don't make me any richer."

"Don't let's fight."

"No…" her voice turns soft. "Don't." She sets the empty plate off to the side and then our bodies are pressed together on the bedroll and horse blankets. She smells of sweat and horse and tastes of sour coffee, and her lips are the sweetest thing I've ever tasted. I can't think when she kisses me like this, the dizzying, head spinning, world tilting kind of kiss that only Belle can deliver. When she's kissing me, especially if she kisses me down there, I don't think that she's a horse thief and I'm supposed to be the law, all I can think is that this is how things are supposed to be, just me and her.

When we were up in the hills, when we were in the water, I remember thinking: this is what love is like.

Her mouth is hard against mine, hot and desperate. She's pushing my clothes out of the way, tugging my shirt from my pants, shoving her tongue down my throat as if she'll crawl inside of me.

"Touch me, Katie." She groans against my neck, biting down and sucking hard enough to leave bruises. Her fingers are working my pants, unbuckling me, struggling to get inside. "Oh god, I need you."

Her words send a jolt through me.

My fingers tangle in her short brown hair and I kiss her back just as ecstatically. I catch her eagerness, her impatience. Her jerky motions have a desperate quality that I quickly adopt, needing that flesh to flesh as badly as she does.

In the intervening times between our encounters, I ache for her. I think that the next time it'll be better, we'll have more time, be able to linger over one another, but every time it's like this—fast and frantic. She falls on me like a ravening thing, sucking, biting, thrusting, as if she can't get enough or quickly enough.

"Slow down," I want to say. "Savor me."

But she's incapable of doing so. And so I assimilate her needs as my own, rocking the heel of my hand against her pelvis as she arches against my fingers, burying them inside her wet heat.

"Oh god!" she cries out, coming like a freight train. She bucks, hammering her hips against my hand, bursting with the wetness of a ripe fruit.

She rolls onto her back, naked on the blankets, and I follow her, leaning over her to take a nipple in my mouth.

She coos, petting the tight twist of my braid.

Her nipple is a pebble against my tongue, warm and hard at once. Sucking her nipples right after she comes almost always makes her come again, almost immediately. And it does this time as well. I watch her fingers, splayed over herself, playing with other nipple, teasing down there, and she comes with an arch of her back and a sigh on her lips. Her eyelids flutter and she gazes at me with a hard-eyed intensity that makes me kiss her mouth, gently this time.

I'm not one driven to say much. Horses don't much care what you say to them, it just matters the way that you say it. I feel compelled to say something now, as she struggles to ease her panting breath, her chest rising and falling rapidly against mine. But I don't know what it would be that I would say. So I stroke her hair and settle for the first thing that comes to mind.

"Easy now," I say. We rest together with our foreheads nearly touching.

Gradually her breathing comes back down, and the sweat on her body cools. She sighs, her body melting against mine, and her eyes close. She has a funny half-smile on her lips as she nestles against me.

"Good girl," I croon, "good girl."

I expect any moment now that the attention will turn to me. I'm still bursting for her touch between my legs, and I'm eager for her to bring me off. But instead of looking to me, she shoves me off and shoots up off the blankets.

"Just what do you think you're playing at?" she asks.

I'm taken aback, don't know what she's talking about.

"You think it's all right and all, for someone like you," she says, "but it's not."

"Belle," I say, "what are you talking about?"

She wraps her arms around her waist, hugging herself. "You think you can just make me feel this way and it's all right?"

I go to her, but she shrugs me away. I try again. I don't have the words, and sometimes, with horses, the touch is enough. She shoves me off again. Tears in her eyes, on her cheeks, she pushes me, until I hit one of the maple trees. She pins me there, the bark scraping my back all to hell, her hand working my swollen cunt so well that I can't tell if I'm gasping for the pain or the pleasure.

"Like this?" she's saying. "Do the boys back home out behind the barn touch you like I touch you?"

I'd made the mistake of telling her about Tommy Houghston and how he'd tried to kiss me. I shake my head, but it's not enough. She thrusts her fingers deeper inside me, stroking me deep until I almost can't take it.

"I can't hear you."

"No!" The word is a wail. "No, they could never touch me like you do."

And I come, I come for her so hard that I see stars, that I black out for long moments so that when I regain my senses, she's eased me down the length of the tree.

"Good girl," she croons, "good girl. I knew you were all mine." She gets me back on the blankets, then kneels to either side of my face, and her parts are there, glistening and swollen for me. I taste her. She moans. The little noises she makes are driving me crazy and I thrust my tongue deeper inside her folds as her hips nudge forward, a gentle rolling canter motion. With a groan, I grip her hips and plant my face against her, licking, sucking, thrusting, hungry for the essence of her, for her moans and squeals, for her gyrating, rocking orgasms that make me feel like a goddess.

I hear slow clapping from beyond the fire and a man struts up wearing a straw boater hat and a tweed suit.

"That was quite the show, darlin'," he says, looking at Belle. "Mind if I help out with the encore?"

I leap to my feet, grabbing for my pistols, but I hear the click of a revolver and freeze. I slowly raise my gaze to look down the length of the man's hog leg.

"Too slow, little missy," he says, then chuckles. "But after what Madam here put you through, I can see why your fast-draw might be a little off."

"What do you want?" Belle asks. And the way she says it, the way she isn't scared, just gets up and picks her clothes up off the ground, shaking off the dirt before pulling on her pants and shirt, that's what sends chills up my spine the way a weapon could never do.

"You think I'd let my favorite flower run off and leave me?" he says. "A little slap and tickle, that's fine, but we killed a man, darlin'."

"Posse's already here," Belle says, pulling on her boots.

He looks at me, chuckles again, really amused this time, and lowers the hammer on his revolver before sticking it back in the holster.

"Well, well," he says, tonguing his big gums, "ain't that somethin'."

"You killed Llewellyn?" They're the first words I've spoken since our new friend walked out of the trees.

Belle and the man exchange a look.

"There were shots fired," she answers. But she won't look at me as she tightens the cinch on her horse's saddle.

Little Joe is restless on his picket, picking up on the charged air in the camp.

"She can come with us," Belle says.

He glances at her, then back at me. Smiles. He crosses the space between them to where she's making meaningless minute adjustments to her saddle and gear. He seizes her by the hair and jerks her back. She scrambles to her feet, cheeks flushed, and he backhands her into the side of the horse. The horse spooks, jerking on the picket, eyes wide in the dimness outside the firelight.

"You see?" he asks me. "You see what a stupid bitch she is?"

I'm still naked, still in a crouch beside my saddlebags. Watching.

"Baby," Belle is saying. "We can just go, ride away from here. She won't tell. Please, baby, Paul, I need you."

Belle is on her knees, blood on her chin from a cut lip, begging, sniveling, snot running from her nose, hands clutching at his trousers, pleading with this... man... not to leave her.

When she and I were in the mountains, she asked me why I was content with her, why I didn't want a man.

I shrugged. "Don't need one," I said.

She'd looked at me quizzically.

"But... it's a man. You have to have a man."

I'd stirred the fire with a stick.

"I don't," I'd said.

"Paul, please," she's begging. "I need you."

And that's when it hits me: she believes this. She believes that men are the keys to the kingdom and that you have to have one to get anywhere in this world. This man, this partner she's blubbering to, she thinks he's the way to success.

That's why she's begging for forgiveness at his knees and not mine.

I've known all along it would come to this. But now, with someone, a friend of mine, dead, with her eyes wild and begging, I know with a cold clarity that no matter how she loves me, she will always be this weak.

Bitterness rises in my throat.

Paul would have jerked around to strike me, but instead he freezes as the barrel of the 1890s Remington pokes against his kidney and he hears the cock of the hammer. Belle rises, breath hiccupping.

"Tie him up," I order.

"Don't do it, darlin'," Paul says to me. "Don't forget what I know about you. What I seen. You're an abomination. A deviant. You really want those rumors spread about you?"

"Shut up," I say.

"Think about it. You let me go, you can have her. We can have her. Everybody wins."

"Yeah," Belle says. "Listen to him, Katie. We can all get what we want…"

She makes to move toward us, hand extended as though to touch my face.

I jerk away from her, wrench his arm up his back and force the Remington deeper into his kidneys. He grunts and I am satisfied. He needs to hurt, like I hurt right now.

"Six rounds makes a lotta holes," I say flatly. And repeat myself, "Tie him up."

Part of me always knew I'd have to give her up eventually, that I'd have to make this choice. She wasn't for me, though she'd become a part of me. A part of me I was no longer proud of. That I loved a woman wasn't the problem. That I loved a woman who was a murderess and a liar—that was. Because no matter what else I might be—a tribad, a rubster, a Sapphic, a silent sinner, a sodomite, or a player of the game of flats—I did not condone liars and theft.

Although I had, by letting her get away time and time again. Even though I retrieved the horses, I'd been party to it.

How many horses had she 'napped in other counties? How many men had she and her consort killed? How much blood lay on my hands for swivving this woman instead of hanging her?

She would never love me, not more than she loved herself. She wasn't capable of that. And it made me feel sorry for her, though it did not soften my heart or my resolve. For all that I might care for her and not wish to see her hanged, for all that it might gut me and leave me a hardened shell of a woman, trying to be with her would hurt more. Because loving someone who isn't capable of loving you back, well that's one of the worst feelings of all.

She has the rope now and sets to binding his hands behind his waist.

"We can be together," she says to me. Her nimble fingers draw the knots tight. Her eyes are shining, maniacal. She's a rabbit in a trap and the coyote's coming. She's desperate for a way out. "We can go away from him…" And she starts up the same patter she just gave her other lover moments before.

I could be free of this, I think, gazing over at her. Free of this taint, free of this claim of hers upon my spirit. She's swearing how she'll be mine, telling me how we could be on our own and free, riding the range, away from the damn dirt and sod-busting and chores.

I think of the boys in the trenches. I think of my brother, raging in his sweated-through sheets with his hallucinations as death claimed him. I think of my father as he pressed his guns into my hand.

"Take care of your mother," he'd said. "Take care of the horses."

I would not kill her, not here and not like this. The law was designed to deal with people like them, and they would be tried and hanged and while I might not ever find another I loved as much as I loved my Belle Starr, I would be a better woman for it. And if I did find another, well then I'd be ready for her. Ready for someone who could give to me as eagerly as I gave to them. Ready for a woman I could lie down beside at night and rise with in the morning and put in an honest day's work beside, who would not mind the laboriousness of work, who would smile at me from beneath her hat, a secret smile just for us, who wouldn't ask me to prove my love by allowing her time and time again to steal and to kill.

"Now unbuckle his belt and get his pants down."

"Oh honey," Paul mocks with a lewd waggle of his tongue. "You'll have to kiss me first."

I remove the revolver from his ribs and rap him a good one upside the head. I hold him by the bonds at his wrists and while he stumbles, he doesn't fall.

"Tie his boots together too," I tell Belle.

She's gorgeous, even with blood and snot and desperation rolling off her in stinking waves. I see her now, really see her. See her desperation and her need. She isn't strong enough on her own. That's why she clings to Paul. She's one of those women who believe they always need a man, to keep them safe, to order them around.

I despise those kinds of women.

She finishes the knots and stands back.

"Fetch me my shirt."

She does and returns with it, wringing it with her rough hands, reminding me of Momma with the checked dish towel.

I kick him behind the knees to get him to drop down, angling a knee into his back to get him down on his belly in the dirt.

"Bring that extra lariat over here," I tell her.

My heart is cold, my mind made up.

"Katie…" Her look is desperate.

I gaze at her shining, tear-stained face, at her wild, manic eyes.

"Lie face down and hands by your ears." I lick my lips and still taste her there, juices drying on my face.

"Baby," she says, "I love you."

How many times have I wanted to hear her say that? How many times have I mouthed those words myself against her hair?

This is not love, I decide, not with Belle. While she might care for me more than she ever had any other person, I was not ready to bet my life, my farm, my future, my mother's future, on heated pledges made in desperation from this common thief.

She's everything I thought I wanted. But she's nothing I need.

Still naked, I stare her down. Slowly, she lies down on her belly. She's shaking as I make the knots. They still hang horse thieves. And this time I'm returning with more than just the horses.

The cats in my stomach are still as I pull on my shirt.

FREEDOM
HARPER BLISS

At first glance, I'm not certain it's Brooke, and once I am, I'm not sure if it's appropriate to approach her.

She makes the decision for me. "Ella, is that you?"

"In the flesh," I say, a stupid joke going nowhere. I put the book I was thinking of buying back on the shelf.

"How have you been?" Brooke is holding a stack of thrillers. She goes through at least three every week.

"Yeah. Good," I mumble. "You know, adjusting to the single life." Instinctively, I want to inquire about Jamie's health, but it still seems to hurt too much to say her name—even to her own mother.

We stand around in the awkward silence that follows for a few seconds.

"Do you want to grab a coffee next door?" Brooke asks. "Catch up?"

I don't really know what to say. Am I still obligated to be polite to this woman? It's not her fault Jamie swapped me for her new colleague after seven years together. "Maybe it's just the seven-year itch," I had tried to tell her. "Maybe you'll regret this in a few weeks." Six months have passed and I've noticed no signs of regret.

"Sure," I say to Brooke. "Coffee would be good."

"Let me pay for these and I'll meet you at the exit in a few." Brooke says it as if we're simply old acquaintances who've run into each other. As if her daughter never broke my heart.

"Okay." I watch her saunter off in her mink coat and heels that are not suited for Saturday afternoon shopping. I never really belonged in the Stevens family, anyway. Too posh for me.

While I wait for her I make up a dozen excuses in my head why I suddenly have to go, but when she meets me at the door, a tote bag full of books in one hand, gently touching me on the shoulder with the other, I meekly follow her. At least, I know Brooke is smart enough to spare me tales of her daughter's newfound happiness.

At the café next door, she insists on buying the coffees. I glare at her from my seat while she places our order at the counter. All long limbs and no trace of a protruding waistline. Everyone in that family is so skinny. Another reason why I didn't belong.

She places the cups on the small round table between us, sits, and slings one leg over the other.

"Thanks," I mumble, wishing I had some whiskey to pour into my coffee.

"After, uh, *it* happened, I tried to call you several times, but I understand why you wouldn't have wanted to speak to me."

It? I remember Brooke's number appearing on the screen of my phone. And how I had to keep myself from picking up and yelling at her for producing such a cruel child, fresh rage still boiling in my blood. "I'm sorry." Inwardly, I scoff at my apology. Does Debby now sit in the chair I occupied at the Stevens' table for Sunday lunch? Do her and Brooke go for coffee together?

"I was so worried about you, Ella. I would have come to see you, but I didn't know where you had moved to and I didn't want to ask Jamie."

"It's fine, really." She has Jamie's eyes—or Jamie has hers, I suppose. Wide and grey-greenish with long,

long lashes. Long lashes and limbs. And cruel hearts. That about sums up the Stevens.

"It's not. I understand things can happen in a relationship, but Jamie didn't handle it very gracefully." Brooke takes a sip from her latte. Some milk froth clings to her lip. She licks it off gracefully. "And this Debby…" She shakes her head.

My ears perk up. This situation may be awkward, but any negative comments about my replacement will surely make it better.

"She's not like you. You knew how to handle Jamie, had a good influence on her. Two party girls together, I'm sure it can't end well."

Does she mean I'm boring? That Jamie left me for someone far more exciting? Me wanting to stay home more was a constant bone of contention between us. I'm thirty-three years old and I think there's nothing wrong with staying in on a Saturday night to watch five consecutive episodes of *Game of Thrones*.

"I tried," I say as the feelings of hurt catch up on me again. "I truly believed our relationship was strong enough to withstand the excitement of meeting someone new, but *bam*, Debby worked there for barely three weeks before Jamie left me." I briefly look into Brooke's eyes, but even that hurts. As I look away, a tear makes its way out of the corner of my eye. I quickly wipe it away, hoping she didn't see.

"Hey." Brooke leans over the table and cups my hand with her palm. "Did you know I sold the house? I live in a flat ten minutes away from here. Why don't we continue our conversation there? I'll pour you something stronger."

I'm not sure I want to go farther down this road. I just wanted to buy some books this afternoon and order a couple of cases of wine to be delivered to my flat downtown. I had not prepared for reminiscing. But maybe it will help. Maybe Brooke can shine a new light on matters. And perhaps she can say more unflattering things about Debby. I also don't want to cry in the middle of this coffee shop. "Okay." I nod and quickly empty my cup. I hope the contents of Brooke's well-stocked bar have survived her move from the suburbs.

The city sidewalks are crowded, so I walk behind Brooke until the ocean of people clears up and we arrive at one of the posh streets alongside the park.

"The house simply got too big. You've no idea of the amount of maintenance a place like that requires, and just for little old me. I was fed up with it." She gestures at a building a few feet away. "I live there now and I can walk everywhere. It's fabulous."

"I bet," I say, as I follow her inside, past an obsequiously nodding doorman.

Brooke occupies one of the lower floor apartments, but the view of the park is still breathtaking.

"Lovely." I scan the living room and recognize some pieces of furniture from the old house. I'm surprised Jamie didn't talk her mother into getting rid of that sofa, considering what we once did in it. Twice, actually…

"Now, for that drink." Brooke shrugs off her coat and heads to a cabinet in the corner of the living room. "Do you still like a good brandy?"

"Oh yes." I perk up at the mention of it.

She grabs the bottle and two brandy snifters, and deposits them on the coffee table, gesturing for me to take a seat next to her.

After pouring us both a generous amount, she hands me a glass and clinks the fat belly of her glass to mine. "You look good, Ella, don't let anyone tell you otherwise."

"Thanks." Immediately, a flush burns on the skin of my cheeks. I wasn't expecting a compliment. The brandy helps. Now both my throat and my cheeks burn.

"How are you coping with being alone?" She draws her lips into a lopsided grin. "As you well know, I'm an expert at that particular activity."

I asked Jamie a dozen times, shaking my head in disbelief, why a beautiful, classy woman like her mother would prefer to remain single for so long after her father's death. "She likes her independence," Jamie would say. "And why don't you ask her yourself if you're so keen to find out?" I wouldn't have dreamed of asking that question back then, and now Brooke practically brings it up herself.

"It sucks." My eloquence has let me down a lot since the break-up. "I mean, I'm not very good at it. How do you, um, go about it?"

"Jamie may have been foolish enough to let you go, but you won't be alone for long, Ella. I'm sure of that." She brings her lips to the glass and sips. "As for me, I just can't seem to find anyone to my taste. Let's just say some of my preferences have changed since Gareth and I got married." She locks her eyes on mine and drags the tip of her tongue across her teeth.

I drink to recover from the sudden intensity surrounding us, from the change of air. What am I doing here, anyway? I look away and my eyes land on a picture of Jamie, all blond and healthy and beautiful. Brooke's hair is blond as well, but more golden and quite probably dyed.

"I should go," I say, suddenly overwhelmed by an alien emotion. I can't identify it as grief or anger—the two main ones I've been suffering from of late. It's more a mixture of apprehension and the rush of being flattered by a member of the Stevens family. I don't get up, though. I remain firmly planted in my seat.

"Stay." Brooke reaches for the bottle and refills my glass, which isn't even empty yet. "I've just remembered something... funny, I guess."

I arch up my eyebrows.

"Remember when we went to the coast a few years ago? The summer of 2010, I think it was."

I nod. "Yeah." We'd stayed in a small house by the beach and all had to share the same bathroom. It was the only time I ever saw Brooke in pajamas and without makeup.

"I overheard a conversation you and Jamie were having on the front porch. I wasn't eavesdropping, I just happened to walk past you girls."

She has my full attention. Somewhere, in the back of my mind, I have an inkling of where this is going, but it hasn't fully registered yet. But maybe I'm wrong.

"You said something like 'I'd do your mother in a heartbeat. She's smoking hot for her age.'"

For an instant, my jaw slackens and my brain stops working. I narrow my eyes and lock my gaze on Brooke's. "I didn't mean to be disrespectful. I was just trying to wind Jamie up."

"I took it as a compliment." A small smile plays on her lips again. "I've always liked you, but ever since then, I've liked you a little more." The skin around her eyes crinkles as her mouth breaks into a wide smile.

If I had to hold up my hand and swear on a bible, I wouldn't be able to claim the thought never crossed my mind without perjuring myself.

"I'm sorry, but I don't quite know what to say to that." I may have said those words—years ago—but she invited me into her home, poured me brandy, and brought them up.

"What's your stance on the subject these days?"

Can't say I saw that one coming. "Seriously?" The brandy is starting to go to my head, and I've been played by members of the Stevens' clan enough to know how to play along.

She sips and nods.

"I stand by my words." I say it with much more bravado than I feel.

"Mmm." She scrunches her lips into a semi-pout, her eyes drawn into slits. "I can only admire that. I'm not getting any younger."

Is she fishing for more compliments? Or is she after something else? Either way, Brooke has barely changed since I first met her about seven years ago. I can't remember her exact age, but I'm guessing late fifties, or perhaps sixty already. She looks at least ten years younger. Because of the direction this unexpectedly strange conversation has taken, the thought crosses my mind again. I immediately reject it. Fantasies are just that for a reason. "You don't look a day over forty," I say, exaggerating, possibly to make a point.

She chuckles. "I'm sorry for making you feel uncomfortable, Ella." She deposits her empty glass on the coffee table and places a hand on my knee. "All I wanted was to cheer you up. Gosh, you looked so sad an hour ago. At least now I can spot a hint of a smile." She squeezes my knee and shoots me a big grin.

My glance drops from her smile to her hand on my knee. She leaves it there, zapping shots of lightning through my flesh, as if her fingers are electrically charged. I haven't been touched by another woman in a long time. Not that it's an excuse for anything, especially not for the thoughts in my mind getting racier by the second. But am I dreaming this or is she coming on to me?

Despite certain body parts starting to throb violently, I say, "I should probably really go now."

"Why?" She scoots closer to me on the sofa, the leather creaking under her legs, her fingers digging deeper into my flesh. "No longer standing by your words?" The light of the late afternoon sun slanting through the window catches in her eyes. She tilts her head and finds my ear with her mouth. "Here's your chance to... do me." After her lips have touched my earlobe briefly, she continues, "I want you to."

"But, what about—" I protest.

"No." Her voice is suddenly stern, still low and gravelly, but harsher in tone. "Don't go there. This is about you and me."

How can she even say that? How can it ever be just about her and me? The only reason I'm even here is because of her daughter. But I know what she means. She's asking. It's my choice. The phrase "consenting adults" springs to mind. Plus the fact that, because of the dismissive way Jamie treated me in the end, I'm in no way obligated to keep her feelings from getting hurt—I'm not her mother. She certainly didn't seem to care a whole lot about my feelings, when it was her time to choose.

I nod, my breath already catching in my throat. I bring my hands to the back of Brooke's neck and pull her close. I stare into her eyes—Jamie's eyes. Is it a twisted sort of revenge? Unexpected comfort? A few words from years ago catching up with me? It stops mattering as soon as our lips connect. I don't need to know her motivation. The kiss crashes through me and destroys at least a little bit of my pain in the process.

The hand she put on my knee earlier travels upward and every tiny movement of it shudders through my flesh. Her other hand is on my throat, her breath in my mouth, her lips on mine.

"Come on," she whispers when we come up for air. She stands and reaches out her hand. I take it and follow her to the bedroom. A brief interlude during which we could both come to our senses. I don't, and by the time she slams the door of the bedroom shut behind us, I'm glad she, clearly, hasn't either.

From the start, it's evident this can only be a one-night-stand, but far from a frivolous, playful one. Strings are already attached. Strings that can never be undone.

She shifts her weight to one leg and starts to unbutton her blouse. In response, I pull my top over my head. In a flash, she comes for me, and I see the need in her eyes. She cups my jaw in her palms before kissing me again. Softly at first, tiny nips at my bottom lip, but soon her tongue darts into my mouth and I start to lose myself again.

I curve my arms behind her back to find the clasp of her bra. Her hands go in search of mine, but my bra closes in the front, so I push myself away gently and show her by undoing one hook. She cocks her head, as if to say, "I think I can manage," and swats my hands away. Slowly, she frees my breasts, my nipples already hard as pebbles, ready for her.

I reach for the button of her trousers next, zipping her down in a frenzy. After stepping out of them, she unbuttons my jeans and pushes them down over my hips.

When she pulls me back in for a kiss, our breasts touch, and we both catch our breath simultaneously. She drags me with her as she walks backward to the bed and crashes down on it, pulling me on top of her. I let my lips wander to the hollow of her neck, her collarbones. I have to taste her nipples. She has her hands in my hair and I could swear she's pushing me down, coaxing me to explore her body.

My lips find her nipple, hard and the darkest of pink. I cup her breast in my hand and suck her nipple between my lips.

She moans and I suck harder while my other hand finds her other breast. How long has it been since Brooke has been touched? I roll her nipple between my thumb and index finger, and the guttural cry that she utters above my head, indicates it may have been a while, but I have no way of knowing and I certainly don't intend to ask.

I feel her hands on my ears and she hoists me up, pressing her lips to my mouth, her tongue dancing with mine. When we break free and I look into her eyes, the desire pooling in them lights a fire under my skin. This time, when my mouth travels down the same path it did before, my hand goes lower, first tracing the waistband of her panties, but soon finding the soaked panel between her legs. Maybe she's been thinking about this since the day she overheard me say she was hot.

My lips clamp down on her nipple again, I let one finger slip under the panel of her panties, more probing than touching.

"Jesus, Ella," a voice above my head says. I barely recognize it.

I push myself up and lock my eyes on hers while yanking down her panties. Brooke Stevens lies completely naked in front of me, her legs already spread, ready for me to take her.

I was only going to buy a book this afternoon. Instead, I ended up here.

I lie down next to her and place a hand on her stomach. Her skin shivers under my touch as I draw a circle around her belly button. I kiss her neck and let my finger go down, slowly, stopping briefly just above her clit.

Brooke has one hand curved under my neck, her fingers on my shoulders, her nails digging deep.

I dip lower, circling her clit, before spreading her pussy lips wide with two fingers. Her hips are already bucking up against me, her head thrown back in the pillows. As slowly as I can muster, I let one finger slip inside of her. Then another. I fuck her gently, controlled, increasing my speed with small increments. When she starts meeting my strokes with thrusts of her pelvis, I push my torso away from her and bend over. The first flick of my tongue against her clit is just a warning shot. Then I get serious. I launch an assault of licks while my fingers drive down deep inside of her.

With her long limbs, she can easily grab a fistful of my hair in her hands. She pulls it roughly, as if losing the last scrap of self-control.

A loud sigh followed by a moan precedes an instant in which her body goes rigid. She yanks at my hair so forcefully it hurts, but I take it easily, because I can feel the walls of her pussy clamp around my fingers as she bucks up higher.

She puffs out a large breath of air as her body relaxes onto the covers. After I let my fingers slide from her I quickly push myself up, eager to read her face. But Brooke's face is entirely covered by her hands and I don't know what to think. I can hardly start feeling guilty now, though.

"Jesus," she says, the sound muffled by her hands.

"Are you all right?" I ask when she peeks at me through her fingers.

"I have no idea." She lets her hands drop down, one of them landing on her chest, the other on my shoulder. "But that was..." Her lips crack into a wide smile, lighting up her face. She narrows her eyes and shuffles around until she's on her side, watching me, elbow bent, her head resting in the palm of her hand.

"Insane?" I offer. "Disturbing perhaps? Or maybe just a little twisted?"

She brings a finger to my lips and presses down. "Shh." Her finger trails down along my chin, in a straight line, until it's just above my breasts. "We're not done yet." Her finger wanders in between my breasts, tracing a line underneath each of them. "And I was going to say wonderful, by the way." She tilts her body until half of it covers mine, her nose buried in my hair.

My skin breaks out in goose bumps as she hitches her body on top of me, her knees spreading my legs in the process. She plants her hands on either side of my head and looks down at me, not saying anything, sinking her teeth into her bottom lip. Then, she bends at the waist, briefly kisses my nipples, before going for the prize.

Brooke Stevens, I think, when her mouth connects with my clit, is about to go down on me. And then she does. The tip of her tongue trails across my pulsing pussy lips, before she sucks my clit into her mouth. I'm so wet, I can feel it trickle along my inner thighs, all the way onto her duvet cover.

And if I ever dreamed of taking things this far, it was only furtively, in unguarded moments just before sleeping or waking, and never with the intention of turning it into reality. But here I am. Legs spread. Brooke's blond head moving between my thighs, her tongue lapping at my most intimate parts. If I close my eyes, it may just as easily be Jamie down there, so I keep them open. I take in my surroundings. This is a new place. A new life. A different person. Both her and me.

I don't say any of the things I used to say to Jamie in the bedroom. I don't need to, anyway. I've already got Brooke where I want her: her lips locked on my clit, her tongue twirling around. What happens next is as much physical as it's emotional. The juices that flow from between my legs, coating Brooke's chin and lips, free me from more than the sexual tension that built up in the course of this afternoon. When my muscles tremble beneath the touch of Brooke's tongue, and the first climax in years not administered by Jamie or myself rushes through me, I burst into tears. The tears are not for Jamie. They're for me. For the joy of this moment. For Brooke's lips on my clit and the way she looks at me when she comes up for air, her face flanked by my thighs, her green eyes sparkling.

And I know all too well this is not the beginning of romance. Only freedom.

ASCENDING AMELIA
ERZABET BISHOP

I see you there, in the shadows of the seating area trying
to be invisible. Your elegance against the dark
background of the club brings me to you like a moth to a
flame. You play with your straw, making little designs
with whatever is left at the bottom of your glass. Your
back is straight and the schoolgirl white blouse you wear
is neatly buttoned and tight against your breasts and
tucked into a short pleated skirt. Not the usual club wear,
to be sure. Not unless it's naughty teacher night. It makes
me chuckle that you would wear the stereotypical
schoolgirl outfit.

Your friends are all dressed for seduction, but you
are different. Unsure. Are you even old enough? I watch
them as they scurry from the table, leaving you alone. My
eyes dart to the Dungeon Mistress across the darkened
room. She too has seen the group leave you. Her brow
furrows in thought and she gives me a nod. It is against
the rules to leave someone unattended who clearly has no
experience. It is as plain as the pert little nose on your
adorable face. I can't leave you for just anyone to acquire.
Given permission, I walk toward you wondering if you
really belong here. You are so young... so pure.

You must feel the weight of being watched. Your
eyes widen in surprise as they meet mine. You flush
beautifully and your gaze stays on me as I walk to your
table, my hips swaying seductively in my new heels and
skintight leather skirt. My breasts push up against my new

corset and I can sense your eyes lingering there. You blush furiously and your eyes dart away. So not impervious to my charms then. Good.

"Is this seat taken?" I ask.

"Not at all." Your eyes meet mine, startled.

"You came with friends?" I ask.

"Yes," you say, awkwardly staring out into the shadows of the crowded room and twisting a piece of long red hair around your finger. A Domme walks by, clad in a leather bustier, her sex bare and unclothed for the world to see. A nude slave collared and leashed trails behind her. Your eyes travel across the sinful curves of the Domme and linger on the cinnamon ass of the slave as she passes. You see me watching you and stare down at your drink glass.

"Is this your first time at Club Ascension?"

You nod, not speaking.

Undaunted, I forge ahead. "Would you like me to show you around?" I offer you my hand.

You hesitate, nervously meeting my eyes, picking at the fabric of the tablecloth.

"We don't have to, if you'd rather not. I couldn't help but notice you sitting here all alone." I reach out and brush your cheek with my hand and watch your lips curve upward in a shy smile. It electrifies me and my pussy begins to tingle. I wonder, does it resonate in yours?

"Please," you say, and stand up. "I let them bring me out here on a dare."

"Really?" My lips twist into a frown. Is she straight then?

You gaze at the floor, completely at a loss for words. Another pulse of desire bursts between my thighs.

"What's your name?" I ask.

"Amelia," you say.

"Are you straight, Amelia?"

"What?" Your eyes go wide.

"I don't want to waste your time or mine. Simply answer the question please," I state, not wanting to mince words.

"I'm not sure." You fumble with the glass on the table, looking anywhere but at me.

"Follow me, lovely schoolgirl."

You move away from the table and we walk together through the crowd and head to the first station.

"I'm not really a student," you say.

"Are you sure?" I pause and look back. "You do seem the type that is up for learning."

You follow, your teeth worrying your lip. Your eyes glance in all directions, unsure of the scenes happening around you. We stop at the first location. I want to see what kind of mettle you have under that short skirt.

"This is a spanking couch." I run my hand across the padded leather seat and gesture to you to do the same.

"What am I supposed to do? If I was going to play I mean?" Your fingers touch the leather and your gaze takes in the wall of paddles.

"Well, usually you would strip in the locker room and come out here with your Domme for the night. Everything is agreed upon before anything ever takes place. Safe, sane and consensual is how we roll here," I say, pointing to the rules posted on the wall. "I am sorry your hosts left you uninformed and unattended. That was very inconsiderate of them."

"Oh, it's fine," you say. "I told them to go have fun."

"No, it isn't actually," I tell you. "You should never be left unattended on your first time in the club. Not without someone watching over you." I purse my lips and frown. I will look your friends up later and have a word. "What about you?" I ask. "What do you do for

131

fun?" I stand closer to you and the scent of your perfume wafts toward me. *Simply lovely.*

"I..." You pause, unsure of how to answer. Your lips part, lightly glossed but so full they make my pulse pound harder between my legs. I want to taste you. To hold you against me, breasts crushed together and straining. I swallow, trying to get myself under control. You are forbidden in many ways. So new to this environment. Inexperienced and fresh.

"Do you want to play?" I look into your eyes trying to gauge if you are just here on a lark, or if there is really a kinkster hiding under that schoolgirl mini skirt. It has to be a costume. No one underage gets into this club. Ever. "We won't do anything you don't want to do," I say, hoping you will take me up on it.

You bite your lip and my body clenches.

"Okay," you say, your breath erupting in a sigh. "Where do I go?"

I point to the door of the changing area. "Go in there and place your items in a locker. There are instructions on the wall. Read them."

You meet my eyes then turn away, heading for the door.

It doesn't take you long to change out of your clothes and come back to me, naked and trembling. High breasts tipped with rosy nipples grace your form, firmly tapering down a taut stomach into a woman's hips. Your neatly shaved mound makes my fingers ache to touch you.

"You're lovely," I say, caressing your hair. You blush again.

"Thank you," you say, bringing your long red hair in front of your body to try and shield your nudity.

I stop you. "Never hide yourself," I say. "Not here."

You look up at me, trembling and unsure. Your eyes are full of innocence but shift into something more subtle.

"Go stand over by the couch while I select our first implement," I say. My heart does a funny little skitter as I scope your heart shaped ass. The smooth ivory curves make me want to paddle some pink color onto them.

"I've read about BDSM in novels. That's why they brought me here," you say, fingering the couch and caressing the leather.

"And what do you think?" I hold my breath, waiting for you to answer. The paddle is heavy in my hands as I make my way back to your side.

"Is that for me?" you ask, eyes wide.

"Yes." I hold it up for you to inspect. It is a simple wooden paddle with the word "slut" carved into the side.

"Is that what you think of me? That I am a slut?" Your voice trembles and you start to back away, a hurt expression on your face.

"Oh, my dear." I grab your hand and give you the paddle. "Slut is a term of pride here. It is freedom to experience another woman's hand on your skin and to relish it without shame." I take hold of your wrist and pull you toward me. I run my hand down the side of your face and gently press my lips to yours.

"Now. Are you here because you want to let that play across your skin, or are you here as a gag for your friends?" I say, staring deep into your eyes.

Your lips quiver and a tear leaks out. "I want to feel," you whisper.

"Then come," I say, pointing to the couch. "Drape yourself across here."

"Yes Ma'am." You bend and lie across the bench on your stomach, your full round ass in the air.

Your body is a delight and I tell you so. You have this lovely habit of blushing that I find utterly refreshing.

"Now, each time the paddle connects, I need you to count for me. Can you do that?" I say.

You nod.

"Here, you will call me Mistress," I tell you, my tone severe. It is a struggle not to reach out and stroke your soft flesh.

"Yes, Mistress," you say, your voice muffled against the smooth red leather of the couch.

I hold up the paddle and massage the lovely ripe mounds of your ass.

Smack!

"One," you say, your voice wobbling.

"Excellent, little one. Now for another," I say.

Smack!

I strike the other cheek. A nice matching pair of pink patches are just beginning to form, the word "slut" striping across your tender flesh.

"Two, Mistress," you rasp.

Smack! Smack!

I strike both cheeks and now your backside is nice and rosy.

"Three. Four." You are sobbing, openly crying. You are not used to impact play. A crowd has gathered and onlookers are admiring your beauty. A burst of jealousy darts through me. I do not want to share. Not yet.

"There now," I say, helping you up from the couch. "You did splendidly." I hand you a tissue from the shelf against the wall and you wipe your face.

"Are you all right?" I ask, brushing some hair out of your eyes. I hand you a bottle of water and a piece of chocolate. You take them greedily and pop the chocolate in your mouth. You twist off the cap of the bottle and take a sip. Your hands are shaking, but the chocolate will help.

I guide you inside one of the private rooms just beyond the main floor. The room is made up like an ordinary bedroom. I chose this one because I think it will make you the most comfortable.

"You may sit," I say.

You do, perched on the edge of the bed with your knees pressed together.

"Is this what you hoped for when you came with your friends tonight?" I ask.

You lower your head, unspeaking.

"No, Amelia. Don't be ashamed of your desire." I walk over and hook your chin with my finger, making you meet my eyes.

"But you. You're... you. I, well, I'm just me," you say, picking up a piece of the sheet and twisting it around your finger. "Boring old me with a fat behind and not much of anything to notice. I barely fit in that schoolgirl outfit. They only asked me here tonight because they thought it would embarrass me." A tear leaks from your eye and I smooth it away with my finger.

"No." I whisper. "Not just boring old you." I sit on the bed and face you. "Do you think that I came to this life any differently? I had a Mistress who taught me that my deepest desires were ones to rejoice in, not to hide away because they made me uncomfortable. The things that live within your heart of hearts will not go away, Amelia. They only fester and grow stronger with time."

I wipe another tear from your reddened eyes and place a kiss on your lips. You groan and ease into it, letting my tongue slip past your lips and explore you. Your breasts press against mine and I understand at once that you need this, but it has to be at your pace. Curiously, I don't mind.

You stare at me, your hands trembling. I unlace the corset that binds my breasts high and firm. They spring free and I take a deep breath. I slip out of my skirt, kicking off my shoes and place my foot on the bed. I am wearing no panties and you stare at the smooth skin of my mound.

"Roll them off," I say and point to the thigh highs.

You take your hands and delicately sweep them down my legs, rolling the nylons as you go. They fall to the floor and I am naked.

"Do you want to touch me?" I ask, standing in front of you.

"Can you close your eyes?" you ask.

I smile. "Yes. Of course. Where do you want me?"

"Here. Change places," you say.

You stand and I sit on the bed.

"Now you close your eyes and lie back," you say. "Please?"

I recline against the mattress and shut my eyes.

You move between my thighs and your fingers flutter against my skin, caressing my legs. A jolt of electricity pulses deep inside and my nipples tighten. Your fingers sweep the soft flesh of my folds and your finger eases inside my pussy. You gasp as the wet heat of me surrounds your fingers.

"You are so beautiful," you whisper. Your breath is hot on my mound and you run your tongue over my clit as you thrust. I want to do this to you. To give you the same gift you have given me.

I moan, trying not to thrust too hard at your face, but as your lips become more ardent in their explorations, I lose myself. Your fingers move in and out of me, and your tongue worships my clit. Electricity flickers behind my eyes and the exquisite rush of pure pleasure rolls me under. I drown in you. In your absolute willingness to be what I needed. Tears prickle against my eyes.

You place a gentle kiss on my belly. Your lips pause and I open my eyes.

"That was wonderful," I whisper, reaching up to brush some hair out of your eyes. You have cleaned your face already and in your gaze I see a peace that wasn't there before. I pause, wondering how much over the age limit you really are.

"Thank you, Mistress," you say.

I move to sit up, and tug you down next to me.

"You know, good little girls who please their Mistresses deserve a reward. Such a good girl." I run my hand down your breasts, outlining your taut nipples with my fingers.

"Did you like wearing the schoolgirl outfit?" I ask.

Your face burns bright. "Yes," you mumble.

An idea forms in my head. "Come Amelia. I think I know of a classroom that needs a very naughty student. What do you think?"

I stand and offer you my hand. You follow, a blazing smile on your lips.

"Yes, Mistress."

"One more thing." I add. "Go get that skirt."

BACHELORETTE PARTY
BETH WYLDE

When Linda unexpectedly shows up at my door the day before my wedding, I know something's up. It's not that Linda never comes to visit me. She does, quite often actually, but she never comes over unannounced. We always make plans ahead of time or she calls to let me know she's on her way. I don't know what she's doing, but I'm getting married in less than twenty-four hours so whatever she wants will have to be quick. I have a lot on my mind right now.

Her hand is poised to knock when I fling open the front door. Her wide-eyed expression shows her shock and it takes a minute for her to regain her composure and slide back into her usual suave butch role.

"Oh... umm, hey Jenny."

"Hey yourself. What are you doing here?" I move aside to let Linda in. She steps past me and stops in the middle of the living room, turning to watch as I shut the door.

"Nothing really. I was just in the neighborhood and thought I'd swing by to see if you're okay."

"Why wouldn't I be?"

Linda shrugs. "You're getting married tomorrow. I thought you might be kind of nervous. Maybe having some second thoughts?"

"Why would I be having second thoughts? Do you know something about Mark that I don't?"

"Lots of brides get cold feet right before their wedding, or so I've heard. I thought you might be one of those."

"Linda Rene Scruggs, you are full of shit. That is the weakest excuse I have ever heard from you, and that's really saying something."

"Since when can't I drop in and say hi without you getting all suspicious?"

"Since never. You always call first. Always! Now spill it. What's going on?"

She holds her hands up in mock surrender. "Okay, okay. I give up. You caught me." Her explanation comes out in such a rush it takes me a minute to interpret it since it sounds more like one long word than several. "Iwanttothrowyouabacheloretteparty."

"Umm... huh?" Once I get the sentence deciphered I'm struck speechless. Of all the reasons I figured Linda might give for her appearance at my door, a pre-wedding party is the last thing I expect. I stare hard into Linda's face to see if she's really serious or if she's just pulling my leg. Judging by her expression she's not joking. "What? Why?"

"There are several reasons."

"Oh, really? Ok, give me one of them."

She deflects my question completely. "Why does the fact that I want to throw you a party seem so unbelievable? We're friends aren't we?"

I nod, unable to form a more coherent reply. Linda hates Mark and Mark hates Linda. She's been vocal from the very beginning about the fact that she thinks I can do better. Mark hasn't kept his hateful opinion of Linda to himself either. It's like being the mediator in a modern day Hatfield versus McCoy feud. Not a great place to be. "You just... You've got to be kidding me. There's no reason for you to..." I lean forward and take a deep breath. I swear I smell whiskey, which is Linda's drink of choice whenever possible. "You've been drinking. I can smell it. Are you drunk?" Intoxication seems like a viable reason for Linda's crazy behavior this evening. I've seen her tie one on more than once during our extended friendship. She's seen me do the same, though somehow I always end up as the one on my knees with Linda holding back my hair as I heave. It never happens in reverse. She's definitely seen me at my worst and the fact that she still sticks by my side after everything really means a lot to me.

Linda takes an indignant step back. "I am not drunk. Nowhere even close to it. I had a couple shots earlier during a game of pool at Anna and Eve. Forget it. I'm sorry I came by."

She turns toward the door and I reach out and grab her wrist. "Wait. Hang on, please. I didn't mean to make you mad. I'm just confused. My mind's a mess and my emotions are all over the place. You're just acting strange and I don't know what to think." She lets me guide her over to the couch. I give a tug on her hand and she plops down next to me. She lands so close that our entire bodies are touching on the left side. With anyone else the arrangement might be awkward but with Linda it's comforting. I lean my head sideways until I'm resting on her shoulder. She sighs and wraps her arm around me, pulling me flush against her body. The only way we could get any closer is if I sat in her lap.

We've always been kind of touchy feely with each other but the current arrangement seems a bit extreme. I'd give anything at this moment to be able to read Linda's mind. "Was that a good sigh or a bad sigh?"

"Why does it have to be either? Maybe I just needed to let some air out."

"You're not the deep breath type."

She pulls back and I'm forced to lift my head or fall over. Our eyes meet and I swear she can see right through me. "What's that supposed to mean?"

"I don't know. You're acting funny. You're always the calm, confident type and this afternoon you seem totally off your game. What gives?"

She gets up and starts pacing the floor. Back and forth, back and forth, until my head swims with the motion. "Linda, stop! Please."

It's the please that does it. She halts in her tracks and looks down at me with blatant anguish in her eyes. "I've screwed this up so badly. I know once you're married we won't be able to hang out the way we have in the past. Mark won't tolerate it." I open my mouth to speak but Linda shakes her head to stop my protest before it even begins. "That's the truth and you know it. He hates my guts and the feeling is mutual. I need you to come with me tonight. I've got the whole evening planned out. I need you to trust me. Come on, Jenny. One last night of craziness. One more wild adventure before you get hitched and leave me behind."

I want to deny her reasoning. Tell her that Mark will never drive us apart, but I know she's right. Somewhere deep inside I've pushed the reality away, hidden it so thoroughly that I've even fooled myself into believing the lie. I know Mark though. Where Linda is concerned, he's so homophobic it's scary.

When Mark and I first started dating he handled my friendship with Linda with casual disinterest. Then as time wore on, he started making little derogatory comments toward her. I don't think Mark liked any of my gay friends, but something about Linda really rubbed him the wrong way. He made sure I knew it too. Eventually he started bitching about our outings. Nothing major at first, just snide remarks to show he hated us hanging out together. I ignored his outbursts in hopes that he'd come to love Linda as much as I do. Eventually I realized why Mark and Linda would never get along. They were both too dominant to ever defer to one another, like two alpha dogs fighting for supremacy. One had to win. They could never co-exist. By the time I figured things out we were already engaged.

The thought that Linda might be thrust out of my life for good in less than a day shatters the last of my reserves. I jump up and grab hold of her like my life depends on it. "I won't let him do that to us. You're my best friend. I need you."

Her arms around me are the anchor I need to calm myself. "I need you too but Mark's going to be your husband. He has to come first, right?"

I know I should say yes immediately. I shouldn't even have to think about it. I drop my arms and pull back, the affirmation is right on the tip of my tongue, but it won't come out. If it really comes down to a choice between Mark and Linda I'm not sure that Mark will win. The sudden realization is an eye opener. "I... I mean, well he should but..."

My indecision seems to be all the answer Linda needs. "Come on." She grabs my hand and starts towing me toward the back of the house where my bedroom is. She pulls open my closet door and tugs me inside. "Pick out something to wear." She looks me over. "Have you had a shower today?"

I shake my head. "No, not yet. I've just been lazing around. Resting up for tomorrow, I guess."

"I'll go get the water started. Grab something to wear and meet me in the bathroom."

There is no time to protest. She's out of the room before I can even open my mouth. I don't really want to argue anyway. The thought of getting out of the house for a while sounds like fun. I still don't believe the party excuse, but being by myself all day has left me thinking about things better left alone right now.

I grab my favorite jean skirt and a pretty white peasant blouse, plus some nice underthings, then dash down the hall to the bathroom. I hope we don't have to leave too soon. It takes me a while to get ready to go out and Linda seems to be on a pretty tight time schedule. She'll have to wait—putting myself together properly takes time.

With Linda helping me along I'm ready to leave in less than an hour. For me that's a major miracle. Linda doesn't seem to see it that way. "I didn't think you'd ever finish getting ready."

"What do you mean? I've never gotten dressed that fast in my life."

Linda laughs out loud as she backs her SUV out of my driveway. "Fast? You call that fast?" She taps the face of her wristwatch. "It took you fifty-four minutes from start to finish. I timed it."

"That is super fast. Normally I take triple that time."

She takes one hand off the steering wheel and places it over her heart like a pledge. "Thank God I'm butch. If I had to go through what you just did to get ready every day I'd go insane."

I fluff the ends of my hair. "My hair is still damp. I didn't blow dry it all the way and I left off half my make-up. I usually curl my hair too once I dry it."

She looks over while we're paused at a stop light. "You look great. You don't need all that goo on your face to make you look pretty and I don't see anything wrong with your hair like that. No one wants to snuggle with someone whose hair is stiff as a board and full of hairspray. I like being able to run my hands through a woman's hair and not having to worry about getting stuck. The clean shampoo smell is nice too."

"I didn't know cuddling with you was in the plans for this evening."

For a second she looks tongue tied. "I just meant, I ummm… I was just telling you why you don't need to go through that whole process to look nice. That's all."

The light turns green and Linda steps on the gas, seemingly flustered over the present conversation. I've never seen her look so out of her element and it's refreshing to see.

All too soon we arrive at the club. The parking lot outside Anna and Eve is packed. As we drive through, looking for a spot to park, I recognize a lot of the vehicles. I turn suspicious eyes toward Linda and she returns my stare with a knowing smile and a shrug. "I told you I wanted to throw you a bachelorette party."

"I thought you were kidding."

She shakes her head and pulls into an empty spot near the entrance marked *Bride's Parking Only!* with a big handwritten sign. "I wasn't." She glances at the clock on the dash and grimaces. "We're twenty minutes late. Let's get inside."

We exit the truck and head up the short sidewalk to the front of the club. I stop her before she can grab the handle to open the doors. "Thank you. I mean it. I don't know what the future holds, but for what it's worth I really appreciate this."

"You're welcome. I wanted to do something cool for you and this seemed like a good idea." She pulls me into a tight hug, her mouth nestled right next to my ear. I can feel her breath as it puffs against my neck, making me shiver with the sensation. Linda pulls back and looks at me. "Are you cold?"

I shake my head and grab for the door. "No. Just nervous I guess. Come on. Let's get my party started."

We spend the next three hours drinking and dancing and having the time of our lives. Linda invited all of my friends in the community and, judging from the big stack of sex toys I got as presents, their credit cards really got a workout. Every time I look at the gift table I blush. I'm not a prude by any means but I have no idea what some of the items are used for and the size of two of the dildos is seriously intimidating. They must be meant as a gag because I'm not sure any woman can stretch that much. Some thoughtful person even included a huge pack of batteries. I may not need Mark after all.

I forgot how much fun going to a lesbian bar could be. No expectations, no judgment, just a building full of women looking to enjoy themselves without recrimination. It's been months since I've been to Anna and Eve with Linda. Mark threw a holy hell fit the last time I went with her so I've ignored her recent invitations, preferring to avoid another big fight with my fiancé. I bet he'd be really pissed off if he knew where I was and who I was with right now. Tough shit. I don't care. The more I think about the situation the madder I get. Why should I have to leave my friends, especially Linda, behind because my future husband is a homophobic asswipe? It's not fair.

Linda slides in beside me on the dance floor, takes one look at my face, and frowns. "Oh no. No, no, no! None of that, little missy. Tonight is all about having fun. Wipe that scowl off your face this instant. You can think about whatever has you so pissed off tomorrow." The lights go down as a slow song comes on and Linda grabs me around the waist, pulling me close as she starts to sway to the beat. "Dance with me, babe."

She smiles down at me as she wraps her arms around my neck. In reply I move my hands to her hips and hang on tight. Her eyes are glassy and her moves are kinda sloppy. She really wasn't drunk earlier but I can tell she's well on her way now. I'm pretty tipsy myself.

We kind of shuffle in place, turning slowly because neither one of us is very steady on our feet. Maybe it's the situation we're in, or the fact that the liquor has really loosened my tongue, but I feel the need to tell her exactly what she means to me and how thankful I am that she came to drag me out of my house today.

I plant my feet in place and our movement stops. She starts to pull away but I clasp my hands behind her back to keep her in place. Her eyes widen slightly and her breathing speeds up the barest bit.

"You'll probably never know how much this party means to me. Despite everything, you've hung in there by my side. I can't imagine my life without you in it. I just can't. I don't even want to think about it. I need you." My hands clench the back of her shirt as the first tears start to fall. I crush my face into her shoulder and start to weep. "Don't leave me. Please."

She squeezes me, her glorious muscles enfolding me tight in her embrace. I've never felt safer or more loved. "Hey. I'm not going anywhere. Mark can kiss my ass." She strokes my hair and rocks me gently. "Look at me. Jenny, I'm serious. Look at me."

Her voice sounds shaky at the end and I find myself obeying her request instantly, wondering if the wavering sound means she's as upset over this as I am. I lift my head and look into her face. The expression of fierce determination lights an answering fire inside of me. Suddenly the whole situation seems crystal clear. I know now why I said yes to Mark. It's not because I'm in love with him. I'm not, and I'm not sure I ever was. It's what he represents that made me accept his proposal.

If I marry Mark my parents will be happy; my life will be simple. My family expects me to marry a guy. To have babies. To do what society finds acceptable. I don't want to settle for acceptable. Been there, done that, got the ring to prove it. There's so much more out there that I refuse to settle for mediocre. I want adventure, excitement. I want to fall into bed with someone who can rock my world and everyone else be damned if they don't find my choice proper.

I want Linda.

The realization is shocking in its clarity, but I finally decide to take the chance. I know I won't regret it. I've made my decision, now I need to help Linda make hers.

Linda is still staring at me, the barest hint of hope and trepidation on her face. I hate the fact that I put that look of worry there, but I'm going to do my best to erase it. I lean forward, keeping my eyes open the whole time as I close the miniscule gap between us. Linda's eyes go wide when she realizes my intentions and for just a second the look of shock is almost comical. Her gaze drops lower, locking on my lips and the fear is replaced instantly by a lustful look that makes my insides twist and my pussy wet. I want this. Oh God, how I want this. "Kiss me. Please just kiss me."

Her lips finally touch mine and the kiss is horribly chaste and brief. Nothing like what I want, and I let her know it. "Kiss me for real."

She licks her lips before she speaks, leaning her forehead against mine until we're so close she only has to whisper. "Are you sure? Don't do this with me if you aren't one hundred percent positive because I don't think I can take it. Losing what I never had is one thing, but if we do this, really do this, and you decide you can't handle it, it just might kill me. I've wanted you for so damn long."

"I'm sure. I'm sorry it took me so long to recognize what's right in front of me. Now please, just kiss me. I want you so much it hurts."

Linda doesn't hesitate any longer. She gives me what I'm asking for and more. Her lips press against mine. There's nothing chaste about what she's doing to my mouth now. She uses everything at her disposal. Lips, teeth, and tongue. It's brutal, primal, everything I expected and beyond.

I press my body as close to hers as we can get and still be two separate people. It's not enough. I want to climb inside her, have her inside me. Suddenly some of the toys on the table make sense.

I pull back only when the need to breathe becomes overwhelming to the point that I'm dizzy. I barely manage to suck in a breath before she's kissing me again. Dear God it's good.

She starts a slow grind against me, sliding one of her legs in between mine as our breasts rub together through our clothing. Her knee hits just the right spot and I have to fling my head back as the pressure against my clit sends a shockwave up my spine. Linda still doesn't let up. She leans over and puts her mouth on my cheek, kissing and nipping her way over to my neck and then up to my ear. She bites the lobe gently and then tugs a bit. There's no pain, only pleasure. Mark has never made me feel half of what I do right this minute with Linda. Sometimes I had to fake an orgasm to get him off of me. With Linda I doubt I'll have to fake anything. I'm close now and we're both still dressed. All we've been doing is dancing and kissing. It's almost more foreplay than I can handle.

"That's it, baby. Move against me. Nice and slow. Does that feel good?"

I nod and groan out a yes, my brain unable to do much more under the onslaught.

Her arms slide down my back until she's cupping my ass in her palms, using her leg and her hands to guide my movements. "Mmmm. God you're so hot. So fucking sexy. I want to take you home and do naughty things to you. Things friends don't normally do with each other."

I widen my stance a bit and press downward. My clit is throbbing and I'm so fucking turned on I wouldn't be surprised if I'm leaving a wet spot on her pants. "Oh God. Don't stop. Please, don't stop. I'm about to come."

She freezes in place. I'm mere seconds from the most powerful climax of my life and the realization that I'm going to be denied is brutal. "What are you doing?" Linda looks furious. I have no clue why. "What did I do wrong?"

She shakes her head and grabs my hand, tugging me through the room and out the front door. I barely register the whistles and catcalls that greet our exit. Apparently our demonstration on the dance floor did not go unnoticed. That's the least of my worries right now though. I want to know why Linda is so pissed.

"Hey, slow down." We reach her vehicle and she unlocks my door and pushes me somewhat roughly inside. Confusion and violent arousal do not mix well. I start to shake. Linda looks over, and noticing my reaction, visibly tries to calm herself. It doesn't seem to be working. "Tell me what happened. What did I do to make you so angry?"

We leave the parking lot in a spray of gravel. Her hands clench tight on the steering wheel. "It's not you I'm angry with. I'm sorry if I didn't make that clear."

"Where are we going?"

She looks over at me, some of her anger replaced by lust. "To my place. We've got some unfinished business."

The scalding heat of her gaze leaves me panting and dizzy. I wiggle in my seat and fight the urge to touch myself. "Oh. I thought maybe you were taking me home."

"Do you want to go home? I told you to be sure before we started. Did you change your mind already?"

I shake my head and scoot closer. "No, but I'm confused. What just happened back there?"

She rakes one hand over her close cropped hair, pushing the longer bangs out of her eyes. "I thought the answer to that was pretty clear. We were making out and you nearly got off."

"I know that. I'm talking about why it made you mad."

She punches the steering wheel. "Because you shouldn't be able to get off that easy. Not if Mark is taking care of you properly. I should have to work harder to make you come."

We pull into her driveway and I have to ask. "Is that a butch thing?"

She whips her head around to look at me. "What?"

"I don't get it. I'd think it would be a good thing to be able to make your girlfriend come so easy. I'm wondering if it's a butch thing. Something I can't understand."

The resulting laughter settles my nerves. I get out of the car and follow her to the porch. As she unlocks the door she starts talking. "I think maybe it's a lesbian thing. I'm not sure. Maybe it's just me. I figured if you were getting good sex with Mark it would take more than some heavy petting to make you come. Maybe you're just really sensitive." She opens the door and leads me inside, locking it behind us. "Is that it? Do you get turned on real easy? Maybe I should try again and find out."

The mood goes from light to intense in a heartbeat. I take a step back instinctively. Something in her gaze makes my stomach flutter. My mind urges me to run, to make her work for what she wants, what we both want. Her next sentence confirms it.

"Go ahead. Try and get away. You won't get far and when I catch you I'm going to fuck you. I'm going to ruin you for anyone else."

I dash down the hall, no idea where I'm headed. I've been in Linda's house a million times but right now my mind is centered on my pussy and the wild throbbing between my thighs that wants her to catch me. To throw me down and take the decision out of my hands. To erase all thoughts of my fiancé and what I had planned for tomorrow.

I fling open the basement door and take the steps two at a time. I can hear her behind me, stalking me slowly. Giving me time to hide before she seeks me out. It's like the most erotic game of cat and mouse ever played. Maybe she's right. Maybe I'm just easy. I know when she catches me that we'll find out for real and I can't wait. I stop in front of the big leather couch in her converted recreation room and wait for her to overtake me.

One minute I'm standing still and the next I'm bent over the back of the couch with my skirt rucked up over my ass and my panties down around my ankles. The forceful domination has wetness slicking my thighs.

Her fingers come into contact briefly with my slit and I know just that small touch has her hand soaked. "Good Lord. You're drenched. Did our game excite you?"

I nod and kick my panties all the way off. "Yes. It did."

I feel her bangs brush my lower back as she leans forward and presses an open mouth kiss to my right ass cheek. "You look so fucking hot. Spread your legs. I'm going to fuck you in a minute, but first I'm going to taste you. I can't wait anymore. You look so good and your scent is driving me out of my mind." I hear a soft thump and picture her dropping to her knees behind me. The next time she speaks her breath blows directly on my cunt. I'm not going to last very long. I'm liable to come the minute her tongue touches me. "I'm going to give you what you came so close to at the club. Is that what you want? Tell me now, Jenny. Do you want this?"

I lean over as far as I can, spreading my legs in a lewd display that shows off everything I have. "Yes. Please. I can't take it anymore."

She hesitates and I want to scream in frustration. "What about tomorrow? What about Mark?"

Thankfully the answer to that question is an easy one. "Mark who? I can't marry him. Not now." I voice my earlier discovery in hopes of making her understand that I don't take this decision lightly. "I don't love Mark. I don't think I ever did. I didn't think I could have you so I settled for him. I don't want to settle anymore."

Two things happen at once. Her tongue licks from my opening to my clit and she pushes three thick fingers deep inside me. I scream at the invasion. I can't help it. I look down between my legs. Linda is kneeling behind me, laving my pussy with her tongue as she fucks me with her fingers. I push back, helping her go deeper. She sucks me into her mouth and crooks her fingers forward, finding that magic spot inside that sends me hurtling toward completion. I don't want to come alone, but I'm in no position to take her with me. It's too late now anyway.

"Oh shit. I'm coming. I'm coming right now!" I let loose with a shout, the pleasure so overwhelming I almost collapse on her face. Linda reaches up and grabs me, lowering me down gently until I'm sitting in her lap. Her chin is shiny with my juices and I chuckle at the sight as I tenderly wipe her face off with my hand. My fingers begin to wander down to her breasts but she stops me before I can reach them. "I want to touch you too. Make you feel as good as I do."

I look into her eyes and she smiles somewhat shyly. "I'm good."

"Huh?" It's far from a witty comeback but I'm pretty sure my brain has melted after such an incredible orgasm.

She shrugs. "Remind me never to tease you about being so sensitive ever again."

"Why not?" Wow, two words this time. Yay me.

"I came when you did without so much as a touch. I can't really pick on you after that."

Now I do laugh, some of my mind starting to come back online. "Yeah, I guess you can't." I snuggle in tighter, leaning my head against her chest to listen to her steady heartbeat. "This is nice."

She puts her head down on top of mine. "Yes, it is."

"I meant what I said earlier about Mark. It's over."

"I'm glad. I don't want this to be a one time thing."

I shake my head. "Me either. I don't do casual sex."

"There was nothing casual about what we just did." Her arms slide under my ass and she lifts me off her lap and up onto the couch. I scoot over to give her room but in order to make it work I end up laying half on top of her again. "Get some rest. I took tomorrow off for the wedding but since there isn't going to be one I guess I'll have to find something else to keep me busy."

Her innuendo isn't lost on me and suddenly my mind flashes to all my gifts that we left at the club in our hasty exit. "Oh crap. What about my presents? Do I have to give them back?"

"I don't think so. I'm pretty sure everyone knew what was going to happen between us when we left halfway through the party. Besides you got some pretty amazing toys. A few of them will really come in handy."

I have to admit my ignorance. "I'm in a bit over my head, I think. There were a few things I got that I have no idea how to use or what they're for."

She pats my back and yawns. "No worries. I'll teach you." She hesitates. "And you should call Mark."

"Not now." I don't want to think about Mark.

"In the morning then. And afterward, we'll go back to the club and pick everything up. You got a really nice purple harness that needs breaking in and I'm just the person to help you do that."

THANKS TO IRENE
NICOLE WOLFE

The rain had nearly flattened Luanna as she ran up the front steps of Amy's apartment building. The umbrella, held before her at an upward angle, acted as more of a sail than a protection against the water driven by Hurricane Irene's approach to Charlotte.

She stabbed the buzzer for Amy's apartment.

"Who is it?" Amy yelled through the intercom speaker.

"It's Luanna! Open the fucking door!"

Dina had called Luanna earlier from the airport.

"I'm still stuck here, baby," Dina had said. "They're cancelling flights like crazy. How close is it?"

Luanna hadn't done much apart from watch the local news reports all day long. "It's still raining, and the wind gets stronger all the time, but they say it still hasn't landed. I don't know if I believe it. The windows have been shaking all day."

"You need to get out of there," Dina had told her.

"But I gotta watch the house," Luanna had said. "I don't want to leave and then come back to find out we've been looted."

"Fuck the house," Dina had said, sending a little jolt through Luanna. "Fuck the TV and all of it. I don't want to come back and find you dead in there because our fucking landlord didn't board up the damn place. Pack up and get out."

"Okay, okay. I'll go to one of the shelters."

Dina had sighed. "Isn't there somewhere else you can go? The shelter's better than nothing, I guess, but they'll be packed. I don't want you stuck outside if they can't let anyone else in."

"Sweetie, they can't just turn me away."

"People get crazy in shit like this. Who do we know that has a safe place?"

"Stuart and Juriel, but they're gone. They're still in Aruba."

There had been such a long pause in the conversation that Luanna thought the call had dropped. She'd been about to ask Dina if she were still there.

"Go to Amy's," Dina had said, although she hadn't sounded happy about it.

Luanna wasn't sure she'd heard right. "Amy's?"

"Yeah, Amy's. Her place is like a damn castle. Go to Amy's. Call me when you get there, and be good."

"You know I will," Luanna had said. "Be good" was their code for "Don't fuck anyone while I'm gone." It was both a joke and their pledge to each other. Luanna had always been good, but if anyone could make her be bad, it was Amy.

The elevator was as cold as an icebox, so she was shivering by the time she reached the seventh floor.

"Jesus, you're drenched," Amy said as she let Luanna into her apartment.

"Ain't no Jesus in this storm," Luanna said. "But thanks for letting me stay here." Amy's apartment was in a solid brick building that was far stronger than Luanna and Dina's rental house near the beach. She and Dina came here often for Amy's professional massages, especially the side-by-side ones that charged them full of "Wouldn't it be hot to double-fuck that white girl?" fantasies they'd discuss later in bed, on the living room floor, or in the shower. They always entailed Dina spanking Luanna and making her admit that she wanted to fuck Amy, but always swearing never to do it and saying that her pussy was Dina's and no one else's. Fucking Amy was always a fun fantasy, but it was never an option. It would shatter their marriage, and they were sure that an offer to "make her the cream in our Oreo," as Dina put it, would freak Amy out, and they'd end up losing a good masseuse.

"You need to get out of those wet clothes," Amy said. "I have some that will fit you."

Amy showed her to the bedroom. Luanna had only ever been in the living room, bathroom, and kitchen. She and Dina had often wondered how Amy's bedroom would look. They'd guessed she had the whole Zen thing going on, with a simple twin bed surrounded by Asian art and incense burners.

They were wrong. Amy's bedroom was decorated with Native American artwork and photos of the southwest, and she had a queen size bed. Amy pulled a hooded black sweatshirt and matching sweatpants, much like the ones she wore, from a dresser and handed them to Luanna.

"These should keep your body warm," Amy said. She opened a door to the bathroom. "You remember where the towels are, right?"

Luanna had used many pre- and post-massage. "Yeah, I remember."

She came out of the bathroom after she dried off and dressed in the sweats. She found Amy curled up on the couch with a cup of tea in one hand and the TV remote in the other. She was watching a live radar image of Hurricane Irene spinning toward them. Rain battered the windows, but Luanna barely heard the wind. Amy's building was like Fort Knox compared to their creaky beach place.

Luanna stood at the window to watch the dark gray skies and horizontal rain as she called Dina.

"I'm at Amy's," she said.

"How was the trip over there?"

"It took me twice as long. It's bad here, sweetie. Real bad."

"It'll be okay, baby. Did you lock the house before you left?"

"Yeah. I even hid the TV in the pantry."

There was another long pause before Dina spoke. "How's Amy?"

Luanna was thankful that Amy had been dressed in sweats and had no make-up on and didn't smell like exotic oils as she always did when they came over for a massage. She looked like she'd just awakened from a nap, and she tried not to think of her in bed.

"She's fine." It was a weak answer, and she knew it.

"Everything's okay there?" Dina asked, although Luanna knew she'd meant "You're not fucking, are you?"

"It's fine. We're okay, sweetie," she said, not talking about her and Amy. She lowered her voice. "I'm being good."

"I know you will be, baby. I know you will."

Luanna thought she heard an odd tone in Dina's voice. It sounded like jealousy, but not toward Amy. It almost sounded more like envy. Was she jealous of her? For being in Amy's apartment without her? Did Dina wish she were in her place?

"Are you going to be good to me when you get back?" Luanna asked.

"I sure am, as long as you're good until I get there."

"When will that be?"

"I still don't know. I'll call you when I know anything."

"I will, too."

The conversation came to the point where the only things to do were ramble about trivial topics or keep talking about how she'd better not have sex with Amy. Neither of them spoke.

"I'm going to check on the flight status," Dina said after a solid ten seconds. "I'm hoping they'll put me up in a hotel instead of having to sleep here."

"I hope they do too. Call me when you're checked in."

"I'll call when I know anything," Dina said again, reminding her that she wasn't going to let her and Amy have a lot of long moments alone. They said they loved each other and hung up at almost the same time, but Luanna was first.

Amy hadn't moved from the couch. She hadn't done anything apart from watch the live radar reports and switch from drinking tea to eating an orange. Luanna put her phone on the windowsill, hoping it would get a good signal there.

"What are they saying?" Luanna asked as she gestured toward the TV.

"The heavy stuff should hit within the hour."

"Shit, it hasn't already?" She sat on the opposite end of the couch.

"No. I hope you don't have anywhere to go soon. Do you want some tea?"

"If it's hot, I'll take it."

She was glad Amy immediately got up because she blushed as soon as the unplanned innuendo escaped her mouth.

"Do you want anything to eat?" Amy said from over her shoulder as she walked into the kitchen.

Luanna could hear Dina in her head: *No you damn well don't.*

"Sure, what do you have?"

"I have some hummus I made yesterday, but I don't know how well that would go with your tea. I have some almond-apricot bars from the market. They're pretty good."

Luanna wasn't sure what hummus was, but eating would keep her busy and not wondering if Amy tasted like apricots.

"Sounds great," Luanna said.

"What did Dina have to say?" Amy asked as she poured hot water into a mug.

Luanna walked into the kitchen. "She's stuck in Philadelphia. All flights along the east coast are delayed or canceled. She won't get back until Irene's moved on. She's hoping they'll put her up in a hotel."

"What are you doing in the meantime?"

Luanna wasn't sure what she meant, but the question became moot once the lights went out.

"Fuck," Luanna said. "That ain't good."

"I have a hand-crank radio, so we can keep up on the news as long as the radio stations haven't lost power. I also have a flashlight in the bedroom. Get that and I'll dig out the radio."

Luanna headed for the bedroom. "Where is it in here?"

"The bedside table drawer."

The bedroom was almost pitch black. Luanna walked slowly with her hands out in front of her waist. She bumped into one corner of the bed and traced the side of it with her fingertips until her hands found the bedside table. She fished through the drawer, found what she thought was the flashlight, but gasped once she pulled it out.

"Did you find it?" Amy asked from the doorway.

"No," Luanna said. "I found something else."

There was silence to match the dark.

"You went to the table on the right side of the bed, didn't you?" Amy asked. She laughed a cute, little embarrassed laugh that made Luanna's pulse throb in her neck. "I meant the left side."

Luanna couldn't resist rubbing the thick vibrator in her hands. "It's nice."

"Thanks," Amy said from the dark doorway. "It does the trick."

Put it away, Dina said in her head. *Put that damn thing away and walk out. Now. Stop touching it and get the fuck out of her bedroom!*

Luanna put the vibrator back in the drawer. "You said the flashlight's in the other bedside table?"

"Yes," Amy said, making Luanna jump. She had moved through the dark room with cat-like silence and was now so close to Luanna that she could feel Amy's breath on her ear. "But I don't think we'll need it."

Luanna's throat tightened. *Walk away,* Dina told her. "What are we going to do?"

"Something we don't need lights for, if you don't think Dina will mind."

I sure as hell will mind! Go to the shelter, baby. Go to the shelter. We'll find another masseuse. You're my wife, baby. Go to the shelter.

Their lips found each other. It was a soft, nice kiss and long enough to help Luanna relax. Amy's strong masseuse hands worked their way up the sweatshirt and over Luanna's perky tits. The shirt came off and Luanna heard Amy's hit the floor as well. Amy took her by the arm and to the bed.

Luanna had wanted to get her mouth on Amy's tits since they'd first met. They were twice the size of hers and she wondered how they'd fit in her mouth. Amy sat back against the headboard and Luanna licked a slow circle around one of Amy's puffy nipples. She moaned and stroked Luanna's long hair as if she wanted to lounge there and do it until the hurricane passed.

Luanna wanted to, had to, feel inside her. She rolled between Amy's legs and Amy lifted her hips so they could get her sweatpants off and throw them onto the floor next to her shirt. She spread her knees and Luanna found her clit swollen and waiting. Luanna rubbed two fingers over it, making Amy jump. She grabbed one of Amy's big tits to keep her from wiggling away.

"Fuck yes," Amy said. "Put your fingers in me."

Luanna slid two fingers in as Amy's head titled back. Amy wiggled on her hand and her mouth tightened as if she was trying to keep the first hot shock from overwhelming her. She let out a belly moan and Luanna thought she could make out Amy's smile through the darkness.

"More," she said. "Faster."

Luanna worked her harder, holding Amy's thigh with her other hand so she wouldn't slide off her fingers. The slap of her hand against Amy's cunt was almost louder than Amy's moans.

"Just like that, that's how I like it," Amy said. "I'm going to come."

Luanna was sure the neighbors must've heard. Amy's scream didn't stop until she pulled Luanna's hand to her mouth and sucked her two fingers like they were popsicles.

Amy used her strong masseuse arms to pull her up for a shuddering kiss and then roll her to the other side of the bed. Luanna heard her fishing around in the dark for the vibrator as she pushed and kicked her sweatpants to the foot of the bed. The buzzing sound ripped through the dark and made Luanna jump before it ever touched her skin. She couldn't see it. She could only hear it coming closer and closer.

She could feel it close to her nipple, then hovering over her belly, and then a half-inch from her cunt. She could see nothing but a vague feminine shape with big tits and her hair pulled back in a ponytail. It was like her bigger bosomed shadow had peeled itself from a wall and was about to fuck her. There was no black girl or white girl. There was nothing in the dark but fingers, tongues, cunts, asses, and tits.

And this vibrating cock that now pumped hard in her pussy while Amy's tongue swirled around her clit. Luanna grabbed at pillows and sheets, fearful she might fall off the bed from the way her body was shaking. Her eyes popped open and she cried out to Amy, God, and anyone else who might've been listening.

Amy didn't take it as a sign to stop. She kept fucking her until the buzzing of the vibrator became a pulsing, meditative hum that lulled Luanna into a strange trance. She remembered how she felt floating on an inflatable raft when she and Dina honeymooned in Key West. The humming, the dark, and her post-orgasm high made her think for a moment that Dina was there between her legs with two fingers in her ass.

Couldn't be good, could you?

But, sweetie, the storm... I'm afraid... I miss you...

What are you going to tell me when I call? How do you think I feel knowing you're there with her? Knowing what you're doing?

I... I'm...

"Thirsty?" Amy asked.

Luanna had to refocus her eyes and ears. It was still dark and the orgasmic fog in her eyes made everything blurry.

"Yes," she said. "I think I am."

"Start with this," Amy said and then stuffed the wet vibrator into Luanna's mouth. Luanna shuddered as intense feelings rippled down from her throat. She pulled out the vibrator and held it between her tits.

"That was better than I hoped it would be," she said.

There was no answer. She sat up and groped around in the dark by her knees for Amy. There was nothing there but bed sheets.

"Here you go," Amy said to her right, making her jump. She not only hadn't felt her leave but she hadn't seen her come back with a glass of water either.

"There's still no power," Amy said. "And the radio says the storm will be with us for most of the night."

"I guess we won't be watching those DVDs I brought, then," Luanna said after draining half the glass of water.

Amy slid back onto the bed and up next to Luanna's hip. "No. So I guess we'll have to figure out some other way to pass the time."

You can still get up, baby. I might forgive once. I don't know about a second time.

The wind howled outside. Rain hard as hail smacked the bedroom windows. Dina might be stuck in Philadelphia for days.

Luanna set the glass on the bedside table and then rolled over to stroke the Other Woman's hip. She had her threesome with Amy after all, but it ended up involving a gal named Irene.

ASH
NIKI CROW

The white hospital corridor, bathed in fluorescent light, is a sickening sight on a Monday morning. I'm tired as hell, and if I weren't the head of my department, I'd have called in sick.

I make my way unenthusiastically to the locker room and undress. More fluorescent lights. They make my body look old and worn-out. I think of Jennie as I look at my face in the mirror. Dark rings, puffy eyes. She's the one who told me I was too old for her. Now I feel too old for myself. I don the green hospital scrubs and reach for a white coat, throwing it over the top.

There are still a few minutes until the start of my shift, and the break room is crowded when I get there. I plot the easiest route to the coffee machine, ignoring my happily chatting colleagues. But then I hear footsteps in the corridor and I remember what is happening today.

"Graham will be here soon," I announce. I nod toward the corridor, and the chattering subsides slightly. "We're conducting job interviews for the position of orthopedic nurse."

Graham is, in turn, my boss, and the most boring man I've ever met. He's in the doorway now, smiling far too widely. Some of the girls greet him with a nod, but as soon as politeness allows, they turn back to their colleagues and the chatting resumes at full force.

How the hell can they all be so cheerful at 7 a.m.?

Ash is the fourth person on the list of possible employees and the last candidate we're interviewing today. I'm sipping what must be my tenth cup of coffee and am making desultory conversation with Graham, when she shows up. She's wearing a black suit and if it weren't for the heavy gauge titanium jewelry, she'd look like a business woman instead of a nurse. She smiles, and an electric impulse travels like a tidal wave along my neural pathways, cerebrum to cunt. It's been a long time since I've felt that way about another woman. I blame Jennie for that too. She could never understand that it's okay to look. I never touched. Seven years together and in that time I never let myself lust after another woman.

But now, in the clinical hospital light, I can almost feel Ash's pale, cool lips around my clit. It makes me want to bend her over my desk and fuck her with whatever I can find that's thick enough to fill her. Right here, right now, and to hell with Graham. He can sit there in his gray suit and be outraged by the lack of self-restraint in his employees, or whatever excuse his moral self can invent. He'd have a hard-on he'd never forget. He's the kind who would.

Instead I gesture for Ash to sit in the chair opposite my desk, and give what I hope is a professional smile. "Hello, I'm Doctor Susan White," I tell her.

Jennie goes away that weekend. Another business trip, she says, but I saw the clothes she packed, and they're not business clothes. Not lounging around a hotel room clothes either. There's a well-known dyke bar in the city she's visiting, and the clothes in her suitcase will make her fit right in.

I'm trying not to care. We are finished, she and I, our seven years together blown away like leaves. What do I care if she's already hunting for my replacement? I think of Ash. Would Jennie like Ash? Then I clamp down on that line of thought. It doesn't matter anymore what Jennie thinks.

I go over to the house where Jennie and I lived for seven years to pick up my last few boxes and to leave the key. It's Jennie's house now.

When the last box is in the car, I walk into the garden. I stare at the pool, dip in a toe. I always wanted to go skinny-dipping but Jennie was afraid of what the neighbors might think. Jennie's not here now. The decision is easy. I leave my clothes in a pile and I stand and plunge headlong into the water at the deep end.

I'm gasping, the water's cold, it's still too early in the season. But I'm enjoying my household anarchy too much to get out just yet. I feel rejuvenated. It's all Ash's doing, even though she hasn't done a thing except show up at the hospital for a job interview.

The air has the illusion of warmth when I get out of the water. I sit in one of the chairs by the pool, legs spread wide to the weak spring sun. Let the neighbors watch if they like. A breeze rustles the trees and touches my exposed pussy. The air is cold and harsh, but I love it. I think of Ash and touch myself lightly; once, twice. The leaves shiver on the trees as I come hard, with Ash's name on my lips.

The following Thursday is Ash's first day of work and I spend the morning looking out my office window, hoping I'll see her. When I do, it's as if she lights up the dullness of the hospital parking lot, bringing it to life.

I watch her disappear from view, collect clipboard and patient notes and get ready to start the morning handover. She's in the corridor when I enter it, stepping out of the locker room with her shirt only halfway buttoned, showing off pale skin and a breast covered in a thin white bra. I find myself admiring her confidence, walking into the corridor half-dressed. The distinct shape of a metal barbell is visible through the fabric of her bra. I wait for her to catch up with me and I know I should turn my head. But I don't. I feel like I've been handed an invitation. She buttons the shirt, quickly.

"You like piercings?" she asks.

I do now. But she doesn't wait for my answer.

"Do you have any of your own?" she continues.

"No."

"You should try it."

"Try it?"

Damn, I want to try it. Not the way she means, though. I want to try hers, I want to suck her nipple and feel the metal on my tongue. I want to roll my lips over that barbell, feel the difference between cold metal and warm flesh.

"It's addictive."

"You have more?"

We've reached the handover room, and there's only time for her to smile at me before we go inside.

I conduct handover mechanically. The professional me is updating the staff on the 82 year old patient with a fractured neck of femur, the 22 year old motorbike accident who's now more steel plate than bone, but the real me—I'm thinking of cold steel perforating nipples, labia, umbilicus, and prepuce. I'm thinking how it might look, how it would taste.

Friday morning is a disappointment. She's not there; she's on the late shift. By lunchtime, it seems my sanity is returning and suddenly I feel silly pining for a girl half my age. I don't even know if she's interested in women, not to mention older women. Not to mention me, the head of her department. She's off limits in so many ways.

Jennie calls me that evening and invites me over, ostensibly because she can't find the key that I left. I know, and I'm sure she knows, that's not the real reason. We have sex that night, and it's a raw fuck. There's the wet slurp of my cunt as she fucks me with her strap-on, low-pitched grunts, and the voice in my head saying this is wrong. I shouldn't be here at all—she's got a new woman, I know she has, and this is no longer my house. But there's the fantastic feeling of a thick cock stretching me, and there's a brutal orgasm building and I can't find it in me to stop her. But the name I want to call isn't Jennie's and I bite my tongue.

I won't go back to this house again.

I drive back to my cabin afterwards, feeling pathetic. It's a windy night, and the skies are gray. A perfect night for making love by the fireplace. I don't light it that weekend.

On Sunday I draw a bath, a bag of dried chamomile flowers under the tap, scenting the water. And I dye my hair, to cover the gray strands.

On Monday, Ash has the early shift, and I take extra care putting on my makeup. A touch of eye shadow and black mascara. Not much, but more than usual. I still smell of chamomile; it's barely noticeable, only if someone comes close enough. And that morning, I do like what I see in the locker room mirror, fluorescent lights be damned. I stand up straight when I button my white coat, and I walk proudly to my office.

I see Ash through the open door a few times, but I'm swamped with paperwork and every time I notice her, it's too late for me to call her in on a pretext; she's already walked past. It's a quiet day for me. No operating list, just ward rounds and outpatients. After lunch, I see her approach my office. I pretend to be engrossed in a patient's chart. She enters without knocking.

"Susan, would you take a look at Mrs. Friedsam," she says. "The drain has dislodged. She may need to go back to the OR."

I look up and she's so close I can see the darker rim of her pale eyes, see the tiny blond hairs on her upper lip. I close my eyes briefly and hope she attributes my flushed cheeks to the warmth of the office.

"Of course," I say, and let her lead me to the patient, but I'm cursing the cowardice that won't let me say anything more.

It's getting dark by the time I make my way back to the locker room, all the ambitions of the morning gone. I stink of hospitals: of disinfectant and hand cleanser, sickness and chemicals. I need a shower. Ash is on my mind as the hot water washes away dreams, mascara, and chamomile.

I hear the locker room door open and close; it must be the cleaner. I reach for the soap. Arms, breasts, and torso. Feet, legs, and I reach for my back.

"Let me do that."

She's there. She takes the soap from me and gently washes my back. I'm afraid to turn and face her, even as sensory input is driving my brain into overkill. I feel as if I might overheat.

"You smelled like chamomile today," she says. "I like it."

Her hands travel on, over my stomach. The soap hits the floor and I watch those hands move toward my breasts. I've never been this horny in my life. The water's too hot; I turn the knob and suddenly it's ice cold. She gasps, laughs, and I finally turn to face her. She's naked, nipples clenching the metal that perforates them. My eyes rake her body. There's a titanium ring in her umbilicus, and I want to push my tongue through it and taste her skin.

"I do like piercings," I say. "I like *your* piercings."

The metal's cool against my tongue, her nipple hard and inviting on my lips. My head spins with the unbelievable wonder of it all. I feel like grinning. I'm having sex with a colleague in the locker room shower. Imagine Graham walking in on us now. Imagine Jennie. But Jennie's face flies from my mind and there's only Ash. Her nipple slips from my mouth and then her face is in front of mine. A kiss, a long kiss, and as our tongues entwine I find another piercing. I'm pushed back against the tile wall. I drop to the floor. She follows, spreads my legs.

"So you like cold water," she says. It's not a question.

She grabs the shower handle and aims the spray at my clit. Her fingers pierce me, fuck me, ruthlessly. I'm in heaven. One, two, three, four strokes... and I come, hard. I don't breathe until it's over; I completely forget.

The aftershocks consume me. Ash is there with me, on the tiled floor of the shower. Her legs are together, but I can see fine blond hair covering her sex. I want to part her lips, explore with my fingers and tongue, see if there are other piercings, secret piercings, hidden away for a lover to find.

I want to kiss her again but she's moved away. Gesturing for me to follow, she grabs a towel.

"I think the cleaner has waited long enough."

The cleaner is outside, waiting for us to finish? I'm blushing again.

"Maybe we could continue this at your house?" she adds.

"Later," I say, recalling our first meeting. "Let's stop by my office first. I'm going to bend you over my desk and fuck you silly."

She smiles and walks toward the door, wearing only the towel. "What are you waiting for?

I think I will light the fire in my cabin this weekend.

THE LAW OF RECIPROCITY
LAILA BLAKE

I just want to be close to her.

The letters were the awkward, hesitant scrawl of the barely literate, written shakily on a scrap of paper. The knuckles of Hannah's fingers were white and bloodless around the feather. They trembled as she held it, and a drop of ink dislodged, painted an uneven circle on the paper. Hannah blinked, watched the writing swim in and out of focus before her eyes.

"Now give it to me," the gypsy woman said. She held out her hand, white, wrinkly, and covered in gaudy jewels. Her wrist jangled with glittering bracelets.

Instinctively, Hannah closed her hand around the scrap of paper and pulled it closer to her body, to protect it, to hide the terrible desire. The gypsy woman raised her brows. There was a mocking quality to her painted face. She was old, and spoke with an accent that Hannah didn't recognize. The woman's accent, her air of mystery, her colorful tent, the golden thread and coins that had been worked into her glittering headscarf, the aroma of spices in the sticky air—all made Hannah dizzy.

"Give it," the gypsy repeated. "Mama Katsu keeps all her little friends' secrets." Almost suggestively, she ran her finger over the small stack of coins on the table: two weeks' wages for a heart's desire.

Hannah pressed her eyes shut as she extended her hand. She could feel the heat of the flame that burned in a little bowl in the center of the table. Then the gypsy plucked the paper from her hand.

"Don't..." Hannah whispered, but it was too late. The old woman's eyes were already scanning her words. The wrinkles on her forehead seemed to multiply, to pile up in ridges and plunge down into crevasses of skin.

Then she tossed it into the bowl of fire. The paper crumpled and blackened. For a second, the words stood out in sharp relief and then everything crumpled to ash. It dispersed in the oil, darkened it.

"Now the name," she said, and Hannah was sure her voice ran colder than just before. A shiver ran down her spine, and she rolled the feather between her thumb and index finger. The second scrap of paper lay on the table before her and Hannah stared at it, at the fraying edges, the beige color, the visible fibers.

The feather scratched on the paper, louder than the old woman's rattling breath, louder than the sound of the fairground outside the tent, louder than the laughing, drinking country folk.

"Give it," the gypsy repeated impatiently.

Again, Hannah reached across the flame. She watched the wrinkled hand approach, watched the firelight dance ominously on the shiny rings and bracelets. They too moved in and out of focus; Hannah felt woozy and sick, and she couldn't breathe, as if the incense were coating the inside of her lungs.

With a last effort, she wrenched her hand from the center of the table and cradled the scrap of paper against her chest.

"I... I changed my mind," she breathed, stumbling to her feet. From the corner of her eye, she saw the old woman slip the coins off the table, and then Hannah made for the tent flap and the open air.

It was almost dark outside. The bonfire threw sparks like stars into the spring air; skirts swished and flew in dancing circles. The music was louder here, so too the laughter and rhythmic clapping.

Hannah fought for air. Someone offered help, pushed a mug of ale into her shaking hand, and the paper fluttered away. She could read it, just for a second, before the wind tore toward the fire.

Lady Rose Talbot.

Lady Rose Talbot sat in the library, hiding among the books. There was nobody else around, and so she could eschew concerns of modesty. She sat in the stacks with her legs crossed and her shoes abandoned a few feet away.

They had visitors, and she couldn't be quite so rude as to stay in her room. But the library was just public enough, just far enough out of the way. Her little sister would distract the young gentleman far better than Rose could have, and Katherine would keep him far, far away from the stuffy shelves and the smells of old paper.

Rose loved that smell, as she loved the dim light and the long lines of cracked spines and fractured gold-leaf lettering. Adventure stories were her favorites, stories with a dashing hero who conquered the damsel's heart.

She closed her eyes, her finger resting between the pages to mark her spot, and leaned her head against the leather spines behind her. She saw the damsel so starkly in her mind's eye—the blushing virgin in the pleasure garden. She was rushing from playful hiding place to hiding place; the exertions driving the blood to her cheeks. Rose would catch up with her in a quiet, shaded corner and touch that heated skin, her lips, the lock of hair that came loose in the chase.

Rose was always the dashing hero in her fantasies.

Shuddering, she opened her eyes again and looked at the gilded pages on her lap. They never said what happened after the hero won the girl.

Distracted, she rubbed her forehead and shut the book. She didn't know what time it was; hours passed differently in the company of books. She rose, dusted herself off, and walked into the hallway to listen for any telltale sounds. There was the jangling of pots down in the kitchen, the usual afternoon bustling of a large house. It would be almost time to get dressed for dinner.

The kitchen was in a state of controlled chaos when Hannah, breathing hard and with aching feet, snuck in through the backdoor. She was late, but not by much and if she managed to get into her apron before the housekeeper saw her, she'd be fine. Her hands were still shaking a little, but the brisk walk up from the village had revived her, had dispelled the smell of incense and the odd accent in the gypsy's voice.

It all felt rather silly now, and Hannah chided herself a fool, brushing her hair and pulling a white cap over the reddish locks. She eyed herself in the dull mirror, and shook her head at her reflection. She thought of the two weeks' wages she'd left in the gypsy's tent, and her brows furrowed deeper.

"You are a fool Hannah Ward. A dangerous fool."

"Hannah? Are you in there?"

She jumped and bit her tongue hard enough to hurt. The taste of copper filled her mouth and she fumbled the knot of her apron at her back.

"I'll be right out. I had to get a new apron, there was a stain—"

"Hurry up. Mrs. Richards wants to see you."

Hannah pulled the apron tight and then rushed along the corridor, past maids carrying flowers and plates and cutlery into the dining room. The smells of roast meat, of cakes and delicacies, wafted from the kitchen into almost every room downstairs.

Hannah brushed the folds out of her skirts and then knocked on the housekeeper's door, trying to keep the guilty expression off her face, trying to calm her breath. Mrs. Richards was a stately woman with streaks of gray in her dark hair. She studied Hannah out of small, suspicious eyes.

"I need you to fill in for Miss Thompson," she finally said, throwing her arms up in an expression of helpless frustration. Hannah's eyes went wide and she shoved her trembling hands into the pockets of her apron. "She appears to have caught the influenza, as have two of the footmen. I know you're not a lady's maid, and under normal circumstances... But Mary is already upstairs dressing Lady Katherine. You will have to take care of Lady Rose, or else this dinner will end in utter disaster."

"I..." She couldn't speak. Couldn't find words. She saw the fluttering piece of paper again, drifting toward the bonfire.

"Now, don't fret and go. Hurry up. I expect you'll need all the time you can get. And don't be a nuisance to Lady Rose, do you hear me?"

From her window on the second floor, Lady Rose could see most of the gardens, the hedges and the flowerbeds, the fountains and statues, all arranged to please the eye. The spring sun had only just driven color to all the flowers, and they burst bright like a fresh print, like the countryside after a cleansing shower of rain.

She had rung the bell for her lady's maid a while ago, but she didn't exactly feel impatient. She was hungry after an afternoon of reading, but she did not relish the thought of the elaborate dinner her mother had planned to entertain their guests. It smacked of hours of laughing at bad jokes and admiring self-serving tales of bravery or skill.

Her sister Katherine was better at that kind of thing. She was the one who often lamented how rarely they entertained, complained of the inherent boredom in being an unwed woman, and who couldn't wait to be married and to run her own house. She would be in her element. Rose wouldn't be. Rose would smile and nod and think of nasty names to call their visitors once they were gone.

Earl Red-Nose and his son, Lord Grabby-Hands, maybe.

She was about to ring the bell a second time, when a timid knock on the door interrupted her train of thought.

"Come in."

"Milady?" A girl stuck her head around the door, looking flushed, little strands of copper hair escaping from her bonnet. "I'm—"

"Hannah, one of the house maids," Lady Rose supplied, and this seemed to take some of the awkwardness out of the girl's posture. She pushed herself through the slit in the door and stood by the wall. "What can I do for you?"

"Milady, please excuse the interruption, but I'm afraid Miss Thompson fell ill and, if it pleases Milady, I was sent up to take her place."

She was a timid thing, Rose thought, pink and soft-voiced, the polar opposite of her lady's maid. Miss Thompson was in her forties, she wore tight buns every day, and always strung Rose too tightly into her corsets.

"Of course," she said, waving the girl into the room. "Come on in. Poor Miss Thompson. I do hope it's nothing too serious?"

The door quietly clicked closed, and Rose watched the girl bite her lip, then smile around her little buck teeth and step closer. She looked a little forlorn. Her eyes wandered to the bed Rose assumed the girl had made in the morning. Her jaw hardened a little and she moved her lips into a brave smile.

"From what I've heard it's just the influenza, Milady. You won't have to put up with me for long."

On closer inspection, Rose realized that it was only her demeanor that made her appear so young. When she stepped into the light, the soft roundness of her face seemed more a personal characteristic than a sign of youth, and it stirred something warm and pleasant in Rose's chest.

"Oh, we'll do fine," she promised, smiling. "I'll show you what to do."

Hannah had tidied the room only that same morning. It was always third on their tour through the house. First Lady Talbot, then Lady Katherine, and finally Lady Rose. Her room always smelled the sweetest. Once, when the family entertained so many guests that the staff had been too busy to go through the rooms two housemaids at a time, Hannah had found herself alone in there. She'd stripped off the pillowcase and pressed it against her face. It had smelled like Lady Rose. It reminded Hannah of her dark hair, her ivory skin, and her cavernous eyes that seemed to go on forever.

Lady Rose Talbot knew who she was—lowly little Hannah Ward. Hannah shivered at the thought, but as hard as she tried, she couldn't feel any less insignificant next to this woman. Everything, from the ease of her voice and her stance, to the very fabric of her skin seemed to proclaim her place in the world. Hannah cringed at the memory of the gypsy's tent, and her stupid, stupid idea. Had it been her wish that had made Miss Thompson ill? Hannah swallowed against the obstruction in her throat and tried to think rationally. She'd had to have been ill before, surely it couldn't come over someone so fast?

"I picked out a dress already," Lady Rose said, nodding toward a hanger by the wardrobe. "If you could help me out of this one."

"Of course, Milady." It was easier when Rose turned around, when her bottomless eyes didn't rest on Hannah's face. She stood like nobody else Hannah knew, straight without stiffness, strong without losing the softness of her waist. Hannah closed her eyes, just for a second, and exhaled a shallow breath.

Little buttons ran down the back of her dress. One by one, Hannah threaded the carved bone out of the fabric, peeled the woman out of her trappings, until she revealed the tight corset and the underskirts.

I just want to be close to her, the paper had read. This was closer than she had dared to dream. So close that she could feel the warmth of the woman's skin radiating against hers, so close that her fingers brushed over Lady Rose's naked shoulder. She smelled like flowers and soap, like books and dust and class.

Even undressed like this, she looked nothing like Hannah. Even in her corset, her shoulders bare, she looked regal, and Hannah had to turn away, folding the dress Lady Rose had worn over a chair. Was it possible to be this close to someone after months of yearning, only to realize that she had never felt this distant, this far removed from her before? It seemed even more stupid now to dream of her, more than stupid, blasphemous almost, to think herself worthy of dreaming so high.

"This one, Milady?" Hannah asked, holding up the evening dress. It was wine red, with an intricate design of glittering pearls worked into the fabric. It was heavy, and jingled very quietly under her hands.

"Yes, thank you, Hannah."

It was the second time she'd called her by her name, and it still went through her like wildfire. *Lady Rose Talbot knew who she was.*

Hannah helped her slip into the stiff fabric, pulled it taut across her arms and then bent to the task of closing just as many little hooks as there had been buttons before. Her fingertips burned with the knowledge of whom she was touching.

For the second time that afternoon, Rose looked up at the sound of a knock on her door. This one had nothing of the careful softness of Hannah's hands, though.

"Darling, are you still in there?"

"Yes, Mother."

Lady Talbot stood in the doorway, looking tense and distraught. She too was dressed in her evening finest, but her hair had come loose and her eyes were wider than usual.

"Good. Good. I want you to stay here." She shook her head tragically. "We had to cancel dinner. Your sister and Lord Hansham have both fallen ill, and so have several members of staff. Your father sent for Doctor Jones, but before we know how infectious this is—"

"Is Kitty all right?"

"Oh, you know your sister. She'll be fine."

Rose bit back a smile. She did know her sister, a trooper if ever there was one.

"Maybe Anna here can bring you up a tray..."

"Hannah," Rose corrected automatically, and she cast the girl a secret little smile. The rise of pink in the girl's cheeks pleased her more than she had expected. It was hard to listen to her mother, to care about their guests or the influenza that seemed to have taken over the house.

Lady Talbot left eventually and Rose's dress jingled softly as she turned to her maid. Hannah was still pale, and Rose remembered that her soft little hands had shaken a little when they'd brushed over her skin.

"Are you feeling well?"

The girl looked almost startled; her eyes widened like a doe's, and Rose wondered if it was girls like this who were routinely saved by dashing heroes. Maybe she had a sweetheart downstairs. One of the footmen maybe, the tall, handsome one all the maids seemed to like so much.

"Y... yes, Milady."

"Are you sure? It's all right, you can tell me."

"No. No, Milady, I'm p... perfectly fine." She licked her lips, wrung her fingers against her spotless apron. "Th... thank you. For your concern."

She stood in the center of the room, stiff and careful, like a skittish young horse. Rose had broken in a young filly before, had touched the peach muzzle and calmed it when it grew too anxious, had held on tight even when it tried to buck. Hannah wasn't like that; she was a beautiful young woman, but she intrigued Rose too, the challenge and the wide timid eyes.

"Do I make you nervous, Hannah?"

The girl visibly gulped and Rose felt bad. A kinder person would let Hannah help her out of the gown and send her down for her dinner tray, when she was so clearly uncomfortable in her presence. But something about Hannah made her pause, something in her eyes, and in her pink cheeks.

"No, my Milady." Hannah looked down, then bit her full lip. "Yes. Milady. A little. I..." She shook her head, and Rose waited. She knew from experience that more interesting answers waited for those who could brave the silence.

"It's just because..." Hannah faltered again, crunching the fabric of her apron between her long, pink fingers. "It's just because you're so beautiful and I'm not. I'm just a maid."

It was as if she'd said too much, and Hannah clamped her mouth shut, then took a step back and bumped against the bed. She lost her balance for a moment, then stabilized herself, breathing fast and shallow.

"Come here," Rose said, and Hannah, meek and careful, obeyed.

Hannah felt her ladyship's fingers on her shoulders. They were warm and so soft, like a summer's breeze. Even as she steered Hannah in front of the mirror, she didn't seem to exert any pressure. Her touch was like a butterfly, or the brush of a feather. Hannah's mouth was dry; her eyelids fluttered and she blinked at her own reflection in the full-length mirror.

"I think you're beautiful," Lady Rose said, and Hannah stopped breathing. She felt her mistress' fingers at the knot of her bonnet, felt her loosen her hair so that it tumbled in copper waves across her shoulders. "See?"

"Milady," she spluttered, hardly daring to move. She'd changed her mind in the gypsy's tent, she'd stopped it all so the old woman couldn't tell anyone, but also, deeper down, she'd feared her magic, feared the events she might put in motion. And now she stared at her ladyship standing behind her, smiling at her through the gilded mirror, and it didn't feel real. It couldn't be real. It had to be magic. Or a dream.

"If I run a house one day, I'll do away with bonnets and gray linen," Lady Rose said, in a bout of raw, hoarse honesty. Her fingers tightened briefly on Hannah's shoulders, gripping so hard that Hannah felt they would leave marks on her skin through the modest gray linen dress. She shivered, stared at Lady Rose, tried to divine meaning from the set of her glittering shoulders.

"Milady?" she asked. Her breath hitched against her throat. Hannah brushed a strand of hair out of her face, but her hand shook too much, ached for the warmth of Lady Rose's skin.

"I don't want to make you nervous, Hannah," she whispered. Her voice was warmer at that volume, deeper than before and it seemed to vibrate somewhere at the bottom of Hannah's stomach, so strong she had to press her legs closer together to stop the tingling. "Just help me out of this monstrosity and then you can go."

Hannah held her breath. She wanted to shake her head, wanted to say something, anything, but then Lady Rose presented her back again. Hannah worked slowly with each hook, savoring the warmth, the contact of skin on skin, the delirious feeling between her legs.

"But don't you want to get married and have children? Live your own life?" her mother had asked when Hannah had decided to search for work as a housemaid. She had never found the courage to admit, not even to herself, that the idea of a husband had always seemed like the greater prison sentence.

Of course there were days when she hated service, when the housekeeper was too stern or the work so hard her muscles ached when she fell into her narrow bed under the eaves, long after the family had lain down to rest. But all of it seemed worth it for this moment, for her fingers on Lady Rose's skin, for the heat of her body so close, for the flowery smell of her hair.

"It's not... It's just because I've..." Hannah stopped, tried to push filters and breaks and walls between herself and the words that were tumbling out of her mouth, but it was too late. "It's just because I've dreamed of serving you, Milady, for so long."

Rose closed her eyes. Hannah's nimble fingers were at the small of her back, almost at the end of the row of little hooks. She could feel the girl's breath on the back of her neck, stirring the fine hairs there, and brushing hot over her skin.

She was a servant. She was a girl. If she talked, if she said one wrong word to the wrong person... A sense of vertigo overcame her; she touched her forehead, and sucked a deep breath into her lungs. Hannah was a servant. She was a girl. It was one thing to read books and to fantasize, but her fingers were real and so were her shaky, uneven breath and her sweet timid voice.

"Milady, are you not feeling well?"

Rose shook her head. She shrugged the jingling dress off her shoulders and watched the gooseflesh rising on her skin as Hannah helped her step out of the fabric. She felt more naked now than she had earlier, more exposed and vulnerable.

"Why have you dreamed of that?" she asked, trying to sound confident, as if this were a conversation she had every day, noblewoman to servant girl.

She could feel Hannah cringing behind her, heard her breath hitch and then she knew, or maybe she merely dared to consider the impossible: that this girl, this beautiful, pink-cheeked girl, was like her. That among a hundred young women she'd met, this was the first who understood the flush of heat, the sudden dizzying realization that she liked the wrong things. The wrong kind of people.

Rose staggered forward and braced herself against her commode. Her fingers found the hard wood and she turned around to look at the girl. Hannah's copper hair was like water under a red sunset, washing down her shoulders.

"Just... just to be close to you, Milady." She looked as if she was about to cry, as if she wanted to sew her lips shut and couldn't. Rose's heart ached for her.

Her body ached for her.

"Would you help me unlace my corset?"

Hannah's tongue was visible for a flash as she moistened her lips. Rose stared, transfixed. Her heart leaped when Hannah nodded, and pounded harder when she didn't look away in shame.

"Y... yes, Milady."

"Rose."

Hannah hesitated, and then a small, careful smile washed over her lips. She nodded again and something passed between the two women, something like a promise, like heat, like the light of distant stars.

Rose turned around again, carefully brushing her hair over her shoulder and out of the way. This time, when Hannah came close, Rose found it hard to breathe. Each loosened string should have made it easier, should have given her lungs more room to expand, but it didn't. The effect was too weak to fight against the dizzying force of Hannah's hands, and the warmth of her breath.

It was wrong, of course it was. But if she stopped her now, then she would never know. She would never be the dashing hero of her stories, and always the meek, obedient girl. That thought catapulted her into rebellion, and when the corset fell away, Rose turned around, one full breast in each hand, her face flushed and her breathing shallow.

The whalebone had pressed deep red lines into Lady Rose's skin. They ran down her side and her quivering stomach.

They were the first things Hannah touched.

She couldn't look at her face, not yet, not anymore, but her shaking fingers traced the pressure marks up her waist to where her arm was pressed against her chest.

When their lips touched, neither of them had made the first step, neither of them had waited to be kissed. Hannah was swept up in the desire that emanated from Rose's body like a highly charged energy field. Rose's lips were so soft, that was the one thing in Hannah's mind, so soft and warm, and before she knew it, Rose's hands were cupping Hannah's face and Hannah had slung her arms around Rose's naked waist.

Rose felt like living porcelain, too precious, too breakable to be real, too fragile to be touched, and yet she pulsed with life under her fingers, and her tongue, hot and wet, pushed harder into Hannah's mouth.

It was Rose who pulled them toward the bed, buoyed up by a swell of bravery. Under that broad canopy, where Hannah had never so much as dared to sit, she now traced Rose's neck with kisses. Rose's encouraging fingers in Hannah's copper hair directed her mouth down to where Rose's bosom swelled in twin peaks from her chest.

In all the nights, all the long working days that Hannah had dreamed of her mistress, she couldn't have imagined this. However often she'd run her hands down her own breasts under the blanket, she couldn't have imagined the texture and the softness of another woman's skin, the thrill of discovery, the jolt of electricity that came with Rose's whimpering breath when her nipples wrinkled into erect little pebbles that disappeared into Hannah's mouth, nudged her tongue.

It was madness, dizzying folly, but she couldn't stop. Not now. Not when she felt Rose's chest expand under her fingers with each breath, so close that the vibration of her heartbeat stirred her skin against Hannah's lips.

"Have you done this before?" Rose gasped.

Hannah shook her head against Rose's breast, took her nipple again and Rose moaned. Her fingers dug harder against Hannah's sensitive scalp and then she found her hand. Their fingers laced together like strands into fabric and when Hannah bit down on Rose's nipple, Rose squeezed her hand and drew it down, down under her voluminous white skirt.

We shouldn't... not this, shot through Hannah's mind as they fought against the puffy material. She saw the gypsy, saw her disapproving frown, saw her piece of paper burning and crumpling into ash. But then there was skin, hot moist skin and wiry hair and the vision disappeared.

Sparks went off behind Rose's eyes. She gasped, held her breath, then pushed out a quaking moan. Her hand was still cupping Hannah's, but the girl moved it of her own accord, moved it up and down Rose's slippery womanhood. Rose cried out each time she hit the nub at the top of her slit, and Hannah learned fast to stay there, and to rub harder even as Rose buried her other hand in Hannah's hair and tore her head back so they could kiss again. She keened her pleasure into Hannah's mouth.

Hannah was her damsel, her beautiful pink-cheeked girl, and she would keep her safe from the dragons downstairs and up. She was her treasure, her bright-eyed miracle, her scandalous novel come to life.

"Hannah," she gasped against her lips."Oh... please don't stop, please..."

When Rose's body contracted in paroxysms of joy, she tasted only Hannah on her lips, and her fragrant copper hair washed over her face. Her miracle sunset. Her body reborn.

SHALLOW END
L.C. SPOERING

The smell of chlorine isn't as sharp at an outdoor pool compared to an indoor one. It competes with the odor of cars on the street, fried food cooked at the overpriced café, sunscreen, coconut, and something like baby powder. The sensation is different too, with the heat of sun-warmed concrete under foot and the same sun beating down on tender shoulders.

I was nineteen, the last summer I worked at the pool. It was situated in the center of the park I'd visited so often as a child, down the block from my parents' house. It wasn't a glamorous job; the rec center was one of the ones built during the boom of the '50s, and it looked it. It was smaller than the ones built after the shine of the '84 Olympics, to cater to every child who thought they too could win a gold medal.

My friends picked up jobs as waitresses that summer, or as clerks at the mall. I'd been a lifeguard in high school, and a toddlers' swimming instructor. Working at the pool didn't pay as much as their jobs, wasn't as cool but, truth was, I didn't think myself graceful enough to be a waitress, and was bad enough at math to believe I'd never manage to count back change. The swimming pool suited me just fine.

I was the only girl. This was before Baywatch, before a swimsuit uniform had any sort of captivation whatsoever. My suit was blue with a white stripe down the left side. The leg holes were cut close to the hips, as was the fashion—at least with women in their forties. The teenage girls who visited the pool to lie out and sizzle under the sun all wore string bikinis, or tank suits with the legs cut high, nearly to the arm holes. My suit made me look and feel shorter, thicker, not much of the racer I'd been on the high school swim team.

Because I was the only girl, I was given the toddlers. I liked the ones that were old enough to have a healthy fear of the water, but were still eager to hop in. Time passed quickly and easily when surrounded by a teeming horde of children.

Swim lesson mothers came, and they stayed. Some lay by the pool with a book, using the hour to furiously indulge themselves in me-time. Others used it as social hour, a swap of gossip like old mother hens, although most of them were no more than five, ten years older than me.

Even though the pool was not open for adult swimmers, some came decked out in their own suits, and those were the ones I watched. My lesson hours were alongside those for the older kids, right after swim team, and those lessons—with the kids who mostly knew what they were doing—were given to the other guards, the ones that all seemed to be named Gary and David and Pete. They were my age, but seemed ageless, and all had broad, hard chests and tans even before summer started. The mothers flocked to them, dressed for them, and arranged themselves on the sun loungers so their cleavage left little to the imagination.

I watched these mothers, taking in glances while I carefully guided their children in circles around the shallow end of the pool, holding their bodies aloft along the surface, muttering almost mechanically that I wouldn't let them drown.

I named the mothers. I only knew their children's names, and so the mothers got new ones from me: Legs, and Slippers, and the one with the mane of red hair, teased up high and proud, Ginger. I was not all that creative, but I could pick them out of a line-up. I thought I could see them out of their poolside costumes and know exactly who they were.

Silver wore a black tank suit with bra cups that pressed her breasts high and forward, as though being served up on a platter. Her legs and arms were tan, but her cleavage remained pale white, as did her neck and face. She wore enormous sunglasses, and her dark hair, pulled up and into a bun, had a single silver streak in it—hence my name for her.

The Garys and Petes and Davids called her Skunk Stripe. They had names for the mothers just as I did, but theirs were far less flattering. The attention they garnered was seen as something both amusing and gross, and they cultivated it, making an effort to swagger as they passed the women, gagging later in the staff room if one of the women had touched them.

I had Silver's son in my class. Even if I'd asked him her name, he was too young to know her as anything but Mommy, and he called for her in abundance, flailing in the water like an eel who had not figured out its place in life.

His name was Timothy, I knew that much. Silver came every Tuesday and Thursday in the pattern of parental duty, and stayed perched on one of the low-slung chairs at the line where the pool dipped steeply from four to six feet. This was at the very edge of our class, and so I only caught glimpses of her as I steered each of the children in turn, my hands under their bellies as they dipped their faces under the surface of the water and kicked against my arms, mimicking strokes to match those of the bigger, stronger kids across the pool.

Silver's tan deepened through the first month. She brought magazines in a large woven grass bag, but didn't seem to read. Her oil-slicked fingers turned the pages like the second hand of a clock, and I knew she couldn't possibly be taking in the stories, only the high gloss photos shining up at her sunglasses. Once class was over, Timothy was redirected to the children's area and, at intervals, Silver unearthed snacks for him: boxes of apple juice, and sandwich baggies of Goldfish crackers.

During July, I found reasons to pass near her, the heat of the concrete under my feet matching the heat of my face the closer I came to her chair. I'd fucked around with my roommate's best friend that spring, but this was years before I came out, before I had a name for the clenching, fluttering feeling I got when around a beautiful woman. That summer, it was just the sensation of the sun staining my shoulders red, and the glint of Silver's streak of hair that made my tongue dry, and my heart lurch at the back of my throat.

It was nearly August before I managed to push my voice out of my mouth to say anything to her other than "Hello", other than "Timothy did great". I stopped at the line, at the divide between four and six feet, shaded my eyes even though I wore white plastic-framed sunglasses. "Looks like it might rain."

She looked up for a beat, and replied, mildly, "You think?"

I spent hours analyzing her response, picking the words apart, and felt like a fool the following week. Rain, indeed. There were exactly two clouds in the sky that day.

It was a childish crush in a lot of ways, an excitement that peaked higher and dropped lower than actual relationships ever had for me. I went on dates that summer, with guys who were not Garys and Petes and Davids, in cars to movies and out to the undeveloped edges of the city, and when their hands wandered down my pants, my mind wandered back to Silver, and her long legs spilling out of her swimsuit.

August dragged its heels. The heat spiked, and the pool was packed day in and day out. I was to return to school at the end of the month, my pockets padded by the salary I'd mostly saved over the summer. My students swam with more confidence in the water that warmed over the day to the temperature of blood. Silver now came every day with Timothy in tow, her skin a bronze color and her toenails painted hot pink.

"I'm Lizzie," I told her one afternoon, as she gathered up her towels and the trash her son had left behind. It was hot enough to see the heat rising off the pavement in waves, turning everything in my vision wavering and liquid, as though I were peering at it from underwater.

"I know," she said, and lifted her fingers to her mouth to whistle for Timothy.

There was no going-away party on my last day of work. All the lifeguards left at some point—it was a seasonal job after all, and paid shit, and we were all students with no sense of loyalty or dedication. I swam my kids through the pool in exhibition, gave away little ribbons and certificates of achievement while the collected parents clapped politely. Silver brought her husband, who looked at his watch frequently; he wore slacks and a button-down shirt, his tie loosened in the heat. He was skipping the first meeting of the day, maybe, to confirm his son could doggie paddle.

I felt ill by afternoon. My bags were packed in my parents' house, and my bus ticket back to school rested on the dresser in my childhood bedroom. The year before, my freshman year, I'd felt only delight, only excitement, and now I stood with a sense of loss that I couldn't put words to, nor did I have anyone to whom I could explain.

"So you're going back to school soon?"

Her voice floated over my shoulder on the bands of heat rising and evaporating from the concrete. It seemed to take forever for me to turn around.

"Friday," I confirmed. She stood with her back to the sun so I could only see her in shadow, a dark outline marked by her curves and the hair that had slipped out of her tidy bun and hung around her heart-shaped face.

"I'll miss you," she said.

My heart seemed to turn into something viscous, something liquid and bubbling, and I bit my bottom lip, and straightened my back so that my breasts strained against the top of my skintight suit. My nipples were clearly visible, but it wasn't the heat that made them stand out.

"Yeah?" I asked, and it was a blessing I couldn't see her face clearly, or my nerves would have crashed right into the pool just with the effort of saying that word.

The locker room where we lifeguards kept our day clothes, our packs of cigarettes, and car keys, was empty at that time of day. We worked in shifts that lasted eight to ten hours, and midday found the majority at their posts, or at the snack bar for lunch. I'd just returned from there myself, and my fingertips were greasy, still stinging from salt. Silver shut the door behind her, and the tile floor felt cool against my feet.

I breathed in the smell of the chlorine that gathered there, the deodorant that lingered in the air. The setting didn't seem to deter Silver, and she rounded on me, forcing me up against the one empty wall in the room, lined with government posters about the minimum wage, which stuck to the backs of my arms.

She looked taller then, somehow more beautiful. My stomach flipped and my knees shook. There was a mixture of excitement as well as fear, and it shot through me with the force of a cannon when she dragged her fingers down my left shoulder and over my forearm, her skin much cooler than mine.

"I've been watching you," she said, and my stomach plummeted again. I wanted to cry, and I wanted to kiss her, but in the end I just nodded mutely, and stood still in an effort to ensure she wouldn't stop touching me.

"Couldn't let you leave without a goodbye, could I?" she said. The question, as rhetorical as it was, hung in the air, and I thought we might remain there—me, her, the question—for all of eternity when her finger slipped under the strap of my tank suit. The fabric immediately sagged as the strap dropped down over my shoulder.

She plucked at the other with the same ease of authority. My suit was not wet, and so it slid a little, and she stepped back just enough that I panicked inwardly for a moment, afraid she was planning to leave.

"Take it off," she commanded me, and I stared at her with round, wide eyes. It took me another second to obey—why wouldn't I?—and I did so with shaking hands.

It was more difficult to remove than a tee-shirt and shorts but the swimsuit peeled away in a surprisingly pleasing manner. I felt her eyes on me as each new patch of skin was revealed. My nipples went hard and pert as soon as they bounced into view, like faces turning toward the sun, eager to behold her.

I wiggled the last few inches of the suit over my hips and then down my legs. I'd never been totally naked in the main part of the locker room before, and it was thrilling in its risk—any of the other lifeguards could walk in at any moment.

She looked me over like someone might assess fruit on a stand. I shivered under her gaze, and found myself straining to keep my back straight, to arrange myself in a way that I'd seen in magazines: alluring, taut, perfect.

Silver touched my chin and lifted it a little. "Relax," she said, as if reading my mind. "If I didn't want you, I wouldn't have brought you in here in the first place."

The muscles of my cunt contracted fiercely, even as the ones around my shoulders and back slackened and sagged with the touch of her fingers. That tiny collection of muscles, that single pulse, made me whimper before I knew the sound was rising in my throat, and Silver flashed me a knowing smile, although she only petted along the line of my jaw and behind my ear as if I were a kitten.

"I'm going to miss you," she informed me, and the words seemed to swim underwater before they reached my ears, and I felt myself blush despite the cool of the room. I shook my head out of instinct, out of habit, and she caught the side of my cheek to still the motion.

"Yes, I am," she said, pushing her thumb over my lower lip. "Don't you tell me how I feel."

My heart tripped over itself, mimicking the sensation of my stomach. I opened my mouth, her finger still there on my lip, but nothing came out.

Her smile was nearly a smirk, and it remained burned on my retinas, like an image left behind on a television screen, even as she slipped from my view.

It took me a moment to realize she wasn't standing in front of me anymore. In the next instant, I felt her breath on my thighs, and her fingers prying them apart. My resistance was only because of my stance, and certainly not because I didn't want her there. It was something I'd craved all summer, since that first lesson when she sat poolside, and all the days after as her skin changed to warm nut-brown.

The first touch of her mouth made me jump, and I jammed my hand over my mouth to keep the squeal behind my lips. I could see her on the floor, smirking up at me, and when my eyes met hers she dipped her head again so her tongue could part my labia to find my clit.

The instant the tip flicked over the sensitive little nub, it was obvious she knew what she was going for, knew, however abstractly, exactly what she wanted—and what I wanted as well. I pushed my hips toward her face so her tongue couldn't stray too far from where I wanted it. It was in my head that the instant I came, she would be gone forever.

She lapped and stroked, and each swipe of her tongue made me wetter and needier. My cunt contracted, grasping for something, anything, to fill it. My fingers found the back of her head sliding between the soft strands of hair. It felt like an animal pelt under my hands. My fingers hooked behind her ears to steer her to the spot that made me quake.

Her hands wrapped around my thighs, squeezing in time with each of my moans, acknowledging them without words. Time melted like ice cream on hot concrete. It could have been years or only a few short minutes, but when I came, it felt like rain.

My legs shook and I gasped, smacking the back of my head against the tiled wall. The orgasm that crashed over me was nothing like any I'd had in my life before: from my own hands, or from someone else's hands or mouth or cock.

Silver chased it, her tongue still relentless on my clit and spasming cunt, until I was sure the only things holding me upright were her strong hands on my legs. Her nails bit into the backs of my thighs, hard enough that purpled crescent moons would remain for a week after.

She licked her lips as she rose back to her full height, her eyes glinting in the artificial light of the locker room. Then I remembered the unlocked doors and I was stunned that no one had heard the noise I made, or walked in on us. But I said nothing.

Her fingers went to her mouth, as if to pat it dry; all that was missing was a napkin. I felt eaten, devoured, and when her eyes went to the door, I felt cast aside.

"I'll miss you," she repeated, and slipped her hair into place, giving me a sly little smile. "You take care of yourself."

Nude, mute, I nodded. What could I have said? You too? I was still processing what had happened, and thought I might keep processing for weeks, years, for the rest of my life.

She left. As she passed through the door, I heard noises from outside, typical late summer pool noises: shouts, splashes, and the occasional lifeguard whistle. The life I led before I walked into the locker room with her, and the life I was pretty sure I would never go back to.

And I didn't. The next summer, I worked at a restaurant where my roommate worked during school. I didn't go home. Some part of me feared seeing Silver again, and staying at my university town made the longing easier to bear. Did she miss me? I liked to think she did.

And now, years later, I wonder does she still think of me when the familiar smell of chlorine rises up in the summer air?

THE FIRST STONE
LISABET SARAI

"You're kinda pretty, for a nun."

The voice was low and throaty, laced with echoes of the ghetto. It dragged me away from the columns of figures marching down the screen in front of me, out of the well-ordered realm of accounting and into the messiness of our inmates' lives. *Our guests*, I corrected myself. Nobody was forced to stay at Serenity House.

"Um—excuse me? Can I help you?"

My interlocutor grinned at me. Her plump, mauve-painted lips framed teeth that were a shocking white in her ebony face. She shook her head. The cheap, brassy earrings dangling from her fleshy lobes swung back and forth over her bare shoulders.

"Just wanted to say hi. Oh, an' to ask if I can stay out past curfew tonight. Heard you were in charge." She extended a hand tipped with hot pink fingernails. "I'm Magnolia. Me and Moonbeam just got here yesterday."

November in Boston, two weeks before Thanksgiving, but Magnolia's skin felt August-hot. The woman's breasts almost overflowed the sequined tube top that constrained them. Below, she wore baggy Boston Celtics sweatpants that didn't hide her more than ample curves. Her feet were crammed into open-toed high heels of scuffed gold-toned plastic. She towered over me. I felt pretty sure that would be true even if I were standing.

"Moonbeam?" Confronted by this apparition, I couldn't seem to manage more than a couple of words.

"My kid." Magnolia indicated a waif-like toddler with kinky pigtails, sprawled on the floor of the common room, surrounded by alphabet blocks. Hard to believe that delicate child was the offspring of this Amazon.

"Ah—um—well, you're very welcome here, Magnolia. We're glad to have you with us." I struggled for the warm yet professional manner I'd learned to adopt with our guests. Rising from my chair, I gave her hand a firm squeeze before relinquishing it. My skin tingled in the aftermath. I'd been right; she stood half a head taller than my five feet six inches, and probably weighed nearly twice what I did. "Have a seat, please. I'm Sister Catherine Patrick, the assistant director. But I guess you know that."

She settled her bottom into the chair I'd indicated. "Yeah, the other gals told me. Pleased to meet you, Sister." Her plucked eyebrows knotted into a frown. "That what I should call you? I ain't had much experience with nuns."

Her obvious concern made me chuckle. "'Sister' would be fine. Or you can just call me Catherine. We don't stand on ceremony here at Serenity House."

"Not like at Baystate Rehab. You forget to call one of the nurses 'Miz' or 'Mister', you lose privs for twenty four hours." She swiped the back of her hand across her brown forehead, which was beaded with sweat. The woman must have a furnace inside.

There was something lush and tropical about Magnolia. Her name fit her. She seemed totally out of place in this shabby office lit by the unrelenting gray of the late autumn sky. I could imagine her wrapped in a rainbow-hued sarong, dancing barefoot on a beach beneath swaying palms. Or swimming naked through the waves under a golden moon...

I hauled my thoughts back to the present. "Is that where you've just come from?" Not all our guests had substance abuse problems, but it was pretty common.

"Escaped is more like it." She giggled. "This place's like heaven after Baystate. Six fucking weeks—oh, sorry, Sister—I mean, six long weeks in that hell hole! Away from my baby, too. 'Course, I deserved it. All the junk I pumped into my veins, not thinkin' about who'd care for her if something happened to me. Then the OD—I really fucked up. Oh, I'm sorry, Sister!"

"Never mind. So you've made yourself comfortable, then? You're happy with your room?" Yesterday had been my day off. Rachel must have done the intake. I reminded myself to check Magnolia's file after she'd left the office.

"It's great. I'm sharing with Lou-Ellen and her little boy. He's only a couple months older than Moonbeam. Food's good, too." She flashed me another grin and glanced down at her generous body. "Not that I need it!"

Her laughter kindled mine. Our eyes met. Hers were espresso-brown, practically black, fringed with mascara-augmented lashes. They snagged me like magnets.

Something jolted through me—a lightning strike, a sudden storm, some personal earthquake. The floor dropped out from under my chair and I found myself suspended in space. My breath caught in my throat and perspiration soaked the armpits of my gray wool sweater. I'd been chilly before—we tried to stretch our donors' generosity as far as possible—but now I burned. I couldn't tear myself away from her gaze, though I knew I'd been staring far too long.

"Are you okay, Sister?" Her husky voice, barely louder than a whisper, wound its way into my stunned consciousness. Her hand hovered above mine, threatening a gesture of comfort.

Don't touch me, I pleaded silently. *Don't.* I pulled back, abruptly enough that I probably seemed impolite, and folded my hands in my lap, a safe distance from the smooth, dark glow of her skin. An almost forgotten ache woke in my belly. The tips of my breasts tingled under my shapeless garments.

"Ah—oh, um—sorry. I—um just felt a bit faint. Most likely it's low blood sugar. I have problems with that sometimes." I fumbled in my desk drawer and found a couple of lemon drops. "These help. Do you want one?"

"I shouldn't," Magnolia replied. But she popped it into her mouth anyway, her lips pursed into a tight O around the candy.

I sucked hard on the sweet-sour nugget, glad for an excuse not to talk while I regained my composure. What in the name of Jesus was going on? Why was I reacting this way? She was a guest, a client. I had a responsibility to her and her child, a responsibility to protect and succor her. To nurture her fragile recovery and send her back into the world stronger, better able to handle the challenges I knew she'd face. To do that, I had to be friendly but a bit aloof. Our women needed the sense of authority that came with my status. They needed the discipline.

As for me—I was a nun, for heaven's sake, sworn to chastity and a pure life of service to others. Lust was a mortal sin.

Lusting after a man would be bad enough. I didn't need to worry about that. Since Tony, I'd had no desire for a man. The body the nuns had snatched from the jaws of death served me and my God well, but my sexual self seemed to have bled out from the razor wounds and down the drain.

Lust for a woman, though... An abomination! I'd been brought up in the Church. The catechism was silent on the question, but of course I knew it was forbidden. Mary Jane, Griselda, and Brigitte had never been more than beloved friends.

"So," Magnolia ventured, peeking out at me from under lowered eyelids, gilded with purple shadow. "Can I stay out past curfew?"

"Ah—that would be rather irregular, especially during your first week with us. Why do you think it's necessary?"

"I gotta go see Ice." Her lips pressed into a thin line of determination. "Gotta tell him we're finished."

"Who's Ice?" I asked, although I had a sinking feeling I knew the answer.

"My pimp. But he never beat me, I swear. And he didn't get me hooked on the junk. That was my own fault." She folded her arms over her ample bosom. I struggled to tear my eyes away from that burgeoning flesh.

"I don't think that seeing someone so involved in your old life is a good idea, do you? Especially not now, when you've just got out of rehab."

"But I owe it to him. He took care of me, through some really bad times. And you know, the hospital wouldn't let him in to see me. Now he's got no notion of where I am—don't even know whether I'm dead or alive. I tried calling him from rehab but his old number's cut off. Down in the 'hood, though, people'll know where he's at. He's got an aunt in Roxbury—might be staying with her."

I racked my brain for a solution. Painful past experience had taught me what would happen if she got together with her pimp. I'd lost other clients to the lure of their pasts. I didn't want that to happen to Magnolia. I wanted to pull her up, up to a higher plane of existence. "Why not write him a letter?"

"I ain't much good at writing. Never paid much mind to school. I was more interested in the boys..." She shrugged and gave me an arch grin. "Maybe you could write it for me, Sister. Bet he never got a letter from a nun!"

Once again her mirth was infectious. The knot of dread and shame under my breastbone loosened a bit. "I could probably do that. You think about what you want to say. We can work on it during free period tomorrow."

I stood up, signaling that our conversation was at an end. I didn't think I could stand it much longer. "So you don't need to go out at all. Stay here and get settled. Get to know some of the other women. We're playing Charades tonight—that's always lots of fun. And tomorrow, you can talk to our social worker, Cheryl, and Ginny, the employment counselor. We need to think about getting you a job."

Magnolia didn't answer, but I saw the doubt in her eyes. I turned back to the computer, fighting the impulse to take her in my arms. "See you tomorrow, Magnolia," I said, effectively dismissing her.

Better for her to think I was impolite or overworked than for her to know the truth.

"Bless me, Father, for I have sinned. It has been a week since my last confession."

"Bless you, my child. Confess your sins and let the love of Christ free you."

"I have had impure thoughts. And lascivious dreams."

"And have you acted on those thoughts?"

"Of course not, Father. I've tried to distance myself from the object of those thoughts. The thoughts persist, though, despite my prayers."

"Thoughts without action are not in themselves sin. And we cannot control our dreams, child. I sense your distress, however. Ask the Lord to cleanse your mind and purify your soul. Dedicate yourself to chastity and to service."

"I will try, Father."

"Be as determined as the saints and the martyrs. God will help you. Say twelve decades of the rosary and six Our Fathers. I absolve you. You are forgiven."

"Thank you, Father."

"God be with you."

"And also with you, Father."

If only it were that simple. I worked six days a week at Serenity House. I tried to avoid Magnolia as much as I could, though I had to fulfill my promise to help her compose a letter to her man. That might have been the toughest hour I'd ever spent in my life. In any case, the place wasn't that big, plus my duties required me to interact with the guests—including the big, boisterous ex-prostitute.

Her pull on me grew the more I saw of her. Magnolia was incredibly popular. I could understand why. From my office, where I was pretending to pay bills or write thank you notes to our benefactors, I'd watch her holding court in the common room. She kept the other women in stitches with her outrageous stories about high times and generous Johns. I never heard her talk about poverty or addiction. But then the other guests knew all about that.

Once she took over the armchair in the corner, the biggest and softest we had, set Moonbeam on her lap, and tried to read to her daughter from one of the donated picture books. Madonna and child, I thought, as winter sun streamed through the dingy windows to light her face. Both my heart and my loins ached as I listened to her stumbling over the simple vocabulary. Moonbeam, a timid, shy little girl—completely unlike Magnolia—gazed up at her mother in adoration.

On Tuesdays, I ran a computer literacy class. We had five second-hand PCs which were more than adequate for teaching the basics of spreadsheets and word processing.

I leaned over Magnolia's shoulder, trying to ignore her intoxicating scent of gardenias and sweat. It might be twenty seven degrees outside on the streets, but as usual she radiated heat.

"Click there, Magnolia. Then choose 'Before text, 0.5 inch', 'First line, 0.7 inch' and 'Single space'."

She honestly tried to follow my instructions. The text jumped right, clumped into a narrow column along one edge of the page.

"Damn!"

"That's okay. Not '5.0 inch', but '0.5 inch'. Half an inch. That's called the left margin. Good. Now select all the text—that's right, drag the mouse, holding down the button. Then go up to the font selection control and choose 'Times New Roman'..."

Somehow she managed to hit the backspace key. The text disappeared.

"Shit! Sorry, Sister..."

"I know, it can be frustrating. You can get it back, don't worry. Just press the 'Ctrl' key and the 'Z' key. See? No harm done."

Magnolia wiped the perspiration from her forehead, leaned back in her chair and sighed. "Hell, don't know why I bother." Her usual equanimity had turned to grouchiness.

"Come on, you know you'll get a better job if you can learn some of this."

She gazed up at me with those liquid chocolate eyes and shook her head. "It's a lot easier being a whore."

A whore. I was in love with a whore. Me, a bride of Christ.

I swore to myself that I'd save her, that I'd teach her what she needed to know, that I'd help her find respectable employment to support herself and Moonbeam. Those vows made me feel slightly less guilty about the damp, fevered dreams I had almost every night, dreams of tropical flowers and dark, succulent flesh.

Kitchen duties rotated among all the occupants of Serenity House, myself included. I was working on supper one night when Magnolia traipsed into the room, wearing a scarlet silk scarf wrapped around her head, leopard-patterned leggings and a Harvard University tee shirt.

"Hi, Sister. It's my turn to help out tonight."

"Good evening, Magnolia. Can you deal with the potatoes?"

"Sure thing." Her breasts hung free underneath her shirt. They swayed hypnotically as she grabbed the peeler and attacked the mound of tubers with her usual energy.

I forced my attention back to chopping garlic, onions and peppers for the meat loaves. I honestly didn't trust myself to look up.

We worked together in silence for five or ten minutes. I sautéed the vegetables, mixed them with ten pounds of ground beef, added eggs, tarragon, basil, massive amounts of black pepper and a tablespoon of Worcestershire sauce, and pressed the mixture into the odd assortment of pans the house owned. Once I had the loaves in the oven, I could escape to my room for an hour.

"Heard you were married once, Sister. That true?"

Oh, God! "Um—yes. More than ten years ago."

"So you ain't no virgin."

Startled, I looked up from the meat loaves. Heat shimmered through me. Despite her tone of levity, she

209

was not smiling. The knowledge I saw in her eyes scared me.

"No. Tony and I—we—" I choked on my own words as tears gathered.

"You can tell me, Sister."

It poured out of me before I could stop myself, the whole sordid story. The fairy tale wedding of Kathy Gallagher and her high school sweetheart Anthony Manzetti, with both enormous families in attendance. The all-too-brief flare of passion. Then Tony's cancer, diagnosed on our second anniversary, and the years of treatment: chemo, radiation, surgery, more chemo. Remissions and the rekindling of hope. Relapses and despair. I'd cared for him through it all: the sweats and the vomiting, the rashes and the sores, the terrible, terrible pain. Everyone praised my strength and courage. A saint, they'd called me.

Two days after his funeral, I'd slit my wrists.

I'd awakened in St. Margaret's Hospital, bandaged and restrained. An elderly nun sat by my bedside, stern and sorrowful. The weight of memory had crushed me.

"Why did you save me?" I'd asked, so weak I could barely whisper. "You should have let me die."

"For shame, child. Your life is a gift from God. How dare you throw it away, when you could be using it to help others?"

"Haven't I done enough, taking care of Tony all those years?"

"Apparently not, since your soul is not at peace."

I shuddered at the recollection. Scalding tears streamed down my cheeks. Magnolia slipped an arm around my shoulder and pulled me against her pillowy chest. Lost in grief and self-pity, I scarcely noticed, at least for a moment.

She stroked my cropped hair. "Poor baby. Seems to me that becoming a nun yourself—well that was a bit much, wasn't it?" A sense of comfort stole over me. Her floral aroma mingled with the kitchen spices. "Maybe you chose wrong."

She pressed her lips to my forehead. Terror and arousal streaked through me in alternating waves. I struggled against her entangling arms. "No, no," I babbled. "Sin—suicide is a mortal sin—I had to atone..."

Magnolia released me with a deep sigh. "Ain't you done enough penance, Sister?"

I rushed upstairs to my room without answering, her scent clinging to my clothing, the mark of her lips branded on my forehead.

I didn't come down to dinner that night, or the next. I made excuses that weren't quite lies and found errands to take me away from Serenity House whenever I could.

When I'd managed several days without running into Magnolia, I relaxed slightly. How immature of me— how irresponsible—to have bared my soul to one of our inmates—our *guest*—as I'd done. They had enough problems without taking on mine.

Next time I saw Magnolia, I told myself, I'd apologize for burdening her with my troubles. And from now on I'd keep a tight rein on my emotions and my hormones. I could be strong. I'd proved that over the ten difficult years since Tony died. Hungers of the body could not undermine the truly committed spirit. I'd rededicate myself to God's work and leave this unpleasant interlude behind.

Two weeks after my embarrassing confession, I found myself in the unheated garage, sorting through the bales of second-hand clothing that had accumulated over the past month. Some of the contents had me shaking my head: tiny string bikinis, blue jeans with more holes than fabric, blouses so faded you couldn't tell their original color. Sure, the inhabitants of Serenity House needed clothes—clothes they could wear to a job interview! After spreading a tarp on the floor, I dumped each bag or box and separated the potentially useful items from the trash.

I could see my breath hanging in the air. My fingers cramped a bit in the cold. Part of me welcomed the discomfort, viewing it as deserved penance. Another part was considering going back to the main house for a warmer sweater, when the door creaked open.

"Hey, Sister."

Fire raced through me, negating the chill. My traitorous nipples tightened into horribly sensitive knots under the sweater. The way the wool abraded them, it might as well have been sack cloth.

As for Magnolia, she was dressed in a tight skirt of electric blue jersey and a lavender top splashed with aqua flowers. Aside from a couple of cheap bangles circling her wrists, her arms were bare.

All I could do was stare. I was melting in the heat she radiated, helpless to speak, to move, to escape.

She stepped closer. I backed away.

"Came to say goodbye, Sister." A rueful half-smile decorated her painted lips. "I'm goin' back to Ice."

"Oh, no! You can't!" Shock and dismay cut through my terrifying arousal. We were losing her, after all my efforts. She'd be swept down into that cesspool of sin and degradation she'd tried so hard to climb out of. "You've been doing so well here, Magnolia. How can you return to that life?"

"That life? You mean hooking?" Her mouth pursed as though she'd eaten something sour. "What the hell else am I goin' do? Honestly? You really see me workin' in some fancy office, Sister? Get real."

"But think about all that time in rehab."

"Oh, I ain't gonna do dope anymore, I swear. I'm clean and I'm gonna stay that way. But Ice—he's my man after all, even if he acts like a piece of shit sometimes.

And he's Moonbeam's daddy." She held out a plump hand. "Don't worry, I'll be fine. Just wanted to thank you, Sister, for your kindness."

I couldn't refuse a hand offered in gratitude.

Our palms touched. Something electric sizzled through me. Her humid scent ballooned around me, drowning out the garage smells of mold and axle grease.

I gazed up at her broad, beautiful face. The ache in my chest swelled until I could hardly breathe. "Please..."

Magnolia's smile was tinged with bitterness. "Please what, Sister?"

I couldn't tell her what I really wanted. "Please don't go back to the streets. Selling your body like so much meat. It's not safe. It's not right. The Bible says..."

She shook her head in exasperation. "Don't you give me no holier than thou, Sister. You been lustin' after me for weeks."

Seizing my shoulders, she yanked my body up against hers. I was swallowed by the lush softness of her breasts. Once she'd trapped me in her massive arms, she bore down on me with that lipstick bright mouth.

"You ain't gonna get away so easy this time, Sister..."

Her lips met mine, silky and firm, with a sweet pressure that stole my determination to fight her. The saints had resisted the corruption of the flesh, but they never faced Magnolia Jones. Before I knew what was happening, she'd plunged her tongue into my mouth and slipped her hot hands under my top. Unerringly, her fingers found the shamefully taut beads of my nipples. I moaned into her juicy mouth when she pinched them. Electric arrows shot down to my sex. The hungry snake of need stirred and coiled in my pelvis. Pleasure washed over me in feverish waves.

"Like that, Sister?" she murmured in my ear before nipping the lobe. Her earrings swung against my throat, chill metal, the only cold in the universe. "Bet you'll like this even more."

In an instant, my sweater was gone, tossed onto one of the piles of second-hand garments, and her lips engulfed my small breast. Searing wetness bathed the skin, even as my naked back broke out in goose bumps. Heat and cold battled for control of my senses. Fear and guilt wrestled with a delirious joy brighter than anything I'd ever known.

I should stop her. I should stop... but oh, by all that was holy, I didn't want to stop. I'd read so much about heaven. This was the closest I'd ever come.

She sucked with single-minded intensity, as if my swollen nipple might burst and flood her with manna. "Oh... oh sweet Jesus... ooh... urrm..." Was that me, moaning incoherently? She grazed her teeth over the aching nub. I yelped, startled by the sharp increment in sensation, then purred as she laved the scraped skin with her scalding saliva.

Just when I thought I couldn't bear any more, she relinquished one nipple to capture the other. Buffeted by sensation, I could scarcely stand on my own, but her powerful arms supported me. Her lips slid down, planting sloppy kisses along my belly. Meanwhile, she unbuttoned and unzipped my bulky, old-lady trousers with a deftness that spoke of extensive experience.

"No..." I panted, as she tugged them down over my hips. My arms were like rubber as I tried without success to push her solid body away from me. "I can't... I don't want..."

"Bullshit," Magnolia growled. She yanked my cotton underpants down into the mess of my outerwear and thrust a finger into my drenched cleft. "You's wet as Boston Harbor, girl."

Sparks raced up my spine. I jerked in her arms as she probed my private parts. *Sin, sin*, the saints and apostles hissed, like the snake in the garden. I closed my ears and let Magnolia Jones lead me into the wilderness.

Melting, undone, I collapsed onto the heaped up clothing. She tumbled down on top of me, burying me under her fragrant, meaty body, and ground her well-padded pubis against my naked pussy while she nibbled at my teats. Her juices leaked through the stretchy fabric of her skirt to soak my skin. Pressure built in my sex, strange and unfamiliar after ten years of denial.

Soft, so soft she was, but hard too, rubbing and pumping against my mons, transferring her inexorable rhythm to the throbbing bead hidden beneath. I clenched my thighs together and arched up to meet her, shameless in my pursuit of more powerful sensations. Magnolia chuckled and slipped her hand down between our legs. When she found my clitoris, I think I screamed.

"That's right, baby. Let it out... You can touch me too, you know. You don't have to be shy..."

Without stopping her rocking movements, Magnolia pulled my hand up to her meaty buttocks. "Go 'head. Squeeze me. Squeeze me hard."

The smooth fullness under my fingers pulsed with heat. My palm tingled as I stroked along the swell of her magnificent rear.

"C'mon. Don't be shy."

Enslaved by sensation, I dug my fingers into the mass of flesh. I was lost, trapped in one of those ripe, forbidden dreams that had haunted me since she'd first appeared in my life. I didn't want to wake up.

"Oh, yeah... yeah."

Her breath came in gasps. Sweat dripped from her brown face onto mine. She kissed me again, grinding our pussies together and twiddling my clit. A climax welled up from my depths, dark and implacable, threatening to spill over and drown me.

Capturing my hand, she brought it to meet hers, in the steamy jungle between my legs. "Fuck yourself, Sister. Fuck yourself till you come."

Her coarseness triggered a twinge of disgust. At the same time, it made me wild. I obeyed, rubbing hard at the magic spot I'd discovered so long ago, rubbing and rubbing, while the pleasure built and built. Magnolia's fingers were busy in my channel, too. Fat and slippery, they twined with mine as we worked together to push me over the edge.

Thank the Lord the garage isn't attached to the house. I tumbled into that whirlpool of bliss, screaming and sobbing, praising God and angels at the top of my lungs. Magnolia's climax was quieter, grunts and growls that nevertheless conveyed her total satisfaction. She collapsed on top of me, her weight providing welcome protection from the icy air around us.

She was the first to stir. While I lay sprawled upon my bed of discarded clothing, limp, totally undone by pleasure, she levered herself onto her hands and knees and climbed to her feet. Her blouse was half off. Her skirt showed a dark patch at the juncture of her thighs, which she brushed ineffectually before giving up with a laugh.

"Hell, Ice knows me. He won't care."

At the mention of her pimp, all my languorous warmth leached away. I shivered and clambered to a sitting position. "You're not really going back to him, are you?"

"'Course I am, Sister." Reaching out, she helped me to my feet. "I can't stay here. Especially now." She didn't have to explain. Especially now that I'd broken my vows and given in to my need.

"But Magnolia..." All at once my arms were around her, holding her fullness tight to my skinny chest. Heat seeped back into my body. I didn't know what to say. All I knew was that I didn't want her to leave.

She let me hold her for a long while, but finally, gently, she disentangled herself from my arms. "He's waitin' for me, hon. I gotta go. But I'll try to keep in touch." She flashed me one of those brilliant, tropical smiles. "Maybe I'll write you a letter."

Magnolia left me there, in the chilly garage, with her lipstick smeared on my bare breasts and her juices painting my thighs. As I tried to repair the damage, I waited for guilt. It never came.

Though I knew it had been wrong, somehow I couldn't regret what we'd done. Oh, I regretted her going back to being a whore, sure, but giving in to my lust? I couldn't honestly say I was sorry. It had been incandescent, a once-in-a-lifetime experience. A lesson, too. Magnolia and I weren't so different after all.

Tomorrow was Sunday, but I didn't think I'd confess what I'd done—what we'd done—today. Really, it wasn't Father Donnelly's business. This was between God and me.

OUT FOR THE COUNT
CHEYENNE BLUE

Linn watches the woman through the two way mirror. Even though the woman is seated, Linn can see she is tall—her upper body rises above the other blackjack players—and slim. The woman's hair is blond and doesn't match her olive skin. Its even color and lack of dark roots tell Linn it's most likely a wig.

The unknown woman has not left her seat at the blackjack table for over five hours. She has waved away the cocktail waitresses, with their trays of watered-down drinks. Instead she concentrates fiercely on the cards.

She's a card-counter, that much is obvious, and going by the steadily growing pile of gaming checks in front of her, she's a good one. Experienced. She kept her nerve through the inevitable losing streak at the start, threw in a few camouflaged hands, and now she's reaping the rewards, winning big as the odds stack in her favor. Linn records a still image from the Eye in the Sky and runs it through the industry database once more. Nothing.

She catches a signal from Raoul down on the floor. She has no trouble interpreting his glare. "Find her in the database. And quickly."

The card counter is obviously disguised, but it's a good one. Linn zooms in with the camera, records a different angle, displays it on her screen. She studies it for telltale signs of a nose prosthetic, or padding in the cheeks, but she can't spot anything unusual.

She calculates from the pile of checks in front of the unknown woman that she's won over $40,000. She'll stop soon, when the shoe runs dry and new decks of cards are used. Linn brings up on screen the image of the ID the woman presented when purchasing her checks. Violetta Pennetta. Violetta exists all right, but Linn is very sure that's not Violetta at the blackjack table.

Sure enough the final hand is played, and the woman who is not Violetta scoops her winnings into her purse and rises from the table. She flicks the dealer a few checks—big ones. Adrian looks happy, as well he might. He's just earned two weeks' money in a few hours.

Linn rises from her post and nods for Sully to take over. Intercept time. She leaves the walkway, going down to the casino floor. She locates the woman who is not Violetta easily enough as she wends her way through the slots. The card counter stops to watch a nondescript woman playing a quarter slot, and Linn's trained eye sees her slip a cloth bag into the woman's purse, which sits open by her side. Linn sucks a breath. Of course. This slot player is the real Violetta. The woman who is not Violetta saunters off, not in a direct line, which would draw attention—few people walk purposefully in a casino—but in a wandering path that takes her past the craps table where she stops to watch for a couple of minutes, before heading for the restroom. Linn twists a smile. After five hours at the blackjack table, she must be bursting. Linn follows her into the restroom, goes into a stall and pretends to pee, but instead she bites a nail until the edge is ragged. When she hears the toilet flush in the next stall, she flushes too and is at the hand basin before the woman who is not Violetta. She pretends to study her nails.

"Damn," she says, and her eyes alight on the woman who is not Violetta. "Excuse me, I don't suppose you have an emery board? I've just torn a nail and it's catching on my clothing."

The blond woman smiles. "I don't think so," she says, "but let me check." Her voice is American, but it's hard to pick the region. If it's possible to have a neutral American accent, then this woman has it. She digs in her purse.

Linn sees the usual mishmash of cosmetics, wallet, comb, cell phone, and keys. She clocks the Lexus symbol on the keys. She will check the CCTV footage from the parking garage later.

"Sorry, the woman says. "No emery board."

Linn smiles. "Not to worry. Had any luck today?"

"Some." The woman does not elaborate.

Up close, the woman is gorgeous. She has wide hazel eyes and clear skin, covered with only a smattering of powder. Linn can't see any prosthetics changing her face shape—the only obvious disguise is the blond hair, which she's still convinced is a wig. The woman is not meeting her eyes—no doubt she wants to get out of there fast, probably to meet the real Violetta, who right now is doubtlessly at the cashier's cubicle, cashing in the checks, using her real ID. It's a common trick, employing some third party to cash in the winnings for a percentage of the takings, but usually it doesn't get this far. Usually the professional gamblers are recognized as they walk into the casino from a match with the industry database, which is shared with casinos all around America. Then an unctuous man in a suit will approach the would-be gambler as they cross the foyer, and, taking their arm, will tell them politely that they are welcome in the casino, please be free and enjoy the facilities. Maybe play some poker, craps, or the slots, but we're so very sorry—we cannot allow you to play blackjack.

Blackjack: the game of the professional, the only game where with sufficient intelligence, skill, and a phenomenal memory it is possible to beat the system by counting cards, memorizing them as they are played from the shoe, and then by calculating the odds it is possible to beat the bank.

Linn wants to keep this woman talking. Maybe she'll learn a snippet, enough to identify her, so that if she attempts to come back, she can apprehend her. "Lucky you," she says. "Did you get lucky on the slots?"

"Poker," the woman says. "My daddy taught me growing up in Indiana."

Good choice, Linn notes. The accent could well be from Indiana, even though she knows the poker story is untrue.

The woman picks up her purse, preparing to leave. She's taut with the thrill of her win, and no doubt she wants to go and celebrate. Wine, good food. Maybe a partner for the night.

Linn needs to keep her there a little longer. She sighs. "I lost again. Maybe I should switch games. But of course no one beats the casino." She puts a confiding hand on the woman's arm. "You're obviously good; I wish you'd teach me."

The woman shrugs. "There are poker schools." But something Linn has said has got through. The woman turns, studies Linn, assessing her. Linn tries to look soft and feminine, unthreatening, although it's difficult in the cotton shirt and pressed chinos she wears for work.

But the woman who is not Violetta must like what she sees, as she says, "Want to come and have a drink with me? I'll give you some tips."

Linn sweeps her eyes down to hide the leap of achievement. Bait taken. There's an invitation in the woman's face, a subtle tinge of amusement carefully hidden. She has taken Linn for a groupie, flirting to maybe earn a handout of $50 or so. But the sexual invitation is also there, open for her to see. Linn's gaydar flares. She hadn't expected this, hadn't clocked the woman's preference through the two way mirror. But now, face to face, she can see the dilated pupils, can see the slight tilt of her hips in Linn's direction.

This is too good to pass up.

She lets her own eyes go wide and ingenuous. "Oh, would you? I'd love that." Deliberately she strokes the woman's arm, enough that it's a response to flirtation, not enough to scare her away if she's reading this wrong. "There's a good bar at the back. We could go there."

"There's a nicer place down the road," the woman says.

"Sure," says Linn, although she's thinking that there are no nicer places down the road. This isn't a huge Vegas casino; this is a small, dusty desert town on the Nevada border, set back from the highway which leads to the brighter lights. Gamblers who stop here are tired overnighters or pensioners on bus trips. Addicts or desperate or bored. So "down the road" means another casino, or else the bar over the border in California, which, although definitely interesting, is not what you'd call a nice place.

"Are you staying here?" asks Linn. "We could go to your room."

"I'm staying out of town," the woman says, "but we can go there, if that's what you want."

She turns the full force of her smile on Linn. No, she's not wrong, there's an invitation, a flirtation. This woman is after seduction, a quick post gambling high fuck. This isn't the first time that Linn has received a proposition like this, but with a jolt, she realizes this is the first time she's seriously considered accepting it.

"I just have to drop by a friend's place on the way. Pick up something. It won't take a minute."

Linn nods. No doubt to collect her winnings. "I'm Linn," she says, and there's a moment of self-flagellation as she realizes she's given her real name. But she's thrown off kilter by this woman. A woman she realizes she desires, for more than the thrill of the chase.

"Francesca," says the woman in return. "I'm very happy to meet you. My car's in the parking garage."

They leave, taking the elevator to the garage. Linn sees Raoul out of the corner of his eye, and although he makes no outward sign, she senses his approval at her tactics. Get to know the punter. Find out what you can about them so that next time they enter the casino there will be the restraining hand on the forearm and the suggestion they don't play blackjack.

The keys she saw in Francesca's purse do indeed fit a Lexus. A silver late-model one. Linn sinks into the leather seat, fakes a wide-eyed look around. "Lovely car," she says, and leans forward to twiddle the radio dial.

Francesca slaps her hand away, and as Linn feigns hurt, Francesca picks up her hand and presses it to her lips, kissing away the red mark.

This time, Linn's gasp is not feigned. The touch of Francesca's mouth on the back of her hand sends a jolt of silver desire along her arm. One touch from the red lipsticked mouth pressing a kiss to her flesh, and she's molten. Wide-eyed she stares at Francesca.

Francesca withdraws. "Did I read you wrong, darling? If I did, it's a first. I thought you knew what you were getting into. You don't want poker tips any more than I want to give them." One side of her mouth lifts in a half smile, and she seems amused.

Caught off balance by the directness, Linn stammers an apology, but Francesca leans across the gearshift and presses her lips to Linn's. She kisses her hard, her mouth firm and assured. Her hand rests on Linn's thighs, pressed protectively together. A shaft of desire pierces Linn's belly. She knows the parking garage is covered by CCTV, she knows that Raoul may be watching this, but right now, she doesn't care. She wants Francesca with a fierceness, an immediateness that equals Francesca's own post win high. It's doubtless going to be a euphoric fuck for Francesca, but Linn is there with her, and if Raoul is watching—well, she will make her excuses to him later.

So she kisses Francesca back, pushing her tongue into Francesca's mouth, and tasting the lust that leaks from her. But she keeps her thighs together; Francesca is probably so high she would fuck here in the parking garage, uncaring of security cameras. But Linn won't go that far. Indeed, she thinks, she will stop this soon. But not just yet.

She breaks the kiss. "Your hotel."

Francesca starts the Lexus. Linn lets her hand settle on Francesca's thigh as they follow the ramps to the exit.

Outside it's dusk, and away from the casino there are only the quiet streets of a town which reeks of desperation. Linn's fingers explore higher, up to the juncture of Francesca's thighs, over her skirt. And then, when that isn't enough, she reverses direction, lets her fingers crawl down to her knee and repeats the process underneath the skirt. Francesca's bare skin is smooth and warm. When Linn's fingers touch the edge of her panties, they are damp.

Francesca navigates quiet streets, pulling up at a small brick house. There are no street lamps here, and the house is the last in the street. Only the straggly mesquite and creosote bush of the high desert are beyond. Francesca cuts the engine.

"I won't be long," she says and she's gone, stepping briskly up the cracked concrete drive to the house.

The door opens before she can ring the bell and the nondescript woman Linn saw earlier at the slots hands her an envelope. Francesca keeps her back to the car, but from her bent head, Linn imagines she's counting the money, handing Violetta her share. She's back at the car within two minutes.

Linn thinks about asking, with the wide-eyed innocence she does so well, if those are her winnings, but she doesn't. Doubts fire into her head, randomly like scattershot. She's never done this before. Sure, she's befriended a card counter, just to ensure they get the right person when next they attempt to enter the casino, but she's never taken it this far. She's never kissed anyone with deception on her lips; she's certainly never contemplated taking it as far as fucking. It's deceptive. It's unprofessional. It's a line she should not cross.

But god, how she wants to.

There's nothing in her contract to forbid this. What would they put? "Fucking professional gamblers will result in termination of employment"? But Linn's own sense of what is right is giving her some uncomfortable moments. Even though she's aware Francesca is using her for her post gambling high, for a quick scratch of the itch, it feels wrong. It feels dirty.

But then Francesca half turns to her with heat in her gaze, and Linn swallows. There's a tension between them, a blaze of heat. And she wants Francesca badly. She pushes down the doubt. Francesca is using her, that's a given. It's an exchange of lust, no more, no less.

Francesca arches a manicured eyebrow. "My room?" she says. "For... poker tips, if you want to call it that. Or some good loving, if you're more honest."

Linn lets her hand drift up Francesca's thigh, scratches one blunt nail over the juncture. "Your room," she affirms.

Francesca is staying at the Ramada on the edge of town. It's a wise choice for a professional gambler: no casino, no security staff to make things awkward. Her room is on the top floor and in the gathering twilight, there's a view west to where the setting sun streaks red across the desert. The mountains are already in silhouette, and the cars on the freeway already have their lights on.

The room is an executive one: wide screen TV, mini-bar, king-size bed, white quilt cover, and a blanket of Navajo design folded on the foot of the bed. Linn sits on the bed and watches as Francesca pulls a bottle of champagne from the fridge. French, she sees by the label, not mini-bar stuff. Francesca has anticipated her winnings. Another checkmark in the professional gambler box.

Francesca pops the cork silently, no flashy explosion, and pours the champagne into two glasses. "Cheers," she says, handing one to Linn. "Here's to new friends."

"To new friends," echoes Linn, "and to winning.'

Francesca smiles a secretive closed in smile. "To winning."

The bubbles tickle the back of Linn's throat, and the champagne is acidic to her taste. She's more of a beer woman. She swallows in great gulps, puts the glass down on the floor, stands and moves across to the window, looks out onto the desert night.

"How long are you in town for?" she asks. "Just tonight?"

Francesca comes up beside her. "Maybe another night as well. It depends on what happens tomorrow."

"On whether you win again?"

A nod. There's a silence. Linn knows she should say something about gambling, try and turn the conversation to blackjack, but she's not interested right now. Right now, she wants to forget she's Linn the Security Guard doing her job, she just wants to be Linn sipping champagne in the hotel room of a beautiful woman. She heaves a deep breath.

"Doubts?" asks Francesca.

"No." And it's suddenly true. Everything is pushed aside, roles, who she really is, who Francesca really is, and it's now only about the moment.

She turns to Francesca, takes her in her arms, aligns their hips and cups her bottom. As a move, it's an unsubtle one, but this whole encounter isn't about subtlety. It's about lust and a fleeting pleasure.

She kisses Francesca, tasting champagne, feeling the pulse of need in her lips. Her tongue sweeps into Francesca's mouth, and she presses tighter, as if by kissing harder she can mold Francesca any way she wants. Her fingers go to the tiny buttons on Francesca's shirt. Silk, she realizes, as the material slips under her fingertips. Her fingers glide over the material, and the buttons work free.

Francesca kisses her in return, and her fingers loosen the front of Linn's cheap cotton shirt. Both shirts come undone at the same moment, and they break the kiss long enough to shrug out of them. Silk and cotton fall into a tangled pile on the carpet. Francesca's skin is olive, the heritage of a warmer climate. She's aging well, but up close Linn guesses Francesca is in her 40s, maybe ten years older than Linn's own 34. Linn's Scandinavian heritage means her skin is white, soft, pale, and lightly freckled. If she stays in the sun too long she burns, but her job means she's indoors most of the time.

Linn traces the line of lace that edges Francesca's bra cups. Black lace, lightly padded. Francesca is slender, skinny almost, and her collarbones stand out in relief. Linn reaches around, undoes the bra and pulls it away from Francesca's body. Her breasts are small, teardrop swellings that rise from her chest. Linn can cover an entire breast with her hand, and she does so, feeling the press of nipple into her palm. Francesca's nipples are long, and when Linn bends to take one in her mouth, she rolls her tongue around it, savoring the tiny peak and Francesca's low moan of pleasure.

She lifts her mouth away from Francesca's breast long enough to ask, "What do you want?"

Francesca's eyes glitter. "I want you to lick me until I come. Then I want you to fuck me, hard. Then, honey, there is all the time in the world for you."

Linn doesn't answer, but her fingers move to the zipper at the back of Francesca's skirt, a designer pencil skirt that probably cost the equivalent of a week of Linn's wages. She lowers the zipper and draws the skirt down over Francesca's hips. Francesca steps out of it, and stands there in black panties that match the bra she so swiftly discarded earlier. The high heels she wears accent her toned legs. Francesca struts to the bed, sits, and kicks off the heels.

"Take off the panties," Linn orders. Excitement pulses in her blood. Francesca is beautiful, and the wrongness of the encounter seeps back into her head. But instead of making her shrink away, it's empowering her. She is giving as well as taking. And when Francesca's panties hit the carpet she wants nothing more than to pleasure her. She pushes her back on the bed. Francesca's thighs fall apart, revealing her pussy, covered with closely cropped dark hair. Even in her excitement, Linn registers more proof that the blond hair on her head is not her natural color. She kneels on the floor, grateful for the thick carpet, and pushes Francesca's knees wider. Her pussy is glistening, the outer lips slick with her juices. Linn bends, uses her elbows to brace herself and puts her mouth between Francesca's thighs. Francesca bucks up, her hips coming off the bed at the first touch of Linn's mouth. All Linn does is put her lips to the other woman's cunt, breathing in the musky aroma of excitement and arousal. Her nose bumps Francesca's mound, and her mouth and chin are damp from the other woman's pleasure. Her lips find Francesca's nub and she suckles it once, briefly, and feels Francesca's thighs clench around her head. Francesca is close to coming already, but Linn wants more than this, so she retreats, runs her tongue around the furred outer lips, flickering in and out of her folds, never touching the prominent clit.

Francesca's juices run slick, and Linn's tongue slides in a glissade around and around. Francesca clenches, pants, and her fingers push into Linn's short hair. "Harder," she directs. "Faster."

Linn complies and her tongue flickers over Francesca's hard clit, quick cat laps, and Francesca comes in a rush and a bowstring arch of body. When her body settles back on the bed, Linn remembers the earlier command, and pushes two, three fingers inside her. Francesca is slick and relaxed and her cunt stretches easily. Linn adds a fourth finger, lets her thumb pass lightly around Francesca's outer lips, nearly, not quite over her clit. She pistons in and out, listening to the soft breath sounds, feeling the clench of pussy around her fingers. Another gush of moisture, and Francesca comes hard in a sudden rush, a sigh like mist on the water even as she spasms around Linn's fingers.

Linn bends, touches her mouth to the soft mound in front of her, withdraws her fingers. Her own pussy flutters like a captive bird. She's still half dressed. She stands and drops her bra, pushes down her work pants, her cotton panties, kicks off her sensible shoes and stands naked. Her pale skin gleams in the dusky light of the room and a sex flush heats her chest.

"Come here," says Francesca.

Linn complies, crawling onto the bed, lying beside Francesca, who takes her face between both hands and kisses her. It's the fleeting peck of a mother bird, then, again, a caress with her upper lip, and finally, she kisses her with the possession of a lover. Francesca pushes her over onto her back, moves down her body. One nipple, then the other receives hot kisses. Francesca's fingers move in sweeping circles over her breasts, her sides, her flat belly, all in light, barely-there touches that have Linn quivering. The pulse in her pussy intensifies—it's now a drumbeat of need, hot and urgent.

All thoughts of the wrongness of this fly from Linn's head. She's not thinking about her job, how she is compromising her professionalism. She's not thinking about the lies she's told—by implication, by words—to get to this point. She's thinking of her body, Francesca's body and how they fit together. And Francesca has told more lies than she. No. Linn's pleasure is of the moment, her thoughts are the chaotic eddying of pleasure, focused down, deep down.

She wants Francesca to use her tongue, her fingers, her fist—she's that wet—and she wants to grind their pussies together. She wants to come and come hard before life and responsibility intrude back in. She knows in her heart they may only have this night. It has to be enough. She will make it enough.

She raises her hips in unspoken invitation, and is rewarded by Francesca's palm cupping her mound, her fingers pushing apart her lips to the sodden valley between. Francesca moves down, enough that her lips can caress Linn's nipple, and she nudges with her knees, so that Linn takes the hint and lifts her legs so that Francesca can curl around her.

Finally, Francesca fucks her, pushing in two fingers and pumping her hard. There are the dual tugs of pleasure from Francesca's mouth on her nipple, her fingers in her cunt, and she flies over the edge into the white light behind her closed eyelids.

The room is dark, cooling as night steals over the desert. Francesca presses a kiss to her nipple, a final kiss on her mouth, then rises and pads to the bathroom. The door closes behind her, and Linn lies back, dreaming the twitching dreams of satisfaction. Francesca exits the bathroom, leaving the light on and the door open. She picks up the warm glasses of champagne and hands one to Linn.

They sip the liquid without speaking. It's warm, flat, and unappealing.

Francesca gestures to the bathroom, and Linn rises, goes to the bathroom, locks the door. She sits and pees and then she sees the curl of hair sticking out of the hastily tidied drawers. She slides the drawer open, looks long at the mess of wigs inside: blond, jet black, auburn, long, short, and cropped. She lifts a strawberry blond wig from the drawer, with its bouncing shoulder-length curls. The next drawer contains various spectacles, make up, and pads that fit in the mouth to alter face shape.

Linn closes the drawer and goes back to the bedroom. Francesca, still naked, lounges against the headboard. Duty sits like a stone in Linn's chest, an unyielding block that tells her what she should do: walk over to Francesca, kiss her on the mouth, thank her and return to the casino and feed Francesca's description to the security guards. Watch out for a tall, slender woman with blond hair. Or red curls. Or a black crop. Watch out for her full mouth, svelte figure, and way of gliding silently across the floor. For a moment, the press of duty fills her mouth with saliva. She's good at her job. Very good. And if she bars Francesca from returning to the casino, she will doubtlessly save the casino thousands of dollars. For Francesca will return tomorrow—that's a given. She will return while the going is good.

Francesca speaks first. "You don't want poker tips."

"And you don't play poker. That's a game of chance."

Francesca nods and her eyes are amused. "I play blackjack. As you well know." She takes a sip of the warm champagne. "Are you cop or security guard? You're obviously one or the other."

"Security guard," says Linn.

"What I do isn't illegal."

"No," Linn agrees. "It's a skill."

Francesca rises from the bed. Even naked her presence is larger than her body, making her taller, more commanding. Although it's only scant minutes since she last came hard, Linn feels the twitch of desire, the pulse in her cunt. She wants Francesca again.

"Thank you," Francesca says.

It's Linn's turn for the amused smile. "For what? For not escorting you out of the casino earlier? Or for this?" The sweep of her hand encompasses the rumpled bed.

"It would have been hard to ask me to leave before. You needed to be sure, in case I was a punter playing on 'intuition'—your best customers, as they always lose in the end. Now you know I'm a counter and that I'll win again. Francesca is my real name. I'm sure that will help you find me in the database." Francesca stands in front of Linn, bends, picks up Linn's clothes from the floor. "I'll be back at the casino tomorrow afternoon. And I'll be here in my lonely bed late tomorrow night."

The invitation is clear. Linn takes her crumpled clothes, and moves away to dress. Her fingers shake as she shoves her feet into the flat black shoes without undoing the laces.

"And after that?" she asks.

Francesca shrugs, and there's a wisp of vulnerability in her eyes. A procession of dinners for one, too bright diners, and long straight highways. "I move on, of course. Another casino. I need to strike while I can."

Linn moves, takes her in her arms, presses a kiss to her lips. Francesca sighs into the kiss and for that moment there's something more than lust between them. Tenderness. Possibility.

"You'll be seeing me," Linn says.

She requests the afternoon shift the next day. She checks the database and finds Francesca. In the photo, her short, dark hair hugs her head, a better match for her olive skin than the blond wig.

Linn is in the foyer at 2.45 p.m. when a woman enters alone. She's tall, but lumpy in her baggy jeans and Denver Broncos sweatshirt. Her hair is long and dark, pulled into a messy pony tail. She looks as if she's here to play the slots, take advantage of some free drinks, enjoy the buffet. Linn eyes her once, lets her gaze move on to the couple who have entered behind her, a couple in expensive clothes who look like high rollers.

She can feel Raoul's frustrated eyes burning into her back. She turns to face the two way mirror where she knows he is watching, and shakes her head once, a sharp short movement.

Nothing.

ABOUT THE EDITOR

CHEYENNE BLUE'S erotic fiction has been included in over 90 erotic anthologies since 2000 including *Best Lesbian Erotica, Best Women's Erotica, Sweat, Bossy,* and *Wild Girls, Wild Nights.* Under her own name she has written travel books and articles, and edited anthologies of local writing in Ireland.

Check out her blog at cheyenneblue.com. She's also on Twitter at @IamCheyenneBlue and on Goodreads.

ABOUT THE CONTRIBUTORS

ERZABET BISHOP is thrilled to learn writing naughty books is a whole lot of fun. She is a contributing author to *A Christmas to Remember, Sweat, When the Clock Strikes Thirteen, Can't Get Enough, Slave Girls, The Big Book of Submission, Gratis II, Anything She Wants, Coming Together: Girl on Girl* and more. She is the author of *Tethered, Sigil Fire,* The *Erotic Pagans Series: Beltane Fires, Samhain Shadows* and *Yuletide Temptation.* She lives in Texas with her husband, furry children and can often be found lurking in local bookstores. Follow her reviews and posts on Twitter at @erzabetbishop.

LAILA BLAKE (lailablake.com) is an author, linguist and translator. She writes character- and issue-driven love stories, co-founded the micro-publishing venture Lilt Literary and blogs about writing, feminism and society. Laila's body of work encompasses literary erotica, romance, as well as the various fields of speculative fiction (dystopian/post-apocalypse, fantasy, paranormal romance and urban fantasy) and she adores finding ways to mix and match. Her short stories have been featured in numerous anthologies, among them *Best Women's Erotica 2014* and *Best Erotic Romance 2014.*

HARPER BLISS (harperbliss.com) has travelled the world in search of sexual satisfaction. She now resides in a hot Asian country and dedicates her time to writing down the stories that have inspired and aroused her.

Harper is the author of the *High Rise* series, the *French Kissing* serial and several other lesbian erotic romance titles.

EMILY L. BYRNE lives in lovely Minneapolis with her wife and the two cats that own them. She toils in corporate IT by day, and writes as much of the rest of the time as possible. Her blog is at writeremilylbyrne.blogspot.com.

NIKI CROW is a Swedish author who lives in a cabin in the forest with her wife and many cats. Under her real name, Niki has published one novel and ghost written another. She is also a successful artist.

Born in Galway, on the windswept west coast of Ireland, RACHEL O. ESPLANADE is named after an intersection in Montreal's bohemian Plateau district. The brainchild of a sexually frustrated software engineer, Rachel's first stories slowly developed in a cold, television-less flat during hot phone calls to a long-distance lover. Rachel's work has been published in the *Ultimate Lesbian Erotica* anthology.

REBECCA LYNNE FULLAN loves stories and plays with them as much as possible. She lives in New York City with her wife, the playwright Charlotte Rahn-Lee. Check out her blog at rebeccalynnefullan.wordpress.com

AVA-ANN HOLLAND is a European mongrel who has written all types of words in all types of contexts for a very long time. She currently resides in the United Kingdom where she spends her days fantasizing about dry land and wet dreams.

SACCHI GREEN (sacchi-green.blogspot.com) is a writer and editor of erotica and other stimulating genres. Her stories have appeared in scores of publications, and she's also edited nine lesbian erotica anthologies, including Lambda Award winners *Lesbian Cowboys* and *Wild Girls, Wild Nights*, both from Cleis Press. A collection of her own work, *A Ride to Remember*, has been published by Lethe Press. Sacchi lives in western Massachusetts and gets away to the mountains of New Hampshire as often as she can.

AXA LEE is an erotica-writing farm girl, who grazes cattle in her yard and herds incorrigible livestock with a cowardly dog. Her work appears in several anthologies. Someday her partner promises to get used to answering weird rhetorical questions that begin with the disclaimer, "So this is for a story…"

JEAN ROBERTA has taught English for a quarter-century in a Canadian university where she has recently begun teaching Creative Writing. Her diverse erotic stories have appeared in approximately one hundred print anthologies, an out-of-print novel, three single-author collections and a novella, *The Flight of the Black Swan* (Lethe Press). More here: JeanRoberta.com.

LISABET SARAI writes in many genres, but F/F fiction is one of her favorites. Her lesbian erotica credits include contributions to Lambda Award winner *Where the Girls Are*, Ippie-winning *Carnal Machines*, *Best Lesbian Romance 2012* and Lammy-nominated *Coming Together: Girl on Girl*. Lisabet holds more degrees than anyone would ever need, from prestigious educational institutions who would no doubt be deeply embarrassed by her chosen genre. She has traveled widely and currently lives in Southeast Asia, where she pursues an alternative career that is completely unrelated to her writing. For all the dirt on Lisabet, visit lisabetsarai.com.

L.C. SPOERING (lcspoering.com) lives and writes in Denver, Colorado. Her work has appeared in anthologies with Cleis Press, Ladylit, and Seal Press, as well as *The Dying Goose* literary magazine. Her first book, *After Life Lessons*, co-authored with Laila Blake, was released in 2014.

NICOLE WOLFE has been published in other girl-girl erotica anthologies and has been writing naughty stories since she was in high school. She was stunned to learn you could get paid for such a thing. She lives in the Midwest with her lovely wife, goofy puppy, and highly tolerant cat. One of the rules she and her wife have regarding forbidden fruit is "It's okay as long as you bring home carry-out." Her story, *Thanks to Irene*, was inspired by a friend who lived in the hurricane's path.

ALLISON WONDERLAND is one L of a girl. Her lesbian literature appears in *Best Lesbian Romance* 2013 and 2014, *Girl Fever, Girls Who Score, Sapphic Planet*, and *Wild Girls, Wild Nights*. Besides being a Sapphic storyteller, Allison is a reader of stories Sapphics tell and enjoys everything from pulp fiction to historical fiction. Find out what else she's into and up to at aisforallison.blogspot.com.

Multi-published erotica author BETH WYLDE writes what she likes to read, which includes a little bit of everything under the rainbow. Her muse is an equal opportunity smut bunny that believes everyone, no matter their kink, gender or orientation is entitled to love, acceptance and scalding HOT sex! Find her online at bethwylde.com